By the Author

Betting on Love

Midnight at the Orpheus

City Kitty and Country Mouse

Visit us at www.boldstrokesbooks.com

CITY KITTY AND COUNTRY MOUSE

by

Alyssa Linn Palmer

2020

CITY KITTY AND COUNTRY MOUSE
© 2020 BY ALYSSA LINN PALMER. ALL RIGHTS RESERVED.

ISBN 13: 978-1-63555-553-0

THIS TRADE PAPERBACK ORIGINAL IS PUBLISHED BY
BOLD STROKES BOOKS, INC.
P.O. BOX 249
VALLEY FALLS, NY 12185

FIRST EDITION: FEBRUARY 2020

CREDITS
EDITOR: RUTH STERNGLANTZ
PRODUCTION DESIGN: STACIA SEAMAN
COVER DESIGN BY TAMMY SEIDICK

Acknowledgments

So many people made this book possible. Many thanks to my partner, Anthony, who is the most supportive person ever. To my good friend Marzena, who helped tease this book from idea through to fruition, you are amazing. To Cathy, my fabulous critique partner, thank you for taking this journey with Kitty & Lucy. To my editor, Ruth, thanks for making this book better. And to my family and friends, your support means the world.

To Anthony, Cathy & Marzena

CHAPTER ONE

The scent of fresh blackberries makes my mouth water.

I won't eat one. It wouldn't look good if the farmer was eating all her own produce while the customers waited. Blackberries are one of our best sellers when they're in season. The farmers' market will open in a few minutes, and I still need to get everything set up. Alice, my partner in crime at Country Mouse Farms, is sick with the flu, so it's just me for the day. I know I'll be run off my feet, but I can't let the market go by. It's mid-spring and people are craving fresh fruit and vegetables. If they don't have or want their own gardens, they come to us. To me.

I lay out the punnets of strawberries, and next to them, the raspberries. The other side is all vegetables: spinach, lettuce, and—a new one this year—dandelion greens. And before I forget, I put out the new postcards Alice had made. The front is a photo of the interior of the greenhouse, with Alice and me standing there, holding baskets of produce, and the back has our website and contact information. They're sharp and professional, and I'm as proud of them as I was of my original business card when I first established the farm as a commercial entity.

Lucy Shen, business owner.

"Five minutes until opening!" The announcement blares over the public-address system. I take a quick look at my stall, circling around the front to carefully align each cardboard box, each price sign, each punnet. Alice always teases me for being so fussy, but I like it looking perfect. Even if it'll be organized chaos by the afternoon.

My first customer arrives within minutes of the market opening. I sell her a punnet each of strawberries and raspberries, and a bag of spinach. Then another pair arrive, one pushing a stroller with a smiley, giggly baby. Two bags of lettuce later, they move on. The morning is brisk business with very few lags. My stomach growls, but I don't have time to eat anything. When it hits one o'clock, there's a lull, and I dig out my sandwich and a bottle of water. I don't like to eat quickly, but not much else for me to do. For a weekday, it's surprisingly busy.

I straighten the punnets once more and spot one of my regular clients, Cindy, making her way through the market. Beside her is another woman, one I haven't seen before. She has her nose in her phone, not paying attention to any of the stalls. She's wearing a blazer with a nice camisole underneath, her hair dark and smooth. Professional. Cindy turns to her, and she looks up briefly before turning her attention back to her phone.

Cindy hurries up to my stall. "I hope you still have a lot left."

"I brought extra today. The raspberries were perfect this morning."

Cindy leans over the table and plucks a punnet from the tray, brings it to her nose, sniffing deeply. "Oh yes, they sure are. I'll take two."

I glance at her friend, who still hasn't looked up from her phone, standing a few steps away.

"What about…?"

Cindy shakes her head. "She's really nice, honestly, but she works too hard."

"Does she like fruit?"

"I think so. It might get her to look up now and again." Cindy leans forward, her voice a whisper. "I'm trying to make sure she does something that isn't work."

I flick my gaze back to her friend. She's frowning, causing a wrinkle in her brow that is somehow charming. She's nibbling on her lip as she does, swiping at her phone. Cindy sighs and reaches out to pull her closer, out of the way of a pair of shoppers bearing down on her with their strollers.

❖

My phone vibrates in my blazer pocket again, insistent, demanding. I pull it out, checking the messages. Fortunately, they're easy to answer. I had two billable hours left this afternoon, yet I'm here with Cindy, my friend and paralegal, following her through a crush of people at the farmers' market. She swears it's the most popular one in the city, and being here now, I can believe it. My phone vibrates again, this time several short buzzes. Emails, or texts. They never really stop. But if I want to make partner, that's how it'll be. And I want that. So much. I put my phone back in my pocket, trying not to let my anxiety play up. But it's hard. I'm so used to answering immediately. Shoving my hands into the pockets of my suit, I duck through the throng to catch up with Cindy, who has finally slowed at a fruit and vegetable stand. She's talking to the vendor, a woman who looks about my age, or maybe a touch older, with jet-black hair and warm dark brown eyes. I check my phone one more time. Nothing new. All right. There's a little flutter in my stomach, and I take a deep breath. Back, anxiety. I can deal with the emails after I leave here. It won't be the first time I've worked late.

"Kitty, come on," Cindy says, tugging at my arm and pulling me up next to her. "Lucy here has the best fruit in the whole market. Luce, I'll take one of each."

I take in the array of fruits—strawberries, raspberries, blueberries, and blackberries, my favorite—and vegetables, all lush and gorgeous in their baskets and punnets. "How can you possibly eat all that?" I ask as Lucy methodically begins placing punnets of fruit into a larger cardboard tray.

"Breakfast on my cereal, lunch in my smoothies, and on my postdinner ice cream," Cindy says, her tone quite serious, though she's smiling. "There's never a bad time."

"What's your favorite?" Lucy asks, and I realize the question is being directed at me. Her gaze is friendly, and something a bit more, something... My stomach flutters again, but there's heat there too. Lucy seems familiar somehow, like I knew her somewhere before. A silly thought, because obviously I didn't, but still, the idea lingers.

I look over her stall, and my gaze continues to be drawn to the small selection of blackberries. Lucy smiles, a gentle, almost delicate smile as her work-roughened hands lift a small blue punnet.

"Try one," she encourages. "Trust me, it's worth it."

I won't ever say no to a blackberry, though it's been quite a while since I've had one. Too long. I pick a large one from the top—it looks almost ready to burst. I pop it into my mouth and bite down, and that's it.

I'm lost. The flavor is luscious, intense, yet it almost melts in my mouth. I close my eyes, savoring that taste. It's summers out at the lake, at camp, the one place my parents let me be in the outdoors, picking the wild berries from along the paths, my fingers and tongue turning dark purple. I can almost hear the buzz of the mosquitos and the bees.

I almost hate to open my eyes, but I do.

Cindy is looking at me almost as if I've grown a second head. We've known each other for years, since school, but I'm pretty sure that even though she's my friend as well as my assistant, she's never seen me outside of my usual work mode. That is me. This, this is something different, something older.

And Lucy, she's as fixed on me as Cindy is, maybe more. I have no idea why. My mind is still on that blackberry.

"I think you need all of these," Lucy says, pressing the small punnet into my hands. Her fingers brush mine, and she has an energy that entices me, a zing I can't deny.

"How much?" I manage to ask.

"Free, this time, since Cindy here bought so many. But if you like one blackberry that much, I know you'll be back." She laughs, and it's as if her face lights up, her eyes glimmering with good cheer. Her smile is wide, open and friendly. Her warmth seems to spread, to envelop me. It makes me want to be around her, to see that smile, feel that warmth.

"Do you deliver?" Fruit to the office, or fruit to the home—it doesn't matter because I can't spare the time to come to the market every week.

Lucy takes a postcard from a rack of them perched in the midst of the strawberries, and our fingers brush again as I take it. "Call me and we can sort something out." On the front of it, she's standing with another woman in a greenhouse. Her girlfriend? Her mom? I don't know. I flip it over, see her contact information and a website. Lucy Shen, Country Mouse Farms.

I tuck the card into my blazer's inner pocket, knowing I won't lose it there. My phone vibrates again and I can't help myself; I pull it out and glance at it.

Ten emails. My stomach drops. All happy feelings drain away.

"Are you all right?" Lucy asks. Her voice seems distant, but maybe it's the blood rushing in my ears.

"Kitty?" Cindy nudges me. "What's up?"

My thumbs flick over the screen and I skim the list. Urgent, urgent, even more urgent. This won't be the way to make partner. I won't impress my boss if I don't get this taken care of ASAP.

"I need to get back to work," I say, showing Cindy my phone.

"None of this can wait." Cindy looks it over, reads the senders and subjects.

"Give us a bit more time here," she says. "I can be ready to go in half an hour. Trust me, you won't be in trouble. Together, we can tackle it in an hour."

I give her a look, *Are you sure?* unspoken. Cindy nods, her hand on my arm. I force myself to take a deep breath. In, then out. And again. And again. After about five or six breaths, some of that worry fades. I put my phone away, though it kills me to do it. And I pick up the punnet of blackberries, taking another from the top. I pop it into my mouth, willing it to put me back into those happy memories.

It doesn't, but my eyes aren't closed this time. I'm looking at Lucy, at her concerned expression. I don't know why she'd worry. We just met.

"See you next week, Luce," Cindy says, hefting her cardboard tray. "I'll need a refill."

Lucy chuckles, but her glance comes back to me.

"Thanks for these," I say, holding up the blackberries.

"You're very welcome. I'll see you soon." Lucy smiles, and that warmth rushes over me once more.

Soon. I'd like that.

Cindy takes me on a tour of the rest of the market, but I'll be the first to admit that my attention is elsewhere. I notice a stand that makes crepes, one that has spices of all sorts, and another that sells homemade dog treats, but my thoughts are on Lucy, and on those blackberries. It's a strain to not eat them all as we walk, a temptation that calls to me. At some point in our half-hour tour, I give in, and when we're at the doors, just about to leave, my punnet is empty.

"You're going to need some more," Cindy says. "Go on, go back to the Country Mouse. I'll wait."

"We don't have time," I say, checking my watch. We're already fifteen minutes past the half hour Cindy promised. "I'll have to wait until next time."

"Call her then," Cindy says, "and get her to deliver. It'll be worth the cost."

I follow Cindy to her car, sliding into the passenger seat and putting my seat belt on. She drives with a speedy intensity I find intimidating, but she'll have us back to the office in no time at all.

We don't talk much on the drive back; I start reading my emails and she focuses on the road. She was right, that most of them weren't quite as urgent as they first seemed, but I get started on replies, carefully double-checking my spelling. Autocorrect is the devil.

I've managed to get two emails replied to by the time we're back at the parking lot. I step out of the car into the surprisingly oppressive mid-spring heat made worse by the dark asphalt. If it was any hotter, my heels would sink into the parking lot's surface. Cindy grabs her tray and we head inside. The air is startlingly cold as we enter the lobby, and I notice a scent I hadn't before, a sort of sterile, disinfectant smell.

"Does it smell funny in here?" I ask her as we head to the elevators.

Cindy sniffs. "Just the usual eau d'office," she says. "Here, smell this instead." She raises the cardboard tray and a whiff of fresh fruit wafts in my direction. We step into the elevator, and I bend to sniff at the strawberries, the rich scent making my mouth water. I would just about kill for another punnet of blackberries. Instead, though, I head back to my office, ducking quietly around corners so no one notices me. As far as they'll know, I've been working all afternoon.

It's research, emails, a few phone calls, and some negotiations with other lawyers in regard to corporate mergers. Usually it's something I love doing, that precise argument, the satisfaction of a victory, however small. But today, my mind keeps wandering, and I can still taste the blackberries. Finally, once I've completed the day's tasks and the rest of the office is nearly empty, I rise to leave. I check my phone once more, reflexively, before I put it into my blazer pocket. My fingers brush a bit of card paper and I pull out the postcard for Country Mouse Farms.

There's no time like the present to get some more blackberries. But when I dial the number, my stomach flutters with butterflies and I find my throat dry. There's no reason for it to be—it's not like I don't talk on the phone for a good portion of my day, and to people far less pleasant than Lucy Shen. This isn't like me.

I finish punching in the number and hold the phone to my ear. There's a ring, and then another, and another, until I wonder if there's no answering machine or voicemail. But finally, the line clicks, and a message plays in Lucy's gentle tones.

"You've reached Country Mouse Farms, and the home of Lucy and Michelle Shen. Please leave us a message and we'll get back to you as soon as we can." There's another stretch of message, but it's in a language I don't understand. I'd guess it to be some dialect of Chinese, given Lucy's looks and her mother's name. The line beeps and I'm caught off guard.

"Hi, Lucy, it's Kitty Kerr. We met this afternoon at the market and my friend recommended your blackberries. Are you able to deliver? Please let me know." I leave her my number, repeating it for good measure. Then I hang up, my breath coming quickly, like I've run a race. My hand is even a bit shaky when I put my phone back in my pocket.

Get a hold of yourself, Kitty. It's only blackberries.

Delicious blackberries.

CHAPTER TWO

I notice the answering machine, a throwback from an earlier era yet still clunking along, blinking when I enter the kitchen, but I'm too tired to care. It's late, and I've just unloaded my remaining fruit—not that there was much—into the farm's walk-in cooler, then done my usual rounds of the greenhouses. I haven't even eaten, unless you count a few berries here and there, and a sandwich during a couple of quiet minutes at the market. My stomach growls as I finally notice the scent of food; I'm pretty sure Mama made my favorite today, the Shanghai rice cakes and a sort of stir-fry. I'd picked up the cakes for her last week. There's nothing quite like my mother's food, especially after a long day.

But before I can load up a plate from the wok, which sits on the stove, the burner on low, I head out to the back porch, where Mama usually sits in the evening, to watch the sun set over the foothills to the west.

She peers through her glasses at me, their large round frames dwarfing her thin face. "Ah, Ming Nhon," she says, "you're home. I left rice cakes for you."

"I'll get some soon," I reply and sit down next to her on the porch swing. It sways gently.

"You are late today," she says.

"It was busy, just me."

"Alice called earlier. She apologized for being sick. I offered to bring her some soup, but she said she wasn't hungry. I hope she is eating."

Mama is always concerned about whether we have eaten enough. It's one of the things I remember as a child growing up—no matter what day, or what was going on, there was always the question, *Did you eat?*

"She'll ask for some when she wants it," I say. Alice is our neighbor as well as being my business partner, and nearly Mama's age, though she'll never admit it. And she doesn't look it, not at all. She's usually hardy and energetic, and this flu is a rare thing for her. I'll have to talk to her later, let her know how things went. But right now, I need food. I'm not used to manning the booth on my own, and I know I'm not the sort who can just jump into the fray and be super-friendly-cheery without it costing me. I rise from the swing and go get my dinner. It's delicious, but I'm so tired that even that doesn't seem to matter much. I pour two cups of tea from the kettle on the stove and bring them outside again, give one to Mama.

"There was a phone call earlier," she says. "I didn't know who, so I didn't answer." She shrugs. "Not local."

"I'll check it tomorrow." I know she doesn't like to answer if she doesn't know who it is. Though she's been in Canada a long time, and my father was English-speaking, she isn't confident in her English and would rather speak Cantonese. He and I always indulged her, and I'm glad I did, because otherwise I might not have known my mother tongue at all. As it is, English flows off my tongue much easier than Cantonese.

"It's a beautiful night, Ming Nhon," she says, squeezing my hand.

"Yes, it is, Mama," I reply. There's nothing quite like this view, looking out over the green hills, past the barn and the greenhouses, the smell of grass and hay and the fresh breeze that comes from the west, off the mountains several hours away.

I only wish I had someone else to share it with, someone who wasn't Mama. As she shared it with my father, I want to share it with someone.

One day.

❖

I wake early, even though I went to bed early with exhaustion, and pad down to the kitchen to put on the coffee, my slippers making little noise on the linoleum. The kitchen window is open and the light breeze is cool, but it helps to wake me up.

From the corner of my eye, the red blink of the answering machine catches my attention. I never checked the messages. While the coffee percolates in its aluminum pot on the stove, I sit down at the tiny corner desk and hit the play button, searching for a pen that works.

"Hi Lucy, it's Kitty Kerr..."

I stop my searching, her voice catching me by surprise. I remember instantly who she is, the woman in fancy office wear, loving my blackberries. Seeing her eating them, savoring them so intensely, it made me wish that she could be *the one*. Most people don't eat food like that. It's a necessary activity. But Kitty, she adored it, took her time, made every bite count. My throat goes dry, and I dig once more for a pen as she repeats her phone number. The message ends, and I finally find one pen that mostly works. I write down her name on a sticky note, but I have to replay her message to get her phone number.

I want to call her back right away, but I check the time. Six o'clock. No, far too early to call. I tuck the sticky note into the pocket of my robe and go back to the stove, check on the coffee, and take down a mug from the cupboard. My heart feels like it's racing, but in a good way. Sort of. Alice would tease me gently about a crush, and Mama would just smile patiently. She thinks I need to find someone, and I told her a few months after Dad died that I liked women, not men, and she'd just nodded. *I knew a long time ago, Ming Nhon*, she'd said. No keeping anything from Mama.

I pour a cup of coffee and take it out onto the porch, looking out over the farm, the sun just above the horizon. It's cool out and a bit damp, but it will be hot later. The sky is clear, and I can already feel the warmth of the sunshine. At this time of morning, when all is quiet, it's easy to let my mind wander.

Kitty's lips closing over the blackberry was one of the most erotic things I've seen. Her lips were lush, and the way her eyes closed, her dark lashes like soot on her cheeks... The desire shivers through me again, like it did yesterday. I tried to hide it then, but I don't bother now. The goose bumps rise on my arms. If anyone saw, I'd excuse it away with the light breeze, but there's only me. And then I feel silly for fantasizing. A city girl like her probably has never gotten her hands dirty, never planted a garden or ridden a horse or even set foot on a farm. Not that she wouldn't, but I've listened to others complain about the city folk and how insular they are. Mind you, these are the same people who, though kind and reliable, also still call my mother the China-lady when they don't think I can hear them. She did pick an English name—Michelle—but her real name is Ai-He.

Dad was one of the community, since his family has been here for years. I remember him telling me about my great-grandparents, Kuo Song and Ru Shi, who opened the first Chinese-Western restaurant in town. They had one daughter, Ming Nhon, who I'm named for. She married Daniel Bennett, to the shock of her family and his. He brought her out to his farm, where I'm standing now, and that was it. Part of the community, yet not part of it.

I would bet that Kitty doesn't care that I'm one-quarter white settler and three-quarters Chinese.

I take a long draw on my coffee, which is getting too close to lukewarm. I need to get dressed and get started on chores. Then I'll go check in on Alice to make sure she's doing better. And then, I will call Kitty.

There's the goose bumps again.

She just wants blackberries. But I'm still hoping for more.

Chapter Three

I'm in a meeting with a client when my phone rings, and the caller ID says *Country Mouse*. I mute the ringer and force my gaze away, focusing back on my client, an older man in an immaculate and expensive suit that likely cost more than my month's salary. He's droning on about stock agreements, and I know I should be fascinated and offering suggestions, but it's like my brain went on hiatus, skipping off to dream about blackberries.

And, if I'm truly honest, about Lucy too.

My client, Mr. Anderson, finishes his speech, and I glance down at my notes. Preferred shares, common shares, portions thereof. I look back up at him, glad that I can still manage to partly listen when I'm distracted.

"We'll get the agreements drawn up and sent over to your office," I assure him. He smiles and rises from his seat, straightening his suit jacket. I rise too and offer him my hand.

"Thank you, Ms. Kerr," he says easily, his baritone likely one that charms all the ladies. I can see it in how he holds himself, how he looks for my reaction. I don't tend to play that game, but he is genuinely friendly, so it's at least easy to be friendly back.

"Can I walk you out?" I offer. He waves me off with a good-natured smile.

"I'll stop by and see Jack on my way"—Jack being my boss, and one of the partners—"since we have a golf game on the weekend. I'll review the agreement within a day." With a wave, he exits my office and I sink back into my chair. My message light is blinking, bright and persistent. Normally I hate seeing my phone blink, knowing that more work looms in my already busy day, but this time is different.

I dial in to my voicemail. Cindy comes to the door but pauses when she sees me on the phone. So much for privacy.

Lucy's voice comes over the line, quiet, calm, but if I'm not mistaken, there's a slight quiver there. My heart skips a beat. She's saying something about berries and then I hear it. "I can deliver to your home or office if you have a larger order, but we are at the Calgary Farmers' Market these next couple of days, and the market out at Cochrane the week after. Let me know what works best for you." She leaves her number and I jot it onto a sticky note.

I save the message. I usually don't, but this time, I want to.

Good Lord, listen to me already.

"Your ten o'clock is here," Cindy says. "Should I show her in?"

"Please. And if you could, look up Country Mouse Farms. I'd like to know their prices on fruit."

Cindy smiles, and it's gleeful and knowing all at once. "Yes, Ms. Kerr," she says, turning to leave. I hate when she calls me Ms. Kerr. It's like being my mother.

❖

After my client leaves, I have a brief bit of downtime. Usually I take advantage and pop out for a sandwich and latte at one of the nearby coffee shops, but today, I stay at my desk and review the printout Cindy has given me with pricing from the farm. Everything seems reasonable to me, but then, when's the last time I actually went shopping? Or cooked? My meals come from restaurants, takeout, or delivery services. Even my groceries. If someone asked me the price of milk, I couldn't even hazard a guess. It never used to be that way. I used to cook. I wish I still had time to cook.

I lift the receiver and dial the farm. The line rings, once, twice, a third time, and then there's a slight click.

"Country Mouse Farms," an out-of-breath voice says.

"May I speak with Lucy, please?" I cringe at how stiff and professional I sound. But I can't help it. I take a deep breath. Go away, nerves.

"Speaking." I hear her take a deep breath too, and I wonder suddenly if that's because of me. Probably not, since she'd been dashing for the phone, but a girl can dream.

"This is Kitty Kerr," I begin, trying to take some of the stiffness out of my voice but failing.

"I was just thinking of you," she says, and my heart shudders and skips in surprise.

"You were?" The words pop out before I can stop them.

"I was tending to the blackberries," she says. "Our crop is almost done for the season, and I was getting the flats ready for the farmers' market."

"How many more do you have?" Anxiety slides into my chest, though it really shouldn't. It's just blackberries, for crying out loud.

"I'll make sure you get some—have no worries on that account," Lucy says. Her voice feels soothing somehow. I take a deep breath. "I can even deliver to your office if you'd like."

I can picture Lucy here, a diamond in the rough among all the starched shirts. I could close my door, give us some privacy. But who am I kidding? My luck with women is abysmal, and the last one I had a bit of a crush on was as straight as they came.

"That would be great," I reply, realizing I've stayed quiet too long. "I have some long days, so whenever is convenient for you."

"Is there anything else you'd like aside from the blackberries? We have a whole range of fruit and veg right now."

"And the more I buy, the less the delivery fee?" I add.

"Basically," Lucy confirms. "But it's not very pricey. Just helps me cover gas."

"Then I'll take one each of strawberries, raspberries, and blueberries. And two or three of the blackberries, if you have enough."

"Consider it done. I'll be coming through the city in a couple of hours so I can get to the market. Should I call ahead?"

I flip to my calendar app. "I'm free at two if you can aim for that."

"I'll do my best," Lucy assures me. "That should work out. Thanks for buying from us, Ms. Kerr."

"Do call me Kitty," I say instantly.

"Of course, Kitty," Lucy says, and is it just me, or did her voice get a bit lower just there, a bit raspy? A bit, dare I hope, attracted? "I'll see you soon."

"Thanks, Lucy." I want to say more, but Lucy says good-bye and hangs up. I set the receiver down reluctantly.

I've never been this excited about fruit. Or anyone, for that matter.

Cindy knocks on the door and lets herself in, as she always does. She places two file folders on my desk, and gives me a good once-over.

"What?"

"You look different," she says.

I have a feeling I know where this is going. Cindy has always had a bit of gentle pressure on me to find a girlfriend. She's happy with her man and she wants me to be happy too. She's been quite up front with that, though the times she tried to set me up were awful failures. She did try, though.

"Different how?"

"You have some color," she says, reaching over the desk to tap my cheek. "It looks good on you."

"It's warm in here."

Cindy chuckles. "No, it sure isn't." She points out the gray cardigan she's wearing over her dress, a brightly patterned summer frock. "If it was, I wouldn't be wearing this, especially not with this dress."

"The combination works so well," I deadpan, and she rolls her eyes.

"Deny whatever you want," she says, "but I know."

"You don't know this," I reply. I pull the folders toward me.

"I do," Cindy retorts, though her tone is cheery as she heads for the door. "Her, you…it's damn near perfect, if I do say so myself. You'll see it eventually."

I know my cheeks have gone red now. She's blunt, but that's what I like about her. I cross my arms and lean back in my chair, still trying to feel nonchalant.

"Pretty sure she doesn't bat for my team."

Cindy turns back and stops in front of my desk, holding out a carefully manicured hand. "Want to bet on that?" Her eyes glint with determination, and probably amusement.

"How much?" I rise to my feet, wanting to meet her eye to eye.

"A spa day?"

"Extravagance is your middle name."

She grins. "You know it. Now, are you in or not?"

"Half-day spa day. I'm not a partner yet." I take her hand and we shake.

"Done. And you'll be partner soon, and then I'll get a full spa day out of you every month."

It's my turn to laugh, and I do, loudly. "Once a year maybe."

"Three times at least," she counters.

"We'll see. I'm not a partner yet," I repeat.

"Pfft. You will be. You work your ass off. Speaking of, you have about ten minutes before your next client. Want me to get you a coffee?"

Coffee. Oh yes. "Please."

"Coming right up, Ms. Kerr," she says with a wink.

Wait a minute. "You weren't eavesdropping, were you?" I'd step around my desk, but Cindy's already at the door.

"Nope, never. But I did hear you tell her not to call you Ms. Kerr. Your voice carried." She grins at me and disappears through the open door.

Now what do I hope for? That I have to pay for a half-day spa, or that I don't?

Chapter Four

K itty.
      I want to chuckle at her name, just because the farm was the Country Mouse. How apt was that? Cat and mouse. I felt a bit like the mouse, being pursued. Though our phone calls were more like tag than chase. But soon I'd be seeing her in person again. I look at the list I'd written down. It wouldn't take long to prepare, and I could finish up the rest of my chores before I left for the city. I'll admit that I won't be making much money on this sale, in comparison to what it will cost me in time, but I'm hoping for more sales later, or word of mouth promotion.

And I have to be honest with myself.

I want to see Kitty again. I need to know if what I'm feeling is just me, or if it's her too. I'd like to think it's both of us. When her voice changed on the phone, it made my heart thrill, and I thought for sure that she was interested.

I don't know why I can't just ask her...Oh, who am I kidding? I know exactly why. Because if I chance it, then I could mess it up, and that'd be the end of everything. So I won't do that. I need more information first. More intel, as Alice says, especially after she's been watching her favorite Tom Cruise action movies.

Speaking of...

I call Alice, dialing her number from memory. She answers, and her voice is still rough.

"Feeling any better?"

Alice coughs. "I've been worse," she replies. "How was it yesterday at the market?"

"I think we have a new client," I reply, "and I sold most of the produce. I have to go into the city today for a delivery before I get to the market. Do you need anything when I get back tonight?"

"This cold to go away." Alice chuckles. "But no. I'm pretty well stocked. But if you can pick up a few magazines at the store, that'd be great. My internet keeps slowing down, and I need my fix of entertainment news."

"That I can do. I'll pop by on my way home."

"You're a dear." I can hear the smile in her voice before she hangs up. Now it's time for me to go to work.

❖

Finding Kitty's office is easy. Finding a parking spot in the crazy-busy downtown is not. I've never been too fond of the hustle and bustle of the city. It's a cliché for the typical farm girl, but it's really true for me. I suppose if I'd grown up here, it'd be different, but I sure don't miss it here once I'm away.

I circle the block several times, being careful to follow all the one-way signs. Finally, finally, a cube van pulls out of a spot just ahead of me, and I can pull in. I turn the key and take a deep breath. Instead of getting out the driver's side, I shift over the bench seat and hop down from the passenger side. I go around to the side and open the door, and pull out the cardboard tray full of punnets. I balance it on one hand as I pull the door closed, then head over to the building. The security gives me a bit of a once-over, but I'm unbothered as I go to the elevator. Twelfth floor. I hit the button and wait. The doors open onto a reception area. Everything's pale wood and gray carpet, minimalist furniture that looks incredibly uncomfortable.

"Hi, can I help you?" A receptionist peers over the high desk, smiling.

"I'm here to see Ms. Kerr," I say, reminding myself to smile. I feel completely out of place here, in my jeans, T-shirt, and work boots. Everything's clean and tidy, but it's not anywhere near fancy enough.

"Just let me call and make sure she's available." The receptionist taps her headset and then speaks a few words and listens. She taps the headset again and then looks back at me. "I'll take you back."

"Thanks."

I follow the receptionist through a maze of hallways, which I'm sure I'll get lost in on my way back. Everything looks the same. Gray and white and splashes of arty color here and there. We arrive at a desk, and I recognize Cindy. She's one of my best customers. It's easy to smile at her, and she smiles back warmly. I feel a bit more at ease.

"Hi, Luce," she says. "Kitty mentioned you were going to be here. Although I think she mentioned that you'd call."

"I completely forgot," I admit sheepishly. I never forget these things.

"No worries. It'll be a good surprise for her." Cindy checks her computer. "She's in the office, and she's free. Let me just pop in and make sure she's not stuck on a phone call." She rises from her desk and turns, opening a door just a few steps behind her. She sticks her head into the office, and I can hear her talking to Kitty, although I can't really make out the words.

My stomach roils with nerves. I take a deep breath. She's just a new customer. No big deal.

Cindy moves back and gestures for me to enter. "She's all yours."

I can feel the heat on my cheeks and can only hope that Cindy hasn't noticed, but by her smile, I think she has. I shift my grip on the cardboard and walk through the open door. Kitty is sitting at a substantial, though minimalist, desk, files stacked on either side of a large blotter. It's almost classic lawyer or, at least, what I think of what a lawyer's desk might look like. A laptop computer sits to one side, its screen glowing.

Kitty rises with a smile, and I suck in a quiet breath. Her skirt suit is much like the day before, but this one has a dark royal blue jacket with a black skirt, and there's something about that color that brings out her eyes and flatters her skin tone and dark hair. Utterly delectable, even more than the blackberries.

"You are a saint for bringing this," she says, rounding the desk. "Do you take plastic, or do you need cash?"

"Whichever you like." I've brought my payment system and it's all set up, but cash is easier still. Kitty moves to a side table and picks up her purse, simple black leather with a long cross-body strap, and digs into it, pulling out a slim wallet. She takes a card from it. I glance around, trying to decide where to set the box, settling on one of the visitor's chairs. She meets me in a few steps, and I take out my phone and the little square payment machine. She leans over my shoulder slightly and watches as I type in her order and get things ready. Then I hand her the machine and she taps her card.

"That was so easy."

"I love new tech." I know I'm blushing again. I'm geeky and just can't help myself as I go into a bit of a spiel about the payment system and how easy it is...And how easy it is to get lost in her gaze. I don't want to be anywhere else but looking at those cool blue eyes. I catch myself and cut myself off before I can get too far into it. "I don't want to bore you."

"I'm not bored." Kitty smiles again. "I just never expected that farmers would have this kind of tech."

"Greenhouses are pretty high tech these days." She can't help being a city girl, it seems. I wonder if she's even been to a farm. Probably not. I imagine her in jeans and a T-shirt, or maybe even coveralls. Coveralls with nothing on underneath. Oh, my.

"I'd love to see them, see how it's done," Kitty says.

"And I'd love to show you."

"You would?" Kitty leans closer, and her tongue comes out to run over her bottom lip. I don't think it's purposeful, but what it does to me...A slight tremor runs through me.

"There's greenhouses and fields, and we have kittens in the barn, along with a couple of pigs and a horse."

"It sounds amazing." She seems almost wistful now, not flirty. A quick change that I'm not sure of.

"Let me know when you'd want to visit." I know I sound too professional, but I just can't let myself open up. It's too risky. She might not be a lesbian. She might not be into me even if she is. I'd rather not have anything than risk alienating this compelling woman. Even if I have had fantasies about her and me and blackberries and a lot of sex.

"Kitty, your two thirty is here. I have him waiting, and you have a few minutes yet, but I thought you should know." Cindy pops her head around the door. "I've given him a coffee too."

Kitty's gaze breaks from mine, darts to the door. "Thanks, Cindy." She looks back to me, and we're close enough that one step would put us to touching. Her gaze is searching, thoughtful.

"Are you serious? About visiting, that is?" Her voice is lower, uncertain.

I squeeze her fingers, cool and delicate under my calloused hand, and to my surprise, she squeezes back, but doesn't let go. "Of course I am."

She smiles then, a truly radiant smile. "One day. Soon."

"Soon," I repeat. What I really want is a set time, the certainty, but I won't push. Where we're touching is warm, and getting warmer, and it feels so right. She squeezes my fingers again, then loosens her touch, dropping my hand.

"I wish I had more time," she says. She rubs her eyes. "A curse and a blessing, this job."

"I'll leave you to it," I say, backing up a step. A very reluctant step.

❖

Cindy takes the berries after Lucy leaves, and she promises to stash them somewhere safe while I finish up my next client. Even as he enters, I can still smell the sweetness of the berries, and the slightly warm, dusty sweet smell of Lucy. Is that even a thing? Most women I've been with have smelled like whatever their favorite body wash was, or whatever perfume they've just put on. Lucy, on the other hand, doesn't carry any of those scents.

When I go to visit her farm, I can find out for sure.

I check my calendar quickly, knowing my next client is waiting. My time is almost fully blocked off for the next few weeks, as solid as it could be without having me work 24/7. A hint of fatigue courses through me, but I straighten and then rise to my feet. Another three hours and I can head home early, and tuck into a good dinner, and some blackberries for dessert. And maybe, just maybe, I'll go to bed early. Early of course meaning any time before one in the morning.

The partnership is in sight, soon.

I'm not that one who is going to quit to have kids, or quit to find herself or quit because she can't handle it. I've seen too many others quit, especially at this firm. I'm going to be the one to tough it out. I know I can handle it.

CHAPTER FIVE

The thought of blackberries is what's kept me going several days running. Tasting those berries after work these past few evenings has kept my life from feeling utterly crazy. And tonight is no different. Once I'm in my apartment, my shoes kicked off, my laptop left in my bag so I can ignore it for a full day, I head straight for the fridge. It's Friday night and I'm supposed to be having drinks with some coworkers, but I fibbed about an appointment and bowed out. I rarely do that, but I feel like I haven't had a moment to myself in ages. As long as my boss doesn't find out, I'm golden.

A bit of dread settles in my stomach and I will it away, opening the fridge door and grabbing the last punnet of blackberries. There are still some strawberries and raspberries, but there are eight blackberries left. I sigh. I'm going to need to pace myself, but tonight, I'll be out of blackberries.

Lucy's card is on my fridge, stuck up by a magnet of an octopus, one my mother bought me when she was on a trip to the west coast. I should call Lucy, but I hesitate. Would it seem over the top to be needing more blackberries now? I mean, she gave me three punnets of them, and it's only been just over three days. That's sad, isn't it?

I pop a blackberry into my mouth and turn away from the fridge. I take a glass from the cabinet and pour myself a small glass of white wine. Not much, because I'm a total lightweight, but just enough to give me a bit of a buzz. I need to come down from all the work, get into a different mindset.

My phone vibrates on the countertop. My work phone.

"Fuck."

I rarely swear, but at the moment, the last thing I want to hear about is more work. But still, I pick up the phone and look at the caller ID.

It's my boss.

Of course it is. Even Cindy knew that I needed downtime tonight. She's the only one who knows that my appointment really wasn't an appointment. The phone keeps vibrating in my hand, and I can't decide if I want to pick up the call or not. I should, since it *is* my boss, yet I just...In another moment, the decision is made for me, as the buzzing stops.

My chest feels tight, my palms clammy. I try to take a deep breath, try to remind myself that it's not a bad thing my boss has called.

Within moments, the voicemail blinks. I can't ignore that, not even if I wanted to. It'd drive me bonkers to have to keep looking at the little icon, and the blinking light. I dial in.

"Kitty, it's Jack. I was hoping to catch you as the rest of my team went home sick with food poisoning. They're working on a file for a top client of mine, and the agreements were to be signed Monday. Please call me immediately."

The message ends, and I delete it.

I should call him. I know I should. I pick up another blackberry. The juice bursts over my tongue, and I close my eyes. When I open them again, I'm still holding my work phone. Dammit. I can't not call. My boss knows me too well, well enough that if I don't call, he'll be certain I'm dead, or close to it. And he's counting on me. He knows I can do the work. And I know that helping out like this is what will get me to partner.

I sigh, looking between the blackberries and my phone.

So much for any rest.

I call.

❖

I get home sometime after midnight. I'm too tired to bother checking the clock. Jack was so pleased when I showed up and saved his bacon. And it's no wonder. The file was a disorganized mass of papers, and I'm surprised I was able to sort it out.

"Kitty, you are a lifesaver," Jack said as he'd sailed out the door. "Email me the finished agreement, and I'll look it over before Monday."

And I did as instructed. All I want to do now is sleep. But I go back into the kitchen for a glass of water and hear a bit of buzzing.

Buzzing?

I flip on the light and see the blackberries out on the counter, and the rising fruit flies. It's been warm in the building and I left my kitchen window open…and forgot to put the berries in the fridge.

My heart sinks. I might be able to wash them off, but they're definitely now overripe and soft, and getting softer. They were on the cusp earlier. As much as I want them still, the flies put me right off. I chuck the berries into the compost, tie off the bag, and trudge back downstairs to throw the bag into the bin. When I get back upstairs, I head straight for bed, stopping only to brush my teeth and strip down.

When I finally sleep, I dream of blackberries.

I pour myself a second cup of coffee, since I've finished my morning chores. It's just about ten o'clock, and the heat of the day hasn't quite hit and the porch is pleasantly warm, the sun shining on the weathered boards. I head for my usual chair and settle in, stretching out my legs, curling my bare toes against the wood. There's no moment more perfect than this.

One of Alice's dogs, a mutt mix that looks sort of like a golden Labrador, bounds up the stairs, jumping up. I lift my coffee away from her reach but scratch her behind her ears so that she lolls her tongue in bliss. Goldie, so named for her coat, is a sweet thing. She rarely leaves Alice's side. I look out over the yard and spot Alice moving slowly toward the house. Thought so.

Goldie leaves me and goes bounding down the stairs, racing back out to Alice, who laughs and pets her once more. Then Goldie races back up again to me. I laugh too. She's the silliest dog.

"I'm hoping she'll wear herself out," Alice calls as she comes closer. "One day, maybe she'll even decide to sleep in."

"She'll need a few more years first." Goldie is only about a year and a half old and still acts like a puppy. She leans up against my knees in a doggy hug, and I scratch her behind her ears again. It's like having my own dog, almost. I wouldn't mind, but with the farm and looking after Mama, I know I don't really have time.

Alice comes up the stairs and sits in the chair next to me. She pats down a few loose hairs from her bun.

"Sorry to leave you in the lurch these few days," she said, again somewhat breathless. "I'm more myself now. Finally."

"Don't worry," I say automatically. "We've been selling well. I think we may have a new delivery client." I tell her about Kitty, but only the basics. Still, I feel my cheeks warm.

"She sounds lovely," Alice says, leaning back in her chair. "Cindy has brought us several newbies." She grins. "But none seem to have made an impression on you until now." Her eyes twinkle. "I wonder why that is?"

Alice, of course, knows my preferences, but we've never really spoken about my personal life before. I don't know how she could sense my interest like that so easily. I like Kitty, I do. But I didn't say anything, and pink cheeks shouldn't be enough of an indication. I sigh.

"She's nice."

"Just nice?"

"There's something about her. I'm not sure what it is." I shrug, feeling a bit helpless, unable to define what I'm feeling.

"I'm sure you'll figure out why." Alice smiles. "You'll have to introduce me."

"It might happen," I say. "She's interested in seeing the farm."

"Now *that*," Alice says, "is promising. When?"

"I don't know. She's pretty busy, a high-powered lawyer type."

"Interesting," Alice says. She looks out over the greenhouses, her gaze in the middle distance. She's thinking, I can tell. What she's thinking about, though, I have no idea. It's not the first time a client has been curious about the farm, about how we do things. Mostly they come, take a brief look around, a short tour, and then it's back to their clean city life, away from the dirt and bugs and hard labor. Would Kitty do that? I really have no idea. She looks like a city girl, in her skirt suits and heels. She's so carefully made up that I wonder if she's ever gotten her hands dirty, let her hair down. Metaphorically, of course, since her hair was down her back, dark and shiny. She's so put together, so unlike me.

"Where'd your mind go?" Alice asks. She's looking at me now, not out at the farm.

I shrug. "The usual place."

"Ah." She nods. "Stop talking yourself down."

She does know me. It's occasionally unnerving, but now, I'm glad she does. I don't want to have to explain it in detail, if I even could.

"You could use a pep talk," Alice remarks. "You're good enough, you're smart enough, and just because she's a city kid and you're a country kid, that doesn't mean it's an insurmountable obstacle. If it even is one."

Kid. Yeah, Alice has known me since I was a little girl. She was the first person to come see my mother when she arrived from China, even though she knew no Cantonese and my mother no English. She's my rock.

"City kids don't usually like to stay out here," I reply. That's been my experience. Usually the farm kids head to the city, and that's it.

"Never say never." Alice rises to her feet. "I'll go say hello to your mother, and then I'll come out to the greenhouse. I know you've had a lot to do these past few days, and I can help you catch up."

"I'll be there," I say. I lift my coffee cup to my lips and drain the rest. The greenhouse beckons, and I set the cup down on the porch by my chair. I'll pick it up later.

I wake with my alarm, but I really just want to sleep. It's Saturday, though, so I hit the snooze button. And again, when the alarm kicks back in. I don't technically have to work today, but I know there will always be something waiting for me. I crawl out of bed and head straight into the bathroom, splashing my face. The cool water makes me feel slightly more alive, but I'm still dragging. Coffee might help. I walk through to the kitchen and see my phone on the counter where I left it last night after chucking out the blackberries.

Damn.

I'm craving those blackberries. There's nothing quite like them. I grab a punnet of strawberries from the fridge, but honestly, they're just not the same. Still delicious, of course. I grab several, then put the punnet back, close the fridge door.

Lucy's card, Country Mouse Farms, is right in front of my nose.

She did say to call.

It's Saturday.

I take down her card, turn it over in my fingers. Should I? I check the clock. It's still early, almost eight. I can't call her yet.

I go back to the bedroom and change into my workout gear, grabbing my sneakers. I'll go for a run, and that will get my energy up, get me feeling a bit more human. And then, when I get back, I'll call.

When I get back, the first thing I do is grab my phone and Lucy's card, but before I can dial the number, I pause. Nervousness makes my stomach churn, and my palms are sweaty. What am I doing? Does she really want me to visit? Am I just being rude, trying to invite myself? I remember my mother's admonishment when I was younger, not to invite myself over just because I wanted to do something. It's kept me from doing quite a bit, but I've never wanted to be an imposition.

Fuck it.

I dial. The phone takes a moment to connect, then I hear the ring. Three times and I'm about to give up when I hear the click, and a voice. "Country Mouse Farms." Definitely not Lucy this time.

"Good morning. May I speak to Lucy, please?" My polite business self takes over, as if I'm sitting in my office, not standing in damp workout gear in my kitchen.

"She isn't here right now," the voice says. "My name is Alice. What can I do for you?"

"My name is Kitty," I say. "I bought some fruit from Lucy the other day, and I was wondering if she still had some more blackberries available."

"Oh!" The woman sounds surprised, yet happy. "We aren't doing any deliveries today, since Lucy is at the Cochrane market this morning, but if you wanted to come out, you're more than welcome. Do you know how to get here?" She rattles off directions, and I grab a scrap of paper and a pen, jotting down what I can. "We'll be here all day," she adds, "so don't feel you have to rush."

"Thank you very much. I'm not sure when I'll get there."

"We're looking forward to seeing you." I hear a voice in the background, and then Alice says good-bye and hangs up.

I set down my phone. My stomach is still churning, but it's a different sort of nervousness now. The farm is an hour's drive south, at least, and I should get moving soon. Time to have a shower.

CHAPTER SIX

I get back to the farmhouse after doing an early morning stint at the Cochrane market just in time for lunch. Mama has made a soup, something hot and sour, and the scent makes my mouth water. Alice is sitting at the table, chatting with Mama while she stirs the soup.

"Ming Nhon, you are just in time," Mama says. She opens the cupboard and takes out four soup bowls, setting them on the table. I notice now that Alice has set out four sets of soup spoons and napkins, and four glasses of water.

"Who's coming over?" I don't remember Mama saying anything about a guest. Mama doesn't pay attention to my question but goes back to the soup, stirring and sniffing, and taking a taste. I turn to Alice. "Who?"

Before she can answer, I hear the wheels of a car crunching over the gravel driveway. I step out onto the porch and see a small hatchback car, one I don't recognize. The sun glints off the windshield, and I can't see the driver. The car stops and the driver kills the engine.

Then the driver steps out.

My heart skips a beat. Or at least, I'm pretty sure it does.

It's Kitty.

She's not wearing her skirt suit—she's dressed in dark wash skinny jeans and a black T-shirt, but I can still recognize her. She's utterly gorgeous. And why she'd be here...? I want to turn back, go inside and quiz Alice and Mama, but I don't. I stand there on the porch and watch Kitty approach. It's easy to admire her as she strolls up the drive, her hips swinging just a touch, her curves delectable. Her dark hair is pulled back into a ponytail, and she pushes her sunglasses up onto her head and smiles at me.

That smile.

I forget all words of greeting and barely even remember my own name. I can feel my cheeks heating, and my mouth is dry, my tongue tied. I shouldn't be like this. I don't ever get tongue-tied over a woman.

"Lucy!" Kitty smiles and waves and then mounts the stairs. I smile back, still not sure what to say. She's here.

"Hi," I stammer out. I sound like an idiot.

Kitty's smile dims. "I'm not imposing, am I?" she asks worriedly. "The lady I spoke to on the phone said it was fine to come out to pick up some berries."

"Of course it is," I manage to say. "I just didn't know you were coming."

Kitty's smile returns, even as she says, "I don't want to be any bother."

"No bother at all." With every word, my equilibrium begins to return. "Come inside—Mama's just made lunch, and I think you're invited." Without thinking, I reach out a hand. Kitty's eyes widen, but she takes my hand, and I bring her into the house to meet Mama and Alice.

❖

Lucy didn't seem very excited to see me here on her doorstep. Maybe I shouldn't have come. But then, Lucy puts out her hand, and I take it, and suddenly it all feels right again.

The farmhouse is all that I'd expected, yet different. We don't take our shoes off at the door—rather, we walk down a hallway, the hardwood floors under our feet battered, the varnish starting to peel. There are pictures hung on the walls, some of them family photos, though they're hard to see in the dim light, and others look like paintings, with Chinese characters at the corner. The hall opens into a large room, both kitchen and living room by the looks of it. It's a classic country kitchen, with an L-shape of cabinets both high and low, and a large kitchen table with mismatched chairs around it. The living room side has two comfortable sofas, a coffee table, and a few side tables with lamps. There's a fireplace, and a pair of beautiful hangings on either side.

My gaze comes back to the kitchen. An older Chinese woman is at the stove, stirring soup, her glasses fogging slightly as she bends over the pot. Another woman, probably the one I spoke to, sits at the kitchen table, in front of a place setting. She smiles at me warmly, and I feel a bit more of my confidence returning.

"You must be Kitty," she says, rising slowly. "I'm Alice."

"It's nice to meet you." I let go of Lucy's hand—albeit reluctantly— and go to shake Alice's hand.

"And over there is Michelle, Lucy's mother. She's the best chef in miles."

"Hello, Kitty," Michelle says. "Come sit down. Lunch is ready." She pours the soup into a large tureen and Lucy lifts it and takes it to the table.

"Come, sit here," Alice says, indicating the seat across from her. "I hope you like hot and sour soup. Michelle makes the best."

"Because you have been sick," Michelle replies as she brings over a large soup ladle to place into the tureen. She turns back to the counter as I seat myself. Lucy pulls out the chair next to me and settles in. We share a brief smile, and I feel Lucy's foot next to mine under the table.

The soup is passed, and it smells delicious. I ladle out a generous portion for myself, and Lucy's mom places a plate of buns on the table, and some butter. My stomach growls, and I flush.

"Eat up," Michelle urges. "You are hungry. And after, Lucy can show you the farm. She told us how you love the blackberries, and I think we still have some left."

I take a spoonful of the soup, and it is quite possibly the best soup I have ever tasted. I don't even have words. It has beef in it, and vegetables, and other things I don't recognize. The flavor of it feels like it burns my tongue, yet it invokes a sort of craving, and I feel like I could eat a lot more.

"This is amazing."

"Have a bun—it'll help cool your mouth down," Lucy says, passing me the plate. I take a bun and place it at the side of the bowl.

"I'll give you the recipe," Michelle says. "It is very easy to make. Then you can make it for Lucy."

Oh. I know my cheeks are warming now, and maybe I can blame it on the spiciness of the soup.

"Mama," Lucy chides, and she looks down at the table, not meeting anyone's gaze. I wonder if she's embarrassed by me, or just generally embarrassed. I'm starting to guess that she's queer, and it seems like her mother and friend also know. What did she say about me to them?

"I'm just being helpful, Ming Nhon," Michelle says.

"Lucy doesn't often have visitors," Alice adds helpfully.

"I do so," Lucy retorts, though quietly.

I rest my free hand on her leg, under the table, out of the way of prying gazes. She rests her hand on mine and squeezes lightly.

"Not often," Michelle says. She turns to me. "So we are very happy to meet you, Kitty."

I can feel the awkwardness radiating off Lucy, and it does suddenly seem that she's younger than her years. I remember my parents behaving similarly whenever I had a boy over, before I told them that I liked girls.

"I'm glad to meet you all too," I say. "I must admit, though, I've never been on a farm before. This is all very new to me." I hope my interest pleases them, that I'm not just some silly city girl. I feel completely out of my element, but I need to push through.

"I can show you around after lunch," Lucy says, and it seems that she is happy to have the conversation directed away from her. I'm glad to oblige if it makes her happy. "We have greenhouses and fields, and though we don't raise animals, we have a few around the place."

"My dogs, mostly," Alice adds. "Goldie and Max spend more time here than at home." She laughs and Lucy smiles.

"They're sweethearts," she says.

"I'd love to see everything," I reply.

"Then you will," Lucy says. She turns and smiles at me, and for a moment I feel like we're the only two people in the room.

❖

I've never been so glad to have a meal over with. Kitty's charming and kind to Mama and Alice, but I know they are watching both of us, knowing that I'm interested in her, and just maybe, she's interested in me too. I don't know if they'll try to play matchmaker, or at least not any more than they already have. It's like being a kid again, having your every move dictated, or at least observed.

We take our bowls to the sink, and I lead Kitty outside, away from the matchmakers. "I'm sorry they're so nosy," I say.

"It's sweet," Kitty says. "And it's lovely that they're so supportive of you. My parents aren't quite like that, I'm afraid. They keep thinking this is a phase for me." She rolls her eyes. "It's been the longest phase. I knew years before I told anyone."

"Me too. Mama figured it out before I could tell her, but she's never minded. And neither did Alice. I've known her since I was a kid. She's always helped us on the farm, even back when my father was with us."

Kitty turns solemn. "I'm sorry that you've lost him."

"It was a long time ago," I say. "Heart attack."

"Still, it's hard to lose someone, especially close family."

I can only nod. My dad was as dedicated a farmer as there ever was, and there's always a twinge of sadness when I think about him.

"Oh my God, what is that?" Kitty has wandered ahead of me, and she's stopped at the greenhouse door, looking up at a metal hummingbird that hangs above it, one of my creations.

"It's a hummingbird," I reply.

Kitty turns to me. "I can see that," she says, sounding amused yet annoyed. "But who made it, and how? I've never seen anything like it."

I step past her and pull open the door of the greenhouse, feeling suddenly shy.

"Me, but it's no big deal." I move into the greenhouse, into the warmth and the smell of dirt and plants and fruit and deliciousness. The hummingbird was an experiment, and I'm still not entirely happy with it. It feels clunky to me, not delicate enough to evoke a real hummingbird.

"No big deal?" Kitty echoes as she follows. "I had no idea you were a sculptor too."

I turn back to her, shrug. "It's not very good."

Kitty's mouth drops open. Somehow she's even more beautiful to me when she looks so surprised. Her brilliant eyes widen, and there's a hint of color over her cheekbones.

"It is so."

"Is not." I can't help the reply, partly true and partly impish. I'm not comfortable with Kitty being so focused on me, just me. I'm not used to it, not used to being anyone's center of attention. I've always been able to slide into the background.

"Is too." Kitty sticks her tongue out. "People would kill for the kind of talent you have," she says. "Trust me on that." She glances back toward the hummingbird.

"It's a hobby," I finally say, walking into the cluster of blackberry bushes that are nearly picked bare. "Just that. The farm is the real work."

Kitty catches up to me. "It's just as impressive," she says, but as I'd planned, she gets distracted by the blackberries and our discussion changes direction. "Is that the rest?"

"That's definitely it for this season," I remark. I pull a small stack of punnets from a cubby nearby. "Want to help me pick the rest? Then we can have some, and you can take some home too."

Kitty takes a punnet from me and starts picking. "You know, I've never gotten to pick berries before," she says. "My parents aren't really outdoorsy people. Lots of big trips, Europe and stuff, but never anywhere farm-like. And no camping, at least not as a family. Too dirty, my mom always said." She rolls her eyes. "I would have loved a weekend camping trip instead of piano lessons. I did get a week of camp one year, though."

"You could camp here. We have a long stretch of fields, and there's a little coulee with a stream and a few trees." I used to hang out there a lot as a kid, when I needed some time alone. No one's ever been there with me. I'm surprised at myself for offering this to her, when I've never offered it to anyone else. Not even Mama, not Dad, not Alice. Not any school friends, not that I had many. It's my special quiet spot.

I want to take back the invitation, wondering at my own easy comfort with Kitty, especially when we hardly know each other. These days, I have many casual acquaintances, mostly customers of the farmers' market, but this is different. *She's* different. I can't quite pin down exactly why.

Kitty sets down one full punnet and starts on a second. I've barely come close to filling mine. "I'd probably drive you nuts. I'm a city girl, through and through. I'd be awake all night wondering if a bear was going to come into the tent."

I chuckle. "Not too many bears around here, at least not often. You'd be more likely to have a coyote visit you. Anvil optional."

Kitty laughs, a real belly laugh, one where her head falls back. "We'd best bring ourselves a roadrunner, then," she quips. "Know where to get one?"

"Acme?"

An image pops into my mind of a metal roadrunner, its feathers made of blades from that old combine out back, the one I've been scavenging from for my current work-in-progress, in the larger outbuilding. I can see it now—the blades, and using other scrap to curve around, make a body. An old steel pipe for the neck.

"What are you thinking?" Kitty pops me out of my reverie.

"A roadrunner," I reply. "Out of scrap."

"I'd love to see that," she says. "We could make it our camp guardian."

"It'd scare off the coyotes."

Kitty laughs. "I hope so."

I can't get it out of my head now. Kitty and me. Camping. Sharing a tent. Sharing…more?

CHAPTER SEVEN

L ucy's cheeks are a bit flushed, and I wonder why, because I'm pretty sure a metal roadrunner sculpture is not what's doing that. I know that my own flush isn't about a sculpture. Or about perimenopausal hot flashes. I'm not quite at that point at thirty-eight. I know what's causing it, and I hope that's what's affecting Lucy too.

Her proximity, her movements, her very being is tantalizing to me. I want to touch her, I want to kiss her, I want…I want her to want me too. I want to be certain.

But of course, nothing is certain. Even law isn't certain, but I can always make an argument. Is that what I need here? An argument? A way to convince Lucy to take a chance on me?

I turn back to the berries and top up my second punnet. The bushes are nearly picked clean, and I know that's going to be it for blackberries for a long while. I turn my head, ready to say as much to Lucy, and she's right there, barely a step away. I didn't even hear her approach.

"Almost done," I manage to stutter out. Barely. My voice is uncharacteristically rough, and my throat feels tight.

"There's not much left," Lucy agrees, but it's a distracted reply. She reaches up, her hand slightly dusty with dirt and work-roughened, and her fingers hover a hairbreadth from my cheek. Her gaze meets mine, her dark eyes uncertain. I know my eyes mirror hers; I'm not certain either.

But there's one thing I'm becoming certain of. This proximity, this brief second, needs just a little push. And I can push.

I turn my cheek just enough that it brushes her fingers, and I lean into her touch. Her hand is warm, and her fingertips aren't as soft as mine, but it's just about perfect. She strokes her thumb over my cheekbone, and our gazes meet. The uncertainty is gone, and I can feel her breath on my face, a delicate caress over my skin that gives me tiny goose bumps. I lean into her touch even more, closing my eyes, taking a deep breath of her scent, of the greenhouse.

And then…her lips brush mine, tentative, gentle.

My eyes open and I step forward, melding our bodies into one, returning her kiss, deepening it. And she responds, her hand at my hip, keeping me there, the hand once on my cheek now sliding under my hair to the back of my neck. A statement if there ever was one, a possession. Our tongues are tangling, our mouths together, our chests and hips aligned. I don't want anything but her, anything but this moment, us here together. Everything else has faded.

I feel the tug on my shirt, then her hand under the hem, skating up my back, splaying between my shoulder blades, pressing me closer still. For someone so quiet, she's taken control, directing me, commanding me, and it makes me weak in the knees. I cling to her, my hands at her waist, fingers through the loops of her jeans, as she ravishes my mouth. This is so much, yet not enough. I need more.

Lucy seems to know somehow, to sense my need, my desperation, my arousal. I feel her fingers now on my belly, then at the button of my jeans, then at the zipper, drawing it downward. Her mouth leaves mine, and we're both panting, breathless.

"Tell me you want this," she says, her voice a gasp. Her lips are swollen from our kisses, and her cheeks are flushed, and she is gorgeous, more beautiful than ever. I've never wanted anything, anyone, more in my life than I do her, right this moment.

"Don't stop," I say, and I take her hand, directing her down into my pants, past my curls, to the wettest, hottest spot. Her fingers curl, stroking, and her hand is pressed to me, the jeans keeping things snug and tight. I drop my head to her shoulder as she strokes, and when she penetrates me, I feel like I am going to collapse, my knees shaking. She feels it, knows it, and she shifts me until we're at the edge of a row of plants, a metal rack behind me. Her fingers plunge in deeper, then out and in again, and I can feel the metal rails against my back, helping me stay upright.

I kiss her then, putting all my need and want into that touch. I'm sure I've soaked her hand and my jeans, and I can feel my end getting closer, nearer, coming to that precipice of pleasure that I've always loved. Then she moves her hand, rubbing against my clit while she's still plunging into me, and that's what it takes.

The orgasm is more than I've ever imagined, more than I've ever experienced. It goes on and on, and I lose any sense of my surroundings beyond her, beyond her body and her hand and her mouth. All I can feel is the pleasure and her.

When I open my eyes again, we're half crumpled against the rack. Lucy eases her hand out from my jeans, triggering a delicious twinge of pleasure, an aftershock.

I snake a hand out, around her waist, under her shirt. She's warm, incredibly warm. And this isn't enough. I want more. I want to be the one to make her come the way she made me.

❖

I did that to her. For her. And it was hot. More than I'd ever expected, ever even fantasized. Kitty's hand is under my shirt now and her touch is all I can focus on, all I want. She leans in close, her lips hovering over mine, her breath warm on my face, still quickened from her orgasm. I shift, feeling the dampness between my thighs, knowing I'm flushed, ready. I kiss her again, and it turns from tender to needy, devouring and delicious. Kitty nudges her leg between mine and it's easy to ride her, the friction hot as I rock against her thigh, the seam of my jeans as tantalizing as fingers in its pressure on my clit.

Kitty breaks the kiss to unbutton my shirt and push down my bra, baring my small breasts and pebbling nipples to her gaze. She dips her head, takes a nipple in her mouth, and that hot, wet sensation is more amazing than I'd ever expected. None of my previous girlfriends ever managed to make it so hot, to have my nipple become a conduit of pleasure to my sex the way Kitty has. Her teeth nip and scrape, her tongue laps and swirls, and then she moves to the other nipple and does the same, until both are swollen and reddened from her attentions. I keep rocking against her, my thighs clamped to her leg. It's a bit like being a teenager again, sneaking those stolen moments, those furtive orgasms.

She tears at my jeans, at the button, then the zipper, and then shoves her hand inside, no finesse, but I don't care. She's where I want her, where I need her, her fingers gliding over my clit, putting pressure and a slight pinch that makes me shudder.

I'm not sure how I'm still standing. She's holding me up, propping me up against the rack, and one of my hands is woven through her belt loops. Not that her jeans are staying put. They've sagged since she never did them up. I can see her tiny panties, rumpled and damp from my hand. And oh God, do I want her. I want her to come again for me, on my hand, on my mouth, again and again.

Kitty presses her fingers into me, the heel of her hand adding pressure on my clit, and I lose all sense of time and space, focusing on her hand, on those fingers, on that rocking against my most sensitive place. She curls her tongue around my nipple, then closes her mouth over it, and then I feel her teeth, harder than before, but it's pleasure, not pain.

And it's enough. More than enough to send me over the edge, coming against her hand, my knees shaking, my head falling onto her shoulder. I've never had it so good. And she drags it out, keeping her fingers in me, stroking, the heel of her hand slowly rocking against my clit. It's amazing, all the little aftershocks, all those pulses of feeling.

I don't ever want this to end. But I remember where we are, and the chances of Alice walking in on us. Or Mama. Even worse.

I lift my head from her shoulder. She smiles at me, and I feel a rush of affection, of lust, of perhaps something a little more. Though it's early, and we've only really just met. But does that make a difference? I don't know. It feels too early, yet not.

"I wasn't planning for that to be part of the tour," I say, straightening, taking her hand as she slides it out from my jeans.

Kitty's expression drops. "You didn't like it?"

"It was incredible," I assure her, and lean forward to drop a kiss on her lips. I take a glance behind us, back toward the greenhouse door. "I just don't want to have company."

Kitty flushes, a beautiful sight.

I let go of her hand, but not before dropping a kiss on her palm. I do up my jeans, straighten my bra and my shirt, and hope that I don't look like I've just had sex next to the blackberries. Kitty does the same, and even slightly rumpled, I think she looks even more gorgeous than she did earlier.

I take a moment to tidy up the punnets, putting the two full of blackberries aside. "We'll come back for those. Want to see more?"

Kitty giggles and the sound is warm, delightful, and surprisingly girlish. "I don't know if anything can top that."

Now it's my turn to flush. I shouldn't really, but I can't help it.

"We have vegetables too." I keep going, because if I don't, I'll want her again, and it's too soon. And Alice might come into the greenhouse. Kitty follows me down the rows, and I feel a tug on my belt loops.

"Just trying to keep up," she says, and I slow, letting her lean right up against me, her warmth delicious. We kiss again, but it's brief, a momentary touching.

I show her the rest of the greenhouse, and she's interested, but when she spots another of my sculptures, this one a pair of mice made from old motorcycle parts and some spare wire, all her attention is on them and away from the plants.

"I still can't believe you do these," she says, as she drops to one knee, looking more closely at the mice. They're not my best work—I probably should have shaped the old clunky carburetors more, made them more organic. One day I might make more of those, but these days, it's the dragon.

"Do you have more?" Kitty asks, rising to her feet. I look out toward the outbuilding, and I know I should just say yes, but…I don't know. Art is vulnerable, more vulnerable even than sex. It's judgment, definitely. Nothing like being called crazy when your art doesn't fit over someone's sofa, or doesn't look like a bunch of dogs playing poker, or Monet's water lilies. I used to put old parts together even when I was a kid, and my dad encouraged it, handing me little bits and pieces. He taught me to weld, against Mama's wishes. That was a boy's work, a man's work, she said. Not a girl's. But she doesn't mind it now. She knows I'm sensible and safe. Although she finds my sculptures quirky. Mind you, I've made her useful things as well. Fixed a few lamps, made her a bed frame when the cheap one failed. That sort of thing. But there's still that fear there, that bunch of nerves.

"Where'd you go?" Kitty asks, and I feel her hand on my cheek. I refocus, and she's looking a touch worried, a bit of a worry line forming between her eyebrows.

"Just thinking," I say, shrugging.

"About what?"

"Art." I take a deep breath. Time for the plunge. "Want to come see?"

Kitty's smile widens, brilliant. "Do I ever."

CHAPTER EIGHT

Lucy seems tentative, somehow worried. I'm not sure why, and I don't quite get it. Her art is incredible. I only wish I could be so creative. I've never been. Always too sensible, always too busy trying to do the right thing. Coloring between the lines. Making sure there were lines. But it's what makes me feel better, makes everything work out. It's safe, of course. And I've had other girlfriends who hated me being safe, but I can't help it.

"We'll head over there," Lucy says, pointing to a larger shed, or small barn, whatever it's called. To me it looks as big as a barn, but I'm just a city girl. Leaving the warmth of the greenhouse makes the outdoors feel chilly, even though it's late May and the weather is gorgeous. Lucy leads me to the shed with purpose, her hesitation of earlier seemingly gone. There's a padlock on the door, older and a bit worn, and the hardware on the door is starting to rust. The wear matches the weathered and gray look of the shed itself. She takes a set of keys from her pocket, flipping through until she finds the right one, and unlocks it, pulling the lock free and tugging the door open. It creaks and squeaks.

"I keep meaning to fix that," Lucy says.

"Better things to do?" I know what that's like, having to rush to finish something instead of taking care of the little things.

"Usually." She seems nervous again, a bit hesitant. She holds the door for me. "After you."

I step inside. There's a smell of oil, of something I can't quite place, maybe...metal? A bit like stepping into my car dealership's service area, I guess. But no smell of rubber. Lucy flicks on the light, and in front of me is a mass of twisted metal. I'm not sure what it's supposed to be, if anything. I feel like I should know.

There's a workbench along one wall, and more tools than I can ever identify, although I can recognize an anvil when I see one. I walk forward and reach out to touch one rounded piece on the work-in-progress in the middle of the shed. To me it looks a bit like a rib, since it's one of several in a row. It's mostly rusted, but I can see where something has been grinding on it, showing through to the metal. And there are marks, maybe solder?

"What is it?"

Lucy steps up next to me and runs her fingers over several ribs. "Not much yet," she says, "but one day, it hopefully is a dragon. I have a lot to do, though. The cleaning and grinding of the pieces takes a while, and then I have to weld it into place."

I'm in awe looking at all her work. I wouldn't even know where to start. "Where do you find all this material?"

"I know a lot of farmers," she says, "and there are a lot of old machines rusting in the fields." She chuckles. "I'm a bit of a one-woman cleanup crew." She points out a stack of metal bars, some rusted, some not. "Those are old plowshares, and they'll be part of the wings, I think. If it works out."

I can't picture it. And I think she knows it.

"It's hard to see," she says, "but it'll get there." She grabs a couple of bars, then takes what looks like a sharp blade from the top of the workbench. "This one's an old scythe," she says, handling it carefully. It's rusted. She lays down a few bars, then the scythe end, and it curls over in a neat arc. "The blade is the end edge of the wing," she says, "and with multiples of these, it'll be like a bat's wing with its bony ridges."

"How do you think of all these things?"

Lucy replaces the scythe on the workbench and shrugs. "I just do. Always have." She wipes her hands on her jeans, leaving a bit of a rusty smear. "It passes the time, especially in the off-season. Though we do grow some things all through the winter."

Lucy's work seems much more interesting than my own. I do like being a lawyer, but there's something about working with your hands, making something that you can see, something that you can eat and enjoy…It's so much more substantial than paper shuffling, signing contracts, and placating clients.

I move around the central mass of metal and spot a few smaller sculptures hidden behind, resting at the far wall. "What else do you have?" I ask, heading closer. I kneel down, resting a knee on the wooden slat floor. The light isn't as good over here. The sculpture closest to me is small, rounded, but it has a head, a body, legs. It's somewhat curled up, and when I carefully shift it, I can see the triangular ears, made of what look like tiny jags of a thin sheet of metal. There's a rounded head, a small, somewhat triangular-shaped nose, and thin wire.

It's a cat! A cute little metal cat, made of metal bits—I can see a few screws, a couple of old wrenches, and other parts I can't identify—and curled up as if in sleep. I love it.

The light's blocked, and I look up.

"I wasn't sure of a home for that one," Lucy says. She's smiling, but her face is in shadow, and I can only really tell by her tone of voice. "But I think I know where it needs to go now."

I rise to my feet, coming face to face with Lucy. "Where will you put it?"

"With a kitty of her own, of course."

It takes me a second to clue in, but when I do get it, I'm grinning. "Really?"

"Really." Lucy bends down to pick up the cat. I reach out for it and she puts it into my hands.

It's heavy. Really heavy. Like, iron doorstop heavy. I have to hold it with both hands against my abdomen to keep from dropping it.

"We'll take it to your car," she says. "You wouldn't want to forget it."

"It'd be hard to miss," I quip, and Lucy chuckles. We head outside and over to my car. Once we're there, I realize a problem. "I can't get at my keys."

"Which pocket?"

"Front right."

Lucy digs into my pocket, and the touch of her on me again warms me to the core. Our gazes meet, and I can tell she's thinking the same thing. Her face is close to mine, but she hesitates, her gaze flitting up to the farmhouse. She gives a small smile. "Maybe later."

She hits the unlock button on my keys and the car beeps, its lights flashing.

"Back door, I'll put it on the seat," I suggest.

"Better on the floor, it might get the upholstery dirty."

I set the cat on the floor mat, then straighten, wiping my hands on my jeans. They leave rusty smears too, but I really don't care. This is my day off, after all.

"Ming Nhon!" I hear a voice from behind us, and Lucy turns. She says something in Chinese to her mother, who smiles and replies in the same language. Lucy turns to me.

"My mother wants to know if you'd like to stay for dinner," she says. I'm not sure what to say. I have feelings for her, and we have spent a lot of time together today, but I don't want to impose. "It's not crashing our party," Lucy assures me. "Mama loves to cook."

"I will, then," I reply. "What are you making?" I ask Lucy's mom. If it's as good as what she made for lunch, then I'm game.

Lucy's mom rattles off a list, but of course, it's not in English. Lucy smiles. "She doesn't know the English names for the dishes," she says, "but it's a good selection of Chinese food. And my favorite dish again. Shanghai-style rice cakes."

"I'd love to stay."

I'm so glad Kitty is staying. I knew our afternoon was starting to come to a close, and I didn't know how to encourage her to stick around. We are only just getting to know each other, and there's no way I want to come across as too needy, too wanting. Rushing only gets you in too deep, and then it hurts even more when it's over. But I love seeing her follow Mama into the house. Like she's a part of the family.

Once inside, in the kitchen, we sit down with cups of tea from the pot Mama has on the stove. It's a bit stronger than usual as it's been brewing for a while, but it's delicious. Mama putters around as she always does, taking out pans and a cutting board and her favorite knife, and starts putting greens and vegetables on the counter to prepare. It's a routine I've seen thousands of times over the years.

Kitty hops up. "Can I help?"

"No need," Mama says.

"I really would like to," Kitty replies, and I can see her hands clasped together, almost like a little kid at Christmas, or in a toy store wanting just that one toy.

"You are a guest," Mama adds.

"I think she wants to cook too," I say to Mama in Cantonese. "She might really like it." Mama turns to me and nods.

"You cook?" she asks Kitty.

"Not as much as I would like," she says. "But I'd love to help out. I used to work in a restaurant kitchen when I was a student."

"Okay." Mama smiles and shows her the knife, and the cutting board, and the carrots she has piled by the sink. "These have to be cut in small sticks." She moves her fingers out to about an inch and a half.

Kitty grins. "I can definitely do that."

She sets to work, and I stay in my seat, sipping my tea. Mama works on her portion of the meal, and she and Kitty together are quite the team, rarely getting in each other's way and moving with a synchronicity that amazes me. In some way, it's like Kitty's always been here. That warms me to the core.

I drink more tea, and Kitty preps more vegetables at Mama's instruction. But it's when the wok comes out that Kitty comes alive, watching Mama intensely at each step, asking questions, and listening carefully to the answers. Mama shows her what to start with, how to cook properly in the wok, when to stir, when to add the next part of the dish, when to add a sauce. I remember learning those lessons myself when I was younger, standing on an old wooden stepstool to reach the stovetop when I was barely old enough for school. But it worked. I can cook all sorts of things now, though I don't often get to. Mama doesn't relinquish control of her kitchen very often.

"Go call Alice," Mama says to me. "She is coming to dinner tonight too."

I rise and go to the house phone, an old push-button phone that hangs on the wall, an incongruity in this age of cellphones. The plastic handset was once white but is now beige, and it's started to crack. I pick it up, dial, and Alice answers after two rings.

"Dinner's almost ready," I tell her.

"Fantastic," she says. "I'll be over in a few. Just have to get Goldie settled. And my son is coming. You remember Adam, right? He stopped by today on his way back down south to Lethbridge."

"I'm sure we'll have more than enough," I say, looking at Mama's progress. She has Kitty at the wok now, stirring with a pair of chopsticks. "Kitty's here for dinner too."

"Lovely," Alice says. "See you soon!"

"Alice is bringing her son," I announce. Mama eyes the food on the go.

"We should have enough. Unless he still eats enough for two."

Kitty laughs.

"As a teenager, he ate more than all of us," I tell her.

"I had cousins like that," Kitty says. "Two or three helpings each, and if you didn't get enough on your first plate, you were out of luck."

"Boys." Mama shakes her head. "They are all the same." She

laughs. "But you ate a lot too when you were younger, Ming Nhon," she tells me.

"I was growing," I reply.

Kitty looks at me, puzzled.

"Ming Nhon is my Chinese name," I explain. "Lucy is my English name. It was much easier for me at school that way."

"Which do you prefer?" she asks, looking a bit confused.

"You can call me Lucy," I reply. I like my English name on her lips, coming from her mouth, in her voice. I'd tell her that, but with Mama around, I'd best not. I'm pretty sure that Mama always understands more English than she lets on.

Kitty looks like she wants to ask me more, but we're interrupted by the entry of Alice and her son Adam. He's tall and broad-shouldered, far larger than anyone I've ever known, and far larger than his mother. Alice told me once that his father had also been a giant of a man, before he'd passed from a heart attack. She joked that Adam hadn't gotten any of her genes. They come into the kitchen, Adam following behind her, towering over her. He's dressed casually, his ever-present flannel shirt with its sleeves rolled up. His forearms have scars from his work as a farrier, but he never seems to mind them showing. I have a few smaller ones myself from the welding, but I always hate people looking.

"Almost ready now," Mama says as she and Kitty take care of things. I get down the plates, and Mama leaves Kitty at the wok and picks out chopsticks for everyone. I grab a few forks as well, just in case. Chopsticks sometimes don't cut it when you're hungry and just want to inhale your food before you pass out from starvation. I'm feeling a bit like that now.

"Who's this new face?" Adam asks, holding out his hand to Kitty.

"Kitty Kerr," she says, taking his hand.

"Adam Kinchloe," he says.

"He looks like no relation," Alice jokes as she slides into her usual place at the table, "but he really is."

Adam grins. "How do you know all these lovely ladies, Kitty?"

"Through Lucy," she says, her gaze moving to mine, a smile gracing her lips. Those lips that I'd just kissed a few hours ago. I have a hunger now, but it's not just about food. "I bought her blackberries."

Adam grins and raises an eyebrow at me. "Lucy's blackberries get all the girls."

"Oh, stop, you," Alice says, lightly smacking his hip, the closest thing to her. "You can't have all the girls."

"Oh, I know."

Adam pulls out a chair and settles in next to his mother.

"Long time no see," I say. "You need to travel a little less."

"A farrier's work is never done," Adam says with a chuckle. "But I'll always come back for Mrs. Shen's food."

"Not mine?" Alice asks.

"Yours too, of course, Mom," he replies. "But no one makes Chinese food like Mrs. Shen."

My mouth is watering as Mama scoops the contents of the wok into a large serving bowl. It looks like a mix of vegetables, and I catch a whiff of teriyaki sauce. Kitty carries another bowl to the table, and it has my favorite again, Shanghai rice cakes. Mama knows it's one of Alice's favorites too. And Adam's, helpfully. We might run out if Kitty takes a liking to it too.

Kitty slides into the seat next to me, and it's a bit snug round the table with this many. Snug enough that her thigh presses against mine, and I certainly won't complain. She sets the bowl down in front of me.

"Guests first," I say.

"Don't mind if I do." Adam reaches over the table and snags the bowl, then scoops a generous portion. He hands it back to Kitty. "Take some now or forever hold your peace."

Kitty laughs, and it's a full laugh, one that, to me, rings like bells. "Thanks for the warning. I bet your mom spent most of her money feeding you, didn't she?"

"You know it," Alice retorts with a chuckle. "Now he gets to feed himself, mostly. It's done wonders for my savings."

"You eat your vegetables," Mama says, setting the other bowl down by his elbow. She goes back to the counter and scoops rice out of the rice cooker and into a third bowl. This time, when she brings it back, she takes her seat. Adam helps himself to the vegetables and to the rice, and when he's done, his plate is heaped. Fortunately, Mama always makes plenty.

I help myself to the vegetables and to a good portion of the rice cakes, and a smaller portion of the rice. Kitty has helped herself to everything, and I watch as she takes her first bite of the rice cakes.

"Oh my God," she says, bringing her hand to her mouth as she chews. Her eyes close, like she's savoring the bite. She opens her eyes. "That's so good—I'm spoiled for anything else."

"Good." Mama grins. "Eat up, everyone."

I start in on my food, but most of my attention is on Kitty.

❖

I don't want to move from my seat after dinner, and then when I half rise to offer to help with cleanup, Mrs. Shen shoos me back to my seat, so I lean back. I should have worn looser jeans. I had no idea I'd end up eating so well.

"I guarantee you'll gain ten pounds," Adam says, noticing my contentment. "The food here is amazing."

I nod. Lucy rolls her eyes. "She's gorgeous just as she is," she says to Adam.

"Of course she is," Adam replies. "So, Luce, how's the project going? Have you showed it to Kitty?" He leans my way and lowers his voice to a stage whisper. "I taught her all she knows about welding."

"You did not, you big liar," Lucy says, snapping him with the tea towel she's holding. "Dad did, and you just helped refine it later."

Adam grins, his eyes twinkling. "That still gets you, even now. Good. So, how's the project?"

"Going," Lucy replies. I think of the scythes spread out with the plowshares. It still blows my mind. I can just picture it, but I know what I'm imagining will be nothing compared to the real thing when Lucy finishes the work.

"Show me later?" he asks.

"You'll see it when it's done," she says, as if she's said this to him a million times before.

"You never let me see it," he fusses, though it's still in jest. I've never met anyone whose demeanor is so jokey all the time.

"No one sees it until I'm done," Lucy says. "That's the rule." She glances at me, and I get the message. Hush-hush.

I sit back, schooling my features as I might do at work. Lucy turns back to the dishes, drying as her mother washes. Alice flits around them, putting away dishes, wiping the counter. I get the impression that this is an everyday thing for the three of them.

"What do you do, Kitty?" Adam asks. It's a question I'm used to getting—my parents' friends always ask, the last girlfriend I had asked that first thing…I realize suddenly that it happens a lot. And always from people who are truly more interested in money than in who I am. Lucy never asked.

"Corporate law," I reply. Short and to the point. Most people stop there. It's rather dull in comparison to criminal law, or even family law.

Contracts and clients, not murderers or full-on Jerry Springer family meltdowns.

Adam nods. "Enjoy it?"

I nod back. "Yup."

"Cool."

"Tell me about being a farrier," I say, trying to keep the conversation going. I have no doubt that it's a far more interesting profession than mine. Just all those horses are more interesting.

"I travel a lot," Adam said. "I trained in England, then ended up coming back here. I like it better than the UK. Less rain. Although sometimes I wish there wasn't any snow. There's always lots of work, though, so I can't complain. Have you ever seen a farrier at work?"

I shake my head. "City girl," I admit.

He launches into a quick rundown of the basics of being a farrier—shoeing horses, trimming their hooves—and how he learned about their physiology. "Nothing wrong with being a city slicker, though."

"Now I know." I feel a bit sheepish. There's so much I don't know about being on a farm. I'll always be a city slicker.

Lucy plops down at the table next to me. "Don't make her feel bad," she says to Adam. "I didn't know what a farrier was either."

Adam shrugs. "Just being educational."

Alice comes over to the table and gives Adam a gentle punch on the arm. "You're talking too much." It's Adam's turn to look sheepish.

"Can't help myself." He stands. "I'll leave you ladies to gab, and I'll go take care of the chores before I turn in. Have to be on the road early tomorrow." He smiles at me, then hugs his mother and bends to kiss Mrs. Shen's cheek. "Fantastic supper, Mrs. Shen," he says. "And great to meet you, Kitty. See you around."

Alice walks him out, then returns.

"That boy. Always looking to show off." She shakes her head, but I can see that she's amused.

Lucy glances at me. "Mama, I'm going to show Kitty around the house."

"Okay." Lucy's mom is putting a kettle on the stove. "Do you want tea?"

"We'll make some later," Lucy says, rising. I rise with her. We leave the great room and kitchen, and Lucy takes me to the foot of the stairs.

"This feels like I'm back in school," I whisper. "Can we go up to your room and play dolls?"

Lucy laughs and takes my hand. "I wasn't thinking about dolls, but I might have a couple you can look at. Anyway, I just wanted some more time. I've been thinking."

"About what?"

Lucy tugs on my hand and gets me up the stairs in a quick jog. There's a long landing at the top and an older wooden rail of carved spindles. Along the wall are a series of bookcases, all stuffed full. I stop in my tracks. I've never been able to pass by a bookshelf. It used to irritate the heck out of my mother, who would be embarrassed when I'd go through the bookshelves of all her friends and all our relatives. I found some interesting books that way. And it was something to do while the grownups talked.

Lucy tugs on my hand but I don't move. She turns back. "What is it?"

"I just have to look."

"Oh." She smiles and releases my hand. "Go ahead. I have a hard time not stopping too. But I warn you, at least half of them are in Chinese."

That doesn't deter me in the least. I skim my gaze over the top shelf, walking slowly along the line as I do. There are some paperbacks, familiar titles popping out now and then, mysteries and thrillers. Lucy has crouched down by one bookcase and has pulled out a larger paperback book covered in a dull plastic. I'm curious, but there are more books to look at. I pull out one that seems different; it's hardcover and looks old, no writing apparent on the wide spine. I flip it open, and Chinese characters look up at me. I replace the book and continue on. There are a few romance novels tucked at the end of one row, and I pull those out. They're not titles or authors I know, not that I get much time to read for pleasure these days, but I take a look.

"I think you'll like this one," Lucy says. I replace the books and turn. She's holding the book with the plastic cover.

"What is it?" The light's a bit dim up here and it glints off the plastic, obscuring the cover.

"Come on, let's go relax, and I'll show you."

I follow her down the hall to a closed door. She turns the knob. "It's not the tidiest up here," she says. "Just to warn you."

"I don't mind." I really don't. I'm feeling almost completely relaxed, and more at home than I've felt anywhere aside from my own apartment.

Lucy flicks on the light and I follow her into her room. It's of a good size, though it's under the eaves, so the ceiling slants on both sides, down to a half wall. The wallpaper is a delicate rose pattern on white, and there's hardwood flooring, though it's mostly covered by a large worn rug with oriental patterning. Under the eaves on one side is her bed, with a brass frame, covered in a mixed pile of quilts, with multiple pillows plumped at one end. She has a long set of bureau drawers under the other side of the eaves, and I spot a small door that must be a closet. Clean laundry is folded and resting on top of the drawers, piled high. And in the other free spaces along the wall, there are stacks of books. One stack looks to be all about farming, another about animals, and more are various kinds of fiction.

Lucy toes off her shoes and pushes them aside. "Make yourself at home."

I already am. She might think it's messy, but to me, this space is cozy, and the bed is inviting and looks incredibly soft. The clutter makes it feel lived in, real. It's rather like how I'd pictured my own room as a child, my dream room. There's even a small lamp clipped to the bed frame. I toe off my shoes and join Lucy as she sits on the bed, scooting up to lean against the pillows. She turns on the lamp, and now I can see the cover of the book she's holding: *Chinese Cooking.*

There's a delectable stir-fry on the cover, and even though we've only just eaten, I feel hungry again already. Lucy pats the bed next to her. "Come on, come sit." I put a knee on the bed and crawl up to her, turning to sit next to her, leaning against the pillows. I can feel the brass rails even through the pillows, but it's not uncomfortable. Lucy shifts, aligning her legs with mine, and her elbow brushes my side. She opens the book.

"I learned to cook with this one," she said, "and Mama brought this one with her when she came from China." She flips to the copyright page. It's in English and Chinese. "Or she had it sent over. Anyway, this book is a gold mine."

We flip through, and she pauses on a page that has a recipe for simmered fish halves. "This is one of the first ones I learned," she says. "My dad told me that his family used to make it all the time because you could find the ingredients locally, even when Chinese food was really unusual."

"It looks delicious." And it did. Fish, garlic, soy sauce, ginger, green onion.

"My great-grandmother would make it with rainbow trout, because the rivers here have the species. It was popular at the restaurant."

"Restaurant?"

Lucy smiles. "Family business, or at least it was. Every small town used to have a Chinese-Western restaurant, and part of my dad's family, the Chinese part, were the owners here. The building is still in town, but it's not a Chinese restaurant anymore."

"So you have chefs in your family." I wish I knew that much about my family, that they did something interesting, but my parents had never really been forthcoming. Just being here, I've seen such a difference. It's not that my parents weren't around—they were—but they spent a lot of time working, and less time doing family things.

"More than a few cooks," Lucy says, "though a lot of it was by necessity. It was either that or a laundry, and I'm pretty sure a restaurant is not as difficult."

She flips the page. "Stir-fry shrimp with vegetables. Another fairly easy dish, although there's a lot of prep work. It's quick. Mama makes this one a lot."

"You're making me hungry," I admit.

"Me too," Lucy says. She puts an arm over my shoulder. "We could go raid the fridge."

"I can wait a bit." It's too nice, sitting here with Lucy.

"After they've gone to bed," Lucy says, a mischievous glint in her eyes. "Hopefully Adam doesn't come back and take all the leftovers with him."

"He'd do that?"

Lucy chuckles. "Not so much anymore, but when he was a teenager? All the time. Mama used to scold him, say that she wasn't a restaurant."

"Her food is good enough for one, better even," I remark. "I wish I had her skill."

"You kept up with her in there tonight," Lucy says. "You're no slouch."

"It's just been so long." My fingers itch to be back there, to be cutting and dicing and watching my creations come to fruition. My university days had been the time for that. I'd get home, after school and cooking at the restaurant, and I'd want to cook some more, experimenting with so many different foods. Sometimes I think I really should have become a chef, but it was too late even then. I was already in school for law, and I didn't want to waste my parents' money by dropping out. But oh, the food. I miss it. These days, it's mostly takeout. Lots of great places in the city, but even the most delicious takeout starts to pale when that's all you're having.

"What's stopping you?" Lucy asks.

"Work," I admit. As if to prove my point, my phone buzzes. Out of habit, I check it. Emails from the boss about Monday and our new client. I sigh. For a few hours, I'd almost completely forgotten about work.

Lucy takes my phone from my hand, places it on the nightstand. "Work can wait, can't it?"

"For now."

"Good." Lucy cups my chin, angles my head. Our gazes meet, and work is the last thing on my mind.

CHAPTER NINE

When Kitty talks about work, she seems to shut down, to pull back. She's the Kitty I first met, on her phone, her attention focused. It'd taken a blackberry to snap her out of it, but I don't have any blackberries right now, at least not with me. But I might be a perfect substitute. I want to see the happy Kitty, the relaxed Kitty. I've only known her a little while, but that Kitty seems to me to be her natural self.

"Think of blackberries," I murmur, and Kitty giggles. I capture her mouth with mine, and her giggles turn to a slight gasp and moan, and I swear she melts into my arms. She tastes sweet, and I can't get enough. We shift on the bed until she's beneath me, her jeans-clad legs around mine. Less clothes would be ideal, but right now, we're so perfect together that I don't want to interrupt this. I deepen the kiss, feel her fingers in my hair pulling me closer. I could lose myself in her, in her kiss.

When we finally part, we're both a bit breathless.

"Why is it like this?" Kitty asks, her voice barely above a whisper.

"I don't know," I answer honestly. "But it's amazing."

"It is." And then she kisses me again, and we're tugging at clothes, taking advantage of our privacy, of the closed door. Once her shirt is off, I break the kiss and bend to her breasts, pushing down her bra so I can tongue her nipples. I take my time, first one and then the other, then again, loving as she arches against me, her nipples pebbling. She's unbuttoning my shirt as best she can, tugging it away, but I don't stop. I trace a line down her stomach, to the waistband of her jeans, undoing the button, pulling down the zipper, tugging them down. She squirms and tries to help and I manage to take them off, tossing them to the floor. And she's there before me, utterly ravishing. Her lips are swollen, parted, and she's looking hungrily at me. I hook my fingers in her panties and tug them down her legs. Once free, she parts her legs for me and I make my way back up, taking tiny tastes and nips of her skin as I go. I pause above her dark curls, dropping a kiss there, watching her.

"Don't stop," Kitty says hoarsely, reaching out to me, her fingers brushing my cheeks, then sliding into my hair. I rest my hands on her thighs, my thumbs resting on the hollows of her inner thighs, lightly stroking. The skin is damp, and I part her lips there, bending to taste her.

She's better than blackberries, better than any of the fruit in the greenhouse. I lick and tease her and she gasps and quivers and I can't get enough.

Just as she seems to be coming toward orgasm, I leave her sex and move upward once more. She accepts my kiss with hunger, and before I know it, she's moved, putting me beneath her, pushing my shirt off my shoulders, unhooking my bra. She pulls it off, throws it away, takes my breasts in her hands, bringing them together and up, her thumbs moving over my nipples, bringing them to peaks. She tastes one, then the other, echoing my earlier movements, until her teeth graze them and she sucks hard. I try to keep from making too much noise, but I know that I did groan before I could stop myself. She nibbles at me, and though I've never come from it before, I just might now. She's nudging my thighs apart with her knee, and it doesn't take long before she's pulling my jeans down and off, my plain black briefs with them.

She cups my sex with her hand, her fingers resting against me. "Tell me what you'd like," she says, bending forward to drop a kiss on each nipple. I put my hand over hers, pressing her fingers past my curls, into me. She moves her thumb over my clit and her fingers inside me press into my most sensitive spot. I see stars behind my closed eyes, and I'm coming before I can stop myself. It's so quick, so easy, so unexpected. The orgasm washes over me, leaving tingles and a hum throughout my entire body.

When I finally open my eyes, Kitty is hovering above me, stroking my sex still, gently, triggering little sparks.

"You haven't come yet."

"No," Kitty says, "but I'm close from just seeing you come."

"Are you?" I slide my hand down her hip, in between her legs. She's drenched, and my fingers slide into her easily. I can feel her tightening around my fingers, and I stroke her as her hips rock against my hand. Her head drops to my shoulder, her breath heating my neck. She's making little gasping noises, and it's making me wet for her again, and I want more.

"Don't stop," she says, reaching down to rub her clit as I stroke her. "More."

She's tightening, clenching, quivering around me and she lets out a breathy *Oh* as she comes, stiffening against me briefly before she sags, boneless. We're sweaty and breathless, and I wouldn't have it any other way.

❖

I don't want to move, but I don't want to crush Lucy. I reluctantly shift off her, but she holds me close, and I settle in next to her, our legs entwined.

"That was incredible," Lucy says. I nod against her shoulder. A glow catches my eye and I lift my head to see her alarm clock on the bedside table. It's getting late. I don't want to go, but I don't think I should stay overnight. What would her mother think?

I shift, starting to get up.

"Don't go," Lucy says, catching my hand. "It's late. Stay."

"I don't want it to be awkward."

"It won't be. Trust me."

I settle back down with Lucy, though I can't imagine how it won't be awkward in the morning. "Your mom won't be mad?"

Lucy shakes her head. "Not at all. Not that I do this often," she adds. "Or at all. But she likes you, and I'm sure she'd be happy to see me with someone."

Being with her is a new idea, but it's one that I like. I can picture us together, spending time together. Cooking. Eating. Curled up in bed together like we are now. I want to take her to my place too, to cook her a fancy meal, have a romantic night.

I tell her my plan, and Lucy kisses me. "You cook all the time?"

"I...well, I used to," I reply, realizing as I speak that I haven't truly cooked in a very long time. I keep meaning to, but coming home so late from work, I have no energy for it. Cooking tonight, with her mom, was the first time in so, so long. I want more of that, want to be creating.

"You should do it more often."

"I should."

"Have you ever considered working at a restaurant?" she asks. "A really nice one?"

I shake my head. Never. It wasn't even an idea when I was growing up. A good job, a steady one, after a full university education. The expectation had never wavered. Cooking was an indulgence, if anything. Working in the restaurant was a stopgap job, shift work to fit around my classes.

"I've always wanted a restaurant," she says, "even though my dad's family struggled to move on from the restaurant in town to do something easier."

"Why don't you?"

"I don't know much about restaurants, and there's the farm to look after. We have help, but it's still hard work. A restaurant is full-time work and then some."

I lie back against the soft mass of pillows, looking up to the slanted ceiling and its delicately patterned wallpaper. I can imagine Lucy bringing in a case of vegetables, imagine myself prepping and cooking, and even imagine her mom joining us. Restaurants are a lot of work. One of my first corporate clients was a restaurant owner who had franchised his operation. Supply orders, staffing, liquor, licenses… it was overwhelming.

"It really is. There are so many things to worry about, so much to do. What sort of food would you have?"

"A mix of things," Lucy replies. Her fingers move through my hair, caressing, a movement that seems unconscious. "The restaurant my family ran had mostly heavier fried foods for their Chinese section, and then stuff like hot turkey sandwiches and fries. You'd be lucky to get a salad or anything green. I'd make a nod to those, of course, because they're classic, but I'd stretch the menu, make it more interesting. Challenge people with things like bird's nest soup, maybe. Or with lotus root salad. Give them new flavors to go with the old. Ginger beef for the diehards, though." She chuckles. "Even though it was invented in Calgary."

"It was?"

"Not a classic dish at all, but a good one."

"I've always liked it. Take-out Chinese is more of a staple than I'd like to admit."

"How come?"

"No time to make my own."

"You work a lot." She tweaks a lock of my hair to show that she's not judging. Her voice is gentle.

"I do."

"Maybe I should come distract you with blackberries more often," she teases. "Or maybe we should open up a restaurant together."

"It'd be crazy."

Lucy chuckles again. "But a fun crazy."

Even as we doze off, I can't stop thinking about it. Cooking tonight was so much fun, and I wish I could do it more. I know I could run a restaurant, but I can't change careers. Not now. I'm too close to my goal. That partnership…I can taste it.

Chapter Ten

I wake the next morning early as I usually do, but I can tell that something is different even before I open my eyes. The birds are chirping, and I can hear Mama shuffling down the hallway from the bathroom, same as ever. But the bed's warmer, and my leg is pinned down. I open my eyes.

Kitty's hair is strewn across the pillow, and she's deeply asleep, her lips barely parted, the tension that's usually in her features relaxed. Gorgeous as the rising sun that slants through the window. I try to keep myself still, but now that I'm awake, I desperately have to pee. I inch my leg out from under hers as slowly as I can. She doesn't wake, but I'm on the side of the bed with the wall, and the footboard is high enough that it'd be incredibly awkward to clamber over. I draw back the covers on my side and try to inch my way down the bed and to stretch over her legs. But the bed squeaks and shudders, and her eyes snap open just as I'm nearly straddling her.

"Sorry," I say as her eyes widen, then relax. She glances around her, seeming to get her bearings. "Didn't mean to wake you."

She rubs her eyes, yawns. "No problem. What time is it?" She scrabbles for her phone, and I finish my trip to the floor and hand it to her.

"Five thirty. It's early yet."

Kitty nods, but when she unlocks her phone screen, her eyes widen again, and she pinches her lips shut, her brows drawing together. "Dammit." She pushes aside the sheets and rises, still naked, just like me. "I'm going to have to get back."

"Breakfast first?" I offer. Kitty looks up at me, away from her phone, and smiles. She leans forward and gives me a gentle kiss.

"If it's quick. It's a bit of a drive back for me."

"Quick, definitely." I'd love for her to stay, but I know that's a lot to ask so early. My bladder twinges again, more urgently this time. "Will be right back."

I grab a light robe from the back of the door and put it on, then open the door and head swiftly down the hallway in a quick two-step. I clean up before I head back to my room, washing my face and hands and brushing my teeth. I dig out a new toothbrush from underneath the sink and leave it on the edge of the vanity. On my way back to my room, I grab a clean bath towel from the linen closet.

Kitty is sitting on the edge of my bed, still naked, tapping rapidly on her phone with both thumbs, biting her lip. She seems to have forgotten she's naked, but I don't mind. I close the door and lean back against it, waiting.

Finally, she looks up. "Sorry. Work. As always." She sighs. I sit down beside her on the bed, laying the towel over her hands and the phone.

"Let it go for a few minutes. They'll wait. The bathroom is free, and you can shower and brush your teeth. I'll get something started for breakfast."

Kitty leans over to me, kissing me again. It's easy to sink in against her, to feel her soft skin against my palms, the heat of her breast, the curve of her hip. It's intimate and domestic all at once, and I dream of doing this every day, waking up with her every morning. It's a big leap, and one I have never made, never wanted to make. Never trusted anyone to make it with. But yet, here I am with her, with Kitty, and I'm ignoring all those old thoughts, old fears. It's not me. And yet it is, somehow. I need to puzzle it through, but right now, I just want Kitty.

The towel falls to the floor, and her hand's on me, sliding inside my robe, cupping my breast, and our kiss deepens. I want her so much. And she wants me.

But she pulls back, and reluctant as I am to stop, I match her movements. We're both panting. Her lips are swollen from our kisses, and I'm sure mine are as well.

"I should shower," she says breathlessly. "It's okay?"

"No one's in there," I say.

"And us?" Kitty says. Her breathless expression, her unhindered desire, has dampened, and a frown crinkles her brow.

"Okay?" I ask. "Of course we are."

A light blush steals over her cheeks. "Of course," she says, as if she should have known. Why wouldn't she know?

"What are you thinking?" I ask. Nothing like being direct. I can do that with her, at least at this moment, in the room's early morning quiet, just us.

Kitty shakes her head. "Nothing, really." She looks at me, searching. "I just...I just don't want this to end."

"Of course it won't." I drop a gentle kiss on her lips. "We're not done yet. Not even close."

Kitty smiles then, rising to her feet and scooping up the towel. I shed my robe and hand it to her, then turn to the dresser, pulling open a drawer. "You'd best get in the shower before Mama takes it over," I say, grabbing my day's clothes. I turn back to her. "Second door, turn left out from my room."

"See you in a few," she says, putting on my robe and gathering up her clothes. She darts out the door, but not before I have the chance to admire her in it, her bare feet and calves visible, and the deep vee at her neck.

Gorgeous. And the perfect wake-up partner.

❖

The shower is heavenly, and it takes away any remaining sleepiness. I make it quick, though. Overnight, my phone has blown up with emails and messages, work that couldn't wait. I want it to be able to wait, but I know I can't put it off. I already put some of it off last night.

I step out onto the worn bath mat and towel off, then hang the used towel on the empty spot of the rack. I dress in yesterday's somewhat wrinkled and messy clothes. Ugh. I've always tried not to be too fussy and prissy, but right now, I am close to throwing a fit from the feel of a dirty T-shirt next to my skin. I look at myself in the mirror, run my fingers through my damp hair. Once it dries, it'll straighten on its own, mostly. I can deal with it. I gaze at myself, and I take a deep breath. And then another. It's a trick I've learned from being really anxious as a teenager: focus on something else, not on the anxiety. Deep breaths. I look at the sink, at the chip on the edge of the enamel, at the two faucets, the blue rubber plug on its chain wrapped around the cold faucet base, dangling into the sink. Everything is just a bit worn, as if it's been here for decades. It probably has, I remind myself. It's a farmhouse, and everything is old, pretty much.

Feeling calmer, I brush my teeth and leave the toothbrush where I found it. I'll come back.

That thought makes me smile, and I leave the bathroom and head downstairs to the kitchen. I can smell something cooking, but I'm not sure what it is. It smells savory, not sweet. And it's not the usual smells I'm used to. Not an omelet, or French toast. I walk down the hall and into the great room. Lucy is moving about in the kitchen, and her mother is sitting outside on the porch, the screen door all that separates her from the great room. There's a light breeze coming in, smelling of hay, of fresh country air.

I wish I could open my windows and have that.

Lucy turns, and when she sees me, her face lights up. "Breakfast is almost ready," she says, turning back to the counter. She's stirring something, and I see sliced green onions on a chopping board, and two eggs whole in their shells. Lucy takes a handful of green onions and sprinkles them over whatever she's working on. I'm too curious, so I move next to her, nudging her with my shoulder. She nudges me back even as she focuses on her work.

There are two bowls that look a bit like porridge, although they don't smell like porridge. The green onions are being sprinkled on top. When she's done that, she takes one of the eggs and a knife, and taps a path around its circumference, cracking it open. It's soft boiled, and the yolk runs out. She scoops the whites out with a spoon and piles them on the porridge. And then does the same with the second egg on the second bowl.

I'm not sure what to think, because this is not like any porridge I've ever had.

"You look confused," Lucy says. "Have you ever had congee before?"

Congee. I rack my mind, but I don't think I've ever heard of it.

Lucy takes up the bowls and I follow her to the table. She's set out a pot of tea, cups, and utensils on the gray Formica.

"It looks like porridge," I say as I sit down in the same place I sat last night. Lucy sets the bowl in front of me.

"It's like that. Just with rice, and savory, not sweet. I have it almost every morning."

I'm sure I look skeptical. I've always tried to hide my emotions, and had to learn to do it for court and for work, but I haven't put up that shield. Not here. I school my features.

"It's a bit different, I know," Lucy says, taking up her spoon. "But try it. If you hate it, I can make you an omelet instead."

I feel a bit like a kid forced to eat a meal they don't like, but I will try it. I can do savory at breakfast. I know I can.

I scoop up a small bite's worth, getting a bit of everything: rice, egg, and green onion. As I bring it to my mouth, I find that I'm salivating, the scent teasing my nostrils. I am definitely hungry. Probably all this fresh air. And Lucy.

I take that bite, and the combination of flavors hits my tongue at once. It's delicious. A bit salty, a bit like a thick soup, almost, but the freshly cooked egg and the raw fresh green onion make it pop on my taste buds. I take another bite, this time more quickly. It feels like it's triggered a craving in me, one I never knew I had.

"I knew you'd like it," Lucy says after I've finished a few more bites. "I've never known anyone who doesn't once they try it."

"This is so good—you should sell it."

Lucy's mom opens the screen door and makes her way inside, going to a pot on the stove. She looks at me, at my bowl. "It's a secret recipe," she says. "From my family."

"Not really secret," Lucy clarifies. "But the broth is a special mix. It's not just water."

"A stock?" I ask. I take another taste, trying to pinpoint the flavors infusing the rice. "Seafood?" And there's a slight spice there, one I've had before. "And ginger?"

Lucy's mom smiles approvingly at me. "You know your food. I thought so, after last night. I make a special stock, and we always use it for congee. It's Lucy's favorite. Mine too."

"We should sell it," Lucy says, "but doing breakfast at a restaurant is a lot of work."

"A restaurant?" Lucy's mom raises a brow. "When are you opening a restaurant?"

"We aren't," I say.

"Not yet," Lucy adds. Our gazes meet, and we smile. Our secret idea, our secret plan. Well, maybe not so secret. It hovers there between us, a shimmering possibility.

"Breakfast is hard," Lucy's mom agrees. "Too many things to choose from, too much to do. But lunch, perhaps, or dinner." She looks directly at me. "You could be the chef. You have enough skill for it."

She does up a bowl of congee for herself, adding the green onions. She doesn't add any egg but instead puts a bit of something else on it, something I don't recognize. "Dried shrimp," she says when she sees me looking. She takes her bowl back out to the porch, leaving us alone in the kitchen.

"You really want to do it?" I ask.

Lucy takes a bite of her congee, savors it, thinking.

"I do. We should do it."

"But how?"

Lucy shrugs. "From the beginning."

CHAPTER ELEVEN

I really don't want Kitty to go.

It blows my mind because she's honestly the first woman I've been with who I haven't wanted to say good-bye to. All the others I could leave easily, or they could, and I didn't feel it like I'm feeling it now. It's so soon, and I should be thinking more reasonably, but I just can't. She's the first one I've really clicked with, who gets me. I get her. She loves food, and she fit in perfectly with Mama and Alice and even Adam. It's a feeling of contentment I've never known before.

After breakfast and a bit more talking about restaurants—it's pie in the sky right now, but it seems like we might really be able to do this—I walk her to her car. It's still early, barely eight, but she gave me a glance at her phone, and I've seen all the emails. She works so hard. But I'm comforted that we'll talk later, and glad my little cat sculpture is going home with her, and the rest of the blackberries. I like to think that it's a little piece of me that will look after her while I'm not there, and the fruit to remind her of where she's been.

"Want to come into the city to meet me for dinner on Wednesday?" Kitty asks, leaning on her open door. She pulls me to her, hooking her fingers in my belt loops. I'm sure Mama's watching from the window, but I don't mind.

"Of course."

Kitty grins and pulls me in for a kiss. When we part, I feel a bit breathless.

"Six o'clock?" she asks. "I'll text you my address."

"Absolutely."

I kiss her once more before she gets into the car, a sweet yet passionate kiss, one I feel to my toes. I'm still tingling as she backs down the driveway and heads down the road. The dust rises in her wake, and I track her until she's out of sight, over the hill.

These few days are going to feel like a year. I miss her already now that she's gone, her enthusiasm, her warmth. More than I expect.

❖

My chest is aching as I drive away from the farm. But I'm a bit giddy too, deliciously overwhelmed in body and mind. Lucy. A restaurant. The food. Oh, the food. And Lucy. Sweet, beautiful, amazing Lucy.

I know Cindy will be dying for an update. She's emailed, but it's been work stuff, not personal. I'll call her soon. She deserves to know what she's started. And I know I should get her something as a thank-you, something incredible.

There's movement at the side of the road, a flash of brown and white.

I slam on the brakes, my heart pounding as the car fishtails a bit on the gravel road. The deer keeps moving across the road and into the ditch on the other side. I rest my head on the steering wheel and try to control my breathing.

I need to get my head out of the clouds.

Once home, I carry the cat and the blackberries to the elevator, heading to the fifth floor and my cozy one-bedroom apartment. It's a high-rise in the center of the city, perfectly convenient for all my needs. Or at least, all my needs before this weekend. When I open the door, playing a balancing act with the cat and punnets, I start to wonder what Lucy will think of this place. It's pretty minimalist, an open-plan kitchen-living room with white walls, gray flooring, and dark blue cupboards. That blue is the only splash of color, but it's not much. The sofas are the same dark blue, angled toward a small flat-screen television I barely watch, and the sliding glass balcony doors. The sun streams in, brightening the space, bringing a warmth to it. Sort of. After Lucy's farm, its easy feel, its rugs and comfortably worn furniture, this place feels a bit sterile.

I look at the cat under my arm. She—for I've decided it is a she—will bring this place some personality. And I'm going to have to work on it. I place the cat on my kitchen bar, where she can survey the space like the queen she is. And I put the blackberries in the fridge where they belong. They'll be my evening treat, with ice cream, while I put my feet up.

As for now…my phone buzzes in my back pocket, and I pull it out. More email, this one from a fellow associate, Joel. He's newer than I am at the firm, just barely out of articling. I feel for the guy, as he's a bit on the shy side, a bit intimidated by the partners.

The email is panicky. I read it over twice, making certain of what he's saying, sure he's making a bigger deal out of this than he needs to. I remember what it was like, questioning my every move once I had my call to the bar, sure that I was going to be found out as a fraud, a kid who shouldn't even be a lawyer.

I kick off my shoes and move toward my laptop sitting on the coffee table. I know I can solve this. This is what I do.

After talking with Joel, walking him through his problem, I am glued to my laptop for far too long, answering emails, reading research, and catching up. I only notice the time when my stomach growls. It's nearly two in the afternoon, and I've been working solidly since ten thirty.

I glance at my phone. Did I text Lucy?

Crap.

I grab my phone, text her my address and a short message. *Work buried me.*

She replies a minute later. *Was worried you didn't get home safe.*

Just fine. Cat's looking after me.

I think she needs a name.

What should it be?

I glance at the cat sitting on the kitchen bar, overseeing the apartment. A name doesn't come to me immediately. I'm not sure what she looks like, what would suit her.

Heimei. Then two Chinese characters.

I stare at my phone, puzzled. *What do you mean?*

Blackberry. In simplified Chinese. :)

Heimei. I try the word out, not sure if I'm pronouncing it right. I take a long look at the cat. I know it's silly, but she seems to brighten somehow, to appear more lifelike.

Heimei it is.

It's perfect.

Of course. Now go eat some.

I will. :)

I get off the sofa, stretching up as if I could touch the ceiling, working out the kinks in my back. I really should get a proper desk, but that'd make it seem too much like the office. I head to the kitchen and take a punnet of blackberries out of the fridge, rinsing them in a colander under the tap. I pop one into my mouth, and the flavor bursts on my tongue, just like it did the first time. I eat another. Close my eyes. Savor it.

When I open my eyes, I'm disappointed to be at home in my own kitchen, not at the farm with Lucy, surrounded by all that real life, that easy comfort. My kitchen seems cold, though I still loved it just yesterday.

With a sigh, I shake the colander, then let it sit in the sink while I grab a bowl and the vanilla ice cream. I scoop out a healthy portion, then let the blackberries fall into the bowl on top of it. It's really more blackberries than ice cream, but I don't mind at all.

I take the bowl and my phone back into the living room, but I don't sit back down on the sofa. I slide my phone into my back pocket and head out to the balcony. It's warm, and the sun is still shining. I stand at the rail, looking out at the city, or at least, what I can see of it. My apartment faces south, but there are more high-rises going up all around my building, and my view is slowly being choked off. I can see all the way to Mount Royal, but I have a feeling I won't be able to for much longer. I try not to look down. It's only five stories, but that's still a bit nausea-inducing for me. Mostly I try not to think about it, and I'm glad I didn't buy any higher.

What I really wanted was one of those tiny inner-city houses, a cute arts and crafts–style place older than my parents. Trouble is, even the fixer-uppers are worth a small fortune. But one day, maybe. I can picture myself putting window boxes full of flowers along the front, having a vegetable garden in the back. Maybe even a little greenhouse.

Lucy flashes in my mind, standing in her greenhouse next to the bushes of raspberries and blackberries. I try to imagine her here, but my imagination can't reach that far. The image of the old house is becoming a bit hazy, but I can picture a farmhouse much like Lucy's, she and I there, puttering about.

I take the last spoonful of my dessert-slash-late lunch and head back inside, leaving the balcony door open. The last juicy berry drenches my tongue. I set the bowl in the sink, then rest my hand briefly on Heimei's head.

The Cat's Paw.

Not a bad idea for a restaurant name, right?

I text Lucy. Time to do some research of my own now. Work can wait.

❖

I get back to the house after an afternoon of weeding the back garden, one of the ones we have that isn't in the greenhouse. There's something about vegetables grown outdoors that makes them so flavorful. Our potatoes and carrots grow back there and our other root vegetables. I remember pulling out baby-sized carrots when I was barely of talking age, rubbing the dirt off on my overalls, and taking a bite. There was nothing quite like it then, to my baby taste buds. This time, though, the smaller carrots in my hand get put under the tap at the side of the house first. I'm a little more sophisticated than I used to be.

I shake the excess water off the carrots and head inside, toeing off my muddy shoes in the entryway. As I come through to the kitchen, Mama comes out of the half bathroom nearby.

"Your phone has been busy," she says, pointing to where it sits on the kitchen table. Just then, it vibrates against the Formica, rattling the salt and pepper shakers in their holder.

"Who?"

Mama shrugs. "I don't read your messages, but I did see Kitty's name." She smiles. "Such a nice girl. She can come visit anytime."

I know I'm blushing, can feel the heat in my cheeks.

"I'm going over to visit Alice," Mama says. She smiles at me and pulls a shawl down from the hook by the porch door. It's fairly warm out today, but she often gets chilly. "Be back later."

I wait until she leaves before I go to scoop up my phone, scanning Kitty's messages.

She wants to do the restaurant.

She has an idea for the name.

The Cat's Paw.

I like it. I really do, but there's something missing somehow. The name makes me think of one of those old-style hanging signs along a boardwalk, carved and square, and painted. Old-fashioned, Western. But not as old-fashioned as the shops at Heritage Park in Calgary. No way I'm wearing some ankle-length dress and a bonnet.

I try to imagine the restaurant as a Chinese restaurant, but I can't really picture myself cooking and serving there, either. The ones I remember, at least the ones that weren't Chinese and Western food, were usually dark wood, with booths along the edges, and quiet. Or very basic, with mismatched chairs and sticky tables.

I want bright, friendly. Simple but elegant, and a bit down-home. Something that can be cozy yet still have that bit of a modern feel. I'm not even sure how to describe it to Kitty. I don't want lace curtains and gingham, but neither do I want stark minimalism. I text Kitty back, because I do like the name. It connects to the farm's name somewhat, and to Kitty herself.

Just thinking of Kitty makes me miss her. It's only been a few hours. I set my phone down and go to the fridge for a Coke, and my phone buzzes again. I don't crack the can until I get back to the kitchen table, and this time I sit down and pick up my phone. Kitty's message is lengthy this time, like she did a huge copy and paste from a website. But it has information on restaurant licensing. Not the most interesting subject.

You're going to put me to sleep here.

Long story short, we can do this! she texts back.

What we need now is money.

Working on it!

What is she going to do?

CHAPTER TWELVE

I finally had to put my phone down last night and charge it, after promising Lucy that I'd look into things. Starting a restaurant is expensive, that's what I know from yesterday's research. I'm feeling pretty disheartened, but I don't want to let Lucy down. Not if I can help it. That's top of my mind as I head into work, stopping at the coffee shop at the bottom of the office tower before I head upstairs. The latte is a double today. I'm going to need that caffeine for sure. I pick up Cindy's usual too, a cappuccino with extra foam. I know she'll know what's up when she sees me. She says I can't hide anything from her. I have no idea how I manage to keep a poker face with clients, but not with her. I try, you know. But it never seems to work. She has that uncanny sense.

When I reach my office, Cindy is nowhere in sight. I leave her cappuccino on her desk right by her keyboard. In my own office, I drop my purse into one of the large bottom drawers of my desk, then pull up my chair. I kick my shoes off under the desk where they'll be hidden from view and flex my toes in their nylons against the commercial carpet.

There's a stack of folders on my desk, and a note on top from Cindy. *Today's!* it says.

I resist the urge to rub my eyes and smudge my makeup. It's going to be a long day. I log on to my computer and open up my calendar, and quickly arrange the folders for review. I'm relieved I came in early to get started. If I'd showed up at my usual time, I'd have been an hour behind schedule already.

Cindy pops her head in a few minutes later, holding up her coffee.

"Thanks for the coffee, boss," she says, drawing out the last word.

I've never had a good comeback for that, but it makes me laugh every time.

"Double just the way you like it," I quip.

Cindy lets herself into my office and closes the door behind her. She slips into a visitor's chair, pulling it close to my desk. She puts down her coffee and props her chin in her hand. "Tell me all about it."

"About what?" I try to play it cool. I don't know why I bother. Cindy laughs.

"You can't play innocent with me," Cindy says. "I know you too well. And I know that Lucy's been here, and you've been chatting. So how was it? How was your date?"

I shuffle a folder over, trying to think of what to say. "It wasn't a date."

Cindy raises an eyebrow, a substantial talent of hers. It says so much without saying a word. She waits.

"It wasn't *meant* to be a date," I clarify.

"Are you sure, counselor?" That eyebrow again. It's waiting, all-knowing.

I laugh, lower my gaze, shake my head. "It was better than a date. Way better." I'd been thinking of, expecting, a one-night stand, but this was much more.

"You didn't even check your email a million times a night, I bet," Cindy observes. She has access to my email as my assistant, and sometimes it really helps me keep on track. She's worth her weight in gold and then some.

"I didn't. I had stuff to do."

"Stuff?"

"Yes. Stuff." I know I'm blushing, but I meet her gaze once more. "Do you know what you've started?"

Cindy grins, wide and gleeful, as she rises. "I don't, but I can guess. I know you need to catch up, so I'll let you get to work. Your nine o'clock had to reschedule, so you have a bit more time with these. And the boss man had to push back your briefing until three. One of his special clients demanded his time."

I glance at my calendar. There's a nice gap around one o'clock. I might actually get to have a real lunch today.

"Lunch at one?" I ask.

"You're asking?" Cindy says. I nod. "Absolutely. Vietnamese? Italian? Sushi? Let me know where, and I can make a reservation."

"Pick one."

"Oooh, I like you when you've gotten laid. I promise I won't break your bank account for lunch. At least not today." She gives me a jaunty wave and steps out, closing my door behind her.

My face hurts from smiling. This is a good day. It was a good weekend. I look over at the pile of folders, the never-ending work. My smile fades a little, but I know I can do this. This is what I signed up for. Every file taken care of is one more step.

❖

At lunch, I sketch out our basic plan to Cindy. She squeals and grabs my hand. "That is brilliant! I'd pay a small fortune to have a meal made from Country Mouse. Chinese food, Western food, whatever. And something sweet and fruity for dessert." She closes her eyes and makes a small moaning sound, even though we've finished our main meals and are waiting on coffee. You'd think she wouldn't even be hungry or thinking about food after the platefuls of pasta we've inhaled.

"I don't know what we'll make," I say. Ideas have been floating around my mind all morning, but I've had to keep pushing them aside to focus on my job. My real job. The one that makes money. The one that pays for my apartment. The one I love. Another few months, and I might even get partner. That job.

Except I keep getting flashes of the greenhouse, of Lucy.

Suddenly I'm craving blackberries.

"You know, I had no idea you could cook," Cindy says. "You always get takeout."

"No time," I admit.

"There should always be time for homemade meals," Cindy says. "My mother, back in Manila, told me that no matter what you're doing, meals are important. It's about love, not just about sustenance."

"What's that saying the guys are always parroting? *I need a wife?*"

Cindy shakes her head. "Those guys are so lazy. And their idea of a wife is stuck back in the 1950s." She rolls her eyes. "But you, Kitty, you need to not work so much."

"I'm not working enough right now for a partnership," I point out. "Jack says he worked hundred-hour weeks or more when he was going for his partnership."

"That's nuts," Cindy says bluntly. "Plain nuts. No one should be working that much. I know I don't."

That's true. Cindy keeps to a pretty set schedule, seven thirty until five, five days per week. There's the odd exception, of course. But they're rare.

I wish I could do that. But I know I can't. Once I'm a partner, I might be able to choose my own hours, but right now, it's all about showing I'm capable.

"I'm not working hundred-hour weeks yet," I note, taking a sip of my water. I know I should be, but I already feel like I don't have much time outside work.

"You work seven days a week," Cindy says. "You need to unplug. To have fun with that gorgeous woman and leave your phone turned off." She shakes a finger at me, and I know she's partly joking, but partly serious. She only ever shakes a finger at me when she's about to quote her mother. "There's nothing more important in life than love."

"Love is great," I admit, "but it doesn't put food on the table."

Cindy lets out a guffaw. "In your case, love might literally put food on the table."

She has a point.

"I'll think about it," I say. "Once I'm done with these clients, I'll have some downtime. But I need to help Lucy with the restaurant idea. We really could do it, Cindy. We really could. I can see it. And I want to have that food."

"Chinese and Western in a new twist," Cindy replies. "I think it's brilliant. Now, how can we help you manage to get that time?"

I pull out my phone and bring up my calendar. The dates are full of little red notes. Meetings, clients, work. There are gaps here and there, and the weekends are partly empty so far.

Cindy takes my phone away and begins to work, looking focused, biting her lip. After a few minutes, she hands me back my phone.

"I've cleared all of your weekends," she says. "No working on weekends. We'll do it all during the week. No client calls, no file reviews. That means you can spend time with Lucy as much as you want then. It's getting closer to the summer, and clients are going to be going on holiday."

I look at my calendar. Pairs of blank days stare back up at me, every weekend clear for the next two months.

"How did you do that?" I ask.

"Priorities," she says as the server brings our dessert. One of the bussers follows with a tray with two coffee cups and all the fixings.

"Ice cream with summer fruit for you both," the server says, setting down two bowls heaped with vanilla ice cream and covered with berries. "Enjoy."

I pick up my spoon. "This looks delicious."

"It really does." Cindy takes a raspberry from the top and pops it into her mouth. She chews, looking thoughtful. "Not bad, but not nearly as good as Country Mouse. I bet these aren't organic."

"I can't tell the difference."

"Try it," she says. "You'll know. You've been eating Lucy's berries for a couple of weeks now, so I'm sure you'll notice."

It's my turn for a raised eyebrow.

"And no, I did not mean that as a double entendre."

"If you say so." I pick up my spoon and take up a couple of raspberries and one large blackberry. As I chew, I notice that the juices aren't as flavorful. The taste seems muted, a shadow of what it could have been.

Cindy was right.

"So?" Cindy asks as I set down my spoon.

"All right. You have a point."

Cindy claps. "Told you."

"I'm ruined for fruit now."

Cindy nods. "Nothing like Country Mouse. Well, I'm sure some are, but not your average grocery store fruit, imported from who knows where."

"I never knew you were so picky."

"You'd be too, if you knew where some of this came from. Half the time stuff isn't even ripe. That's why it's so flavorless. It looks ripe, but it isn't. It comes from some refrigerated truck that's driven all the way from Mexico or California." She makes a face. "BC fruit is better, but only in season. Country Mouse is the tastiest I've had, outside of being on Vancouver Island at the height of the season."

"What's so much better then?" I ask.

"Peaches," she says. "All throughout BC, at every farmers' market. Whole cases of them." She closes her eyes, her lips turning up in a smile. "They're amazing. Melt in the mouth."

"Maybe you should help with the restaurant too," I remark.

Cindy opens her eyes. "Not me," she says. "I like my free time. But I'll be your taste-tester. Every good restaurant needs one, right?"

"You're in." We will need a taste-tester once we start on menus. Everything seems so intimidating as I think over all that we'll need.

And menus are only one part of it. Appliances, licenses, somewhere to host it all…

"Don't overthink it just yet," Cindy says.

"I'm not."

"You are so," Cindy says. "I know that look. I've seen it many, many times before. Trust me on this, Kitty. Take things as they come. Between you and Lucy, it'll be the best restaurant ever."

❖

I make it home to the apartment at a sensible time for once. I'm sure Cindy has pulled some strings with her magical calendar rescheduling trick, but at six o'clock, I find myself in my kitchen, staring at my empty fridge.

No wonder I always eat out.

I head into the bedroom, kick off my sensible pumps, and make quick work of my skirt suit, hanging it back in the closet. I change into skinny jeans, Converse, and a T-shirt that says *Time to Smash the Patriarchy*. Simone de Beauvoir's on it, and I love it. Cheeky, a statement, but also a bit obscure, because she's not exactly a household name here. I grab my purse on my way out the door, and my car keys. Time to hit the grocery store. I'm not quite sure what I want, but I know that anything has to be better than the sad bottles of condiments in my fridge. A girl can't live on ketchup, Dijon mustard, and a half bottle of expired Caesar dressing.

Ick.

Instead of going to the closest grocery store, I take a longer drive, going to the Asian grocery in the northeast part of town. It's huge, and I've only been here once or twice before, and not in the last few years. I grab a rolling basket just inside the entrance, and then I start off on my sojourn.

And it is a sojourn. The place is packed, and it's huge. There are so many things here, and it's mind-boggling. I start in the frozen section, snagging some shrimp dumplings. I know I have a steamer somewhere in a cupboard that I could use. And if I feel lazy, they'll be perfect with a salad. I move into the sauces, picking up a few I don't have and a fresh bottle of soy sauce. From there it's to the rice aisle for a bag of jasmine rice, then to the cooler section for a bit of milk and some fresh rice noodles, and then to the meat section. I snag some chicken drumsticks, but then my eye is caught by the live fish in the tank, and the lobster.

I leave those behind, though, after I come to the realization that there's no way I can kill either creature myself. Just thinking about it makes me shudder. Sad, perhaps, since I'm definitely no vegetarian. But I go into the frozen fish section and pick up some light basa fillets and some frozen shrimp. After I take a round of the produce section, picking up lettuce, salad fixings, green onions and ginger, and some Shanghai bok choy, I drag my full basket to a checkout.

I don't quite know yet what I'll make, but I have a few ideas. One of the recipes in Lucy's book caught my eye, a steamed fish with onions. My stomach growls. I look down at my basket.

I really shouldn't shop when I'm hungry.

Once out of the store and back home, I lug my bags up to the apartment and put everything away. The basa is frozen solid. I frown. They put two fillets to a package, and I only need one. I wrap both naked fillets in plastic, then put one into the freezer and the other into a bath of warm water in the sink.

My stomach growls again. I take down a cutting board, trying to ignore the noises as I chop up the green onions and mince the ginger.

I close my eyes, picture the recipe page from Lucy's book, skim down the list of ingredients and instructions. I can't normally remember that much detail, but I went over this recipe at least half a dozen times. I take out the soy sauce and pour some into a small bowl. And it's there that I stop, trying to picture the page. Usually I can remember something exactly, but not today. What else was in the sauce?

I pull my phone from my back pocket, dial Lucy. She picks up on the third ring, and the line is crackly.

"This is a nice surprise," she says, sounding a bit out of breath.

"Did I catch you busy?"

"I was in the shed, figuring out this dragon. I only just heard the ring. What's up?"

"I miss you," I say. That wasn't my first intention, but hearing her voice, a small ache has started in my chest. I want to be there with her, watching her work on her dragon. Not just talking to her on the phone.

"I miss you too," she replies, her breathy voice starting to return to normal.

"I also was hoping you might be able to check something for me."

"What's that?" I hear a slight clanking in the background.

"Remember that book you showed me? There's a recipe in there for steamed fish. I'm trying to make it, but I can't remember all the ingredients."

"You're making a recipe you've never made before, from memory?" Lucy sounds startled.

I look at the counter, full of ingredients. "I am."

"I'm impressed. I'd never do that. I can't even imagine trying something without having the book in front of me, or having at least made it a few times. How do you remember it all?"

I chuckle. "Thing is, I *can't* remember it all. At least, not this time. The sauce is stumping me. I knew about the fish, and the green onions, and the ginger, but the sauce? I know there's soy, but I feel like there's something I'm missing."

"Oil for the pan," Lucy says. "I know that for sure. And a good sealing lid for the pan too."

"And the sauce?"

"Definitely the soy." Lucy hums to herself. "I'd better check the book. You should do it the regular way the first time. See how you like it, and then you can get all fancy."

"My mother used to say that," I say "when she was around. My nanny did too, but only for really complicated stuff."

"You had a nanny?"

I hadn't thought about Mrs. Chadwick in a long time. "I did, at least until I was about eleven or twelve. She was the best."

"Where was your mom?" Lucy asks. I can hear the creak of the shed door, and I assume she's heading toward the house.

"Working. She's a doctor. And Dad's a lawyer."

"I never had that," Lucy says. "A bit more old-fashioned here, I guess." I hear her footsteps against the wood porch. "Almost there. I think I left the book in my room." She says a hello to her mother, then I hear her breathing growing heavier. She lets out a breath. "Took the stairs at a run."

"Wish I'd been there to see it," I say. I can picture her doing it, though, taking the stairs two at a time, maybe more.

"All right, here's the book." There's a brief pause. "Soy sauce and a bit of rice wine."

"I was so close."

"You were. Do you have rice wine?"

I go to my pantry and open the door, scan the bottles. Damn.

"Nope."

"Sake?" Lucy suggests. "It doesn't have to be Chinese rice wine. Although, if you have really nice sake, I don't know that you want to waste it on steaming when you could be drinking it instead."

"I think I do." I reach up, push aside a couple of bottles. There it is. It hasn't been used in a while. It's not often that I eat in Japanese. "Got it."

"All right. It's half a cup of sake, one-third cup of soy sauce."

"Perfect." I rattle off the rest of the directions to her and Lucy confirms them.

"You have a scary good memory, you know."

"I'm a bit weird," I admit.

"Not weird," Lucy says. "You."

That statement makes me want Lucy here even more than I already do. I'm not very sentimental, or at least, I've never thought I was, but my heart aches.

"Want to come for dinner?"

❖

My heart skips a beat. In an instant, I'm calculating how long it would take, how much driving it would be, how I could do it. The answer, though, is that it's not really possible, at least not tonight. There's too much distance.

"Not tonight," I reply, reluctant to even say the words.

"Still Wednesday, though?" Kitty asks.

"Yes. Absolutely." I can do it. I think. There's a lot to do here, but I can manage it somehow.

"Fantastic." Her voice is low and warm and emotional.

"Too bad you don't live closer."

"Or that there isn't better tech to get us there," Kitty adds.

"*Star Trek*? Beam me up, Kitty." I chuckle.

"I didn't really watch that," Kitty admits. "Sci-fi isn't really my thing."

"Favorite TV show?"

"Um…"

"*Laverne and Shirley*? *Who's the Boss*? *Full House*?" I rattle off a few from when we were kids. Well, that first one not so much. But reruns, maybe. "*MASH*? *The Flintstones*?"

Kitty laughs. "When I was a kid I loved the Smurfs."

"Smurfilicious!"

Kitty keeps laughing. She tries to say something, but she can't stop. I love that I can get her to do that.

I have an idea. I move into the kitchen, to the junk drawer, and pull out a small pad of paper and a pen. As I wait for her to stop her giggling, which is turning breathless, I sketch out a Smurf, and then think of how I could make one. Or maybe something else.

"Sorry…" Kitty takes a long breath. "Better now. It's just…I didn't expect that."

"We can be smurfy anytime you want."

"Oh, don't, I won't be able to stop." Kitty sounds like she's muffling more giggles.

"Careful, you don't want to turn blue," I chide. Now I'm having a hard time holding back laughter.

"My face hurts," she confides.

"Mine too." I've never smiled this much.

"I'm so glad I met you."

The statement is heartfelt, and it makes my knees weak. I sink into one of the kitchen chairs. I'd thought this could be casual, but maybe it's a bit more.

"Me too," I reply, at a bit of a loss for words. What's to say to that that isn't over the top?

There's a silence on the line between us, almost as if we've somehow overstepped, or somehow exposed too much of ourselves.

"What should I bring tomorrow?" I ask to break the silence. "And what's the best way to get to your place?"

"I'll text you directions," she says.

"I have a pen."

"Oh. Right." She gives me the address and the best route there. "I'm on the fifth floor."

I wince. More downtown. Traffic and chaos. But for her, I'll do it. "Is there parking?"

"Street parking. Text me your license plate and I'll put it into my account and can set you up so you don't have to pay. Way easier than using the machines."

"I think I can be there around six. How's that work?" I can do my chores early, and maybe Alice can take some of the others.

"Perfect." I can picture her smiling.

"I should let you get back to your cooking. Let me know how it goes."

"If it goes well, we could put this on our menu," she says. "It seems easy enough and quick enough to cook."

"And it is delicious," I add.

"I'll text you a photo too," she says.

"I'll be waiting for it."

There's another pause, a silence. I don't want to say good-bye, and I have a feeling that she doesn't want to, either.

"You hang up first," I say.

Kitty giggles again. "What are we, twelve?" she teases.

My turn to giggle. I do feel younger, like there's a new energy. "Maybe. Now hang up."

"No, you hang up."

"No, you."

Kitty snorts, a sound I've never heard from her. I love it. "We'll count to three, do this the sensible way," she says.

"All right. One..."

"Two..."

And we say together, "Three."

Reluctantly, I hang up the phone.

Just then, Mama comes into the kitchen, carrying a woven basket with some vegetables from the back garden.

"Kitty called," she guesses.

"How'd you know?"

She shakes her head. "I'm your mama," she says. "I know. But your smile is so wide it might fall off your face." She pats my shoulder as she walks by to the sink. "I love seeing that."

I touch my cheek, tight with the smile.

I love it too.

CHAPTER THIRTEEN

Alice has promised she'll take care of the evening chores, so after I finish my work for the day, I shower and get dressed in my nicest jeans, the most stylish of the mostly outdated clothes I wear. I pick a clean white button-down shirt with tiny red flowers. To me it feels elegant, but I know in the city I'll look out of place. I shouldn't care, but I always have. I've always been the one out of place here. Not many Chinese faces in this small town, in the rural areas in this part of the world. Maybe one family per town, if that. You'd think I'd be used to it. I know Mama doesn't care much, though she doesn't get to town all that often. She prefers the farm, says it reminds her of her home back in China, on her father's plot of land. A lot of the Chinese greens we grow come from her family back in China. I'd like to grow more of them in the greenhouse, but we've focused mostly on Western fruits and vegetables, things we know will sell. But in the next year, I'd like to grow and sell gai lan. The greens are versatile, and the stalks thick, so you can chop the stalks for stir-fry or have the greens in many ways.

I take a last look in the mirror. Clean, presentable. But hardly ready to go into the city. I'll do it, though. It's been too long since we've seen each other. It sounds silly saying it, thinking it, since it's only been a few days, but still…every moment feels an eternity.

I head downstairs and pack up a selection of fruits into a cooler bag, then take a shopping bag of greens with me too. We haven't specifically planned anything for dinner, but I don't want to show up empty-handed. I put the food in the back of my little car, an older Ford Taurus that we use for quick jaunts, when I don't need to use the truck. Mama waves from the porch.

"Don't come back too early," she calls to me.

"I won't," I call back as I slide into the driver's seat.

The miles fall away as I sing along to the radio, listening to CKUA. The mix tonight is a good one, some old, some new, and I sing along to John Prine and then to David Bowie, T. Buckley, and Sarah Jane Scouten, all in a row. Singing keeps me from being nervous, at least until I hit the city limits. The traffic increases exponentially, and I have to make several turns and merges that I hate, the city drivers seeming too aggressive, too impatient. I'm sure if I drove this route every day, I'd be fine, but right now, in the thick of evening rush hour traffic, I'm starting to wish I'd held off coming to see Kitty until the weekend.

But I wouldn't have lasted that long. At the next red light, I let my hands drop from the wheel, then flex and stretch my fingers, loosening some of the tenseness there. I'm getting closer, and soon I'll be able to park and then relax at Kitty's place.

I take the exit into downtown and follow Kitty's directions, which I've written on a small piece of paper and stuck near the dashboard. Once I get to Tenth Avenue, the traffic slows to a crawl. That's fine, because I'm scanning for a parking spot along the street. I see Kitty's building at the corner, but the parking lane is packed solid. I come up to a set of lights, and I put my signal on. I'll go around the block. Maybe something will open up. I follow the traffic, then turn again onto a one-way street, but there's nothing here either. I continue on until the next light, turning right again. The side street has no parking either. I turn right at the corner when there's a pause in traffic, and still, there's nothing in front of Kitty's building.

Once more around the block, then on the next go round I get lucky, and an SUV pulls out of a spot just in front of me. I signal and pull in quickly, giving a sigh of relief. It felt like I was going to be out there forever, circling again and again, like a hawk looking for a mouse.

As it's after six in the evening, the sign says parking is free. One small blessing. I take my food from the back seat and lock the doors, heading into Kitty's building. I find the directory and key in her number. Two rings, and she answers. I reply.

"Come up!" There's a buzz, and I pull open the inner door, then head across a lobby with slate floors and cool gray walls to a bank of elevators. The place looks brand new, or nearly brand new. I press the button for the elevator. A minute later, the doors open, and a couple dressed in suits, one man with a carefully styled beard, the other with short, spiky hair, exit in a cloud of cologne, talking loudly. They don't seem to see me at all. One laughs as they head outside into the evening.

I step into the elevator and hit the button for the fifth floor. The elevator is a fast one; my ears pop and the door is opening on to a bland gray corridor. I step out and look left and right. Neither way indicates whether it is correct, so I choose one, turning to the left. I seem to have chosen correctly, because I'm soon at 505. The door is cracked open, so I push it inward and step into a small entryway. There's gray laminate flooring and a floor-to-ceiling mirrored closet that unkindly reflects my frazzled self back at me. I set down my bags and run a hand through my hair, though I don't know if that helps.

"Kitty?" I call out.

Kitty appears from around the corner, and she squeals when she sees me, then rushes forward into my arms. I catch her in an embrace, walking back a step to cushion myself from her exuberance.

"Finally," Kitty whispers against my ear. She loosens her grasp and we come face to face. "It felt like forever."

Every stressful moment, every time around the block, falls away as I take in her eyes, the arch of her eyebrows, the smile on her lush lips.

"I'm here now," I say.

Kitty takes my face in her hands, and then we're kissing, a locking of lips that is intense, needy, desperate, as if we've been apart months. I don't want to it to stop, but we eventually do come up for air. I'm not sure how much time has passed, but it doesn't matter. I'm here, she's here, and we're together. Finally.

"I brought food," I say, indicating the bags. "Fruit and greens."

"I've been experimenting," Kitty says, pulling me with her down the hall and into the kitchen. The place looks spotless, or almost. Gleaming stainless steel appliances, granite countertops, elegant white cupboards with brushed metal pulls. Like out of a magazine. I almost don't want to touch anything for fear of leaving fingerprints.

Kitty takes the bags and plunks them on the pass-through bar. I notice my little cat sculpture sitting on the bar, overlooking the living room. I touch a finger to it, a stroke down the nose. It's cool to the touch and smooth.

"I thought that was the best place for Heimei," Kitty says. "She can see everything in the apartment." She opens the bags, starts pulling out fruit. "It's going to take us a while to eat all this," she says.

"We don't have to eat it all tonight. But I thought I could cook the greens for you tonight, if you want."

"Sounds great." Kitty hooks her fingers through my belt loops and pulls me close. It feels entirely natural to rest my hands on her shoulders. "I have chicken thawing, but no absolute plans."

"Want me to make up something?" I ask. "I don't get much chance to cook at home, unless I'm helping Mama with her meals."

"She likes to cook?"

"Always. And she finds it easier to do than some of the farm chores."

Kitty takes out the greens from the second bag, laying them on the counter. "She does seem a bit frail. How old is she?"

"In her late sixties," I reply. "But she was born in rural China, and during that time she was growing up, there was famine. She never quite recovered from it. And girls weren't nearly as important to the family." I shrug. Mama's always been matter-of-fact about her upbringing.

"How awful. I didn't even realize that there had been famine."

"Policies of the government, and some natural disasters. She told me once that she was just happy to have survived. A lot of her family didn't. And here, she says we have so much, she never has to worry again."

"What's it like growing up on a farm?" Kitty asks. I take up the greens and take them to the sink, running water to rinse them. Kitty takes out a clean tea towel and I lay the cleaned greens on it.

"Mostly good," I reply. I have to think about what I like about it. Not many people bother to ask me about myself, about the farm, and especially not Mama. "I used to complain, of course. It wasn't very exciting. But I got to roam all over the farm and farther. And I learned a lot. My dad's family have always been farmers, so he learned it from the best. And the land has been passed down for several generations. I think my dad's grandfather came from Eastern Europe somewhere. Might have been Germany, or Prussia at the time. I can't recall."

"So your dad was white?" Kitty asked.

I am not surprised at the question. That's usually one of the first when someone finds out about my history, my family. "Nope, not entirely. His father married a Chinese woman, my grandmother. It caused quite a bit of fuss in town, and especially in the family. But they fell in love and he had his heart set on her. He told me once that he'd seen her in the Chinese and Western food diner, bringing a bowl of soup to a customer, and he thought she was the most beautiful woman ever."

"That's amazing," Kitty says. "And such a story. So romantic."

She smiles, her gaze moving off to the middle distance, probably imagining what it would have been like.

"I think his family eventually accepted her," I say. "She wasn't going anywhere. And he said she cared for his parents in their old age. I never met them, my great-grandparents. And my grandparents always seemed quite old. But I guess most adults do to a child."

"I grew up in the city," Kitty says, "daughter of two high achievers. And I have an older brother. He's off in the army. I don't know that they have a big love story like your grandparents."

"Your mom never told you anything?"

Kitty shrugs. "She was always busy working. I had a nanny growing up, Helen Chadwick. She was more my mom than Mom was. And my dad's always been busy too. But we get together for dinner now and again, in between all our crazy schedules."

"You should ask them at the next dinner," I say. "Maybe there is a big love story there, but they just haven't told you."

"Maybe," Kitty says. "But your mom and dad…was there a story there?"

"Sort of. To improve his language skills, his mother got him to write to her aunts back in China, and word got around that he was an eligible bachelor. One of the aunties got my mother in touch with him. They wrote back and forth for a couple of years before the marriage was agreed upon and Mama immigrated. And she insisted upon keeping her maiden name, though my paternal grandparents disagreed. That's why I'm a Shen when I should have been a Bennett."

"She could write a book about it," Kitty says.

"I don't know that she would," I reply, "but it's a neat story. We're still in touch with her side of the family. It helps me keep up on my language skills too. Aside from Mama, I don't get much opportunity, after all."

"I don't know that I could even attempt Chinese," Kitty says. "The sounds are so different."

"It's not a Western language, that's for sure. But I could teach you a few words here and there." I pat the greens dry. "Do you have some canola oil?"

Kitty goes to a closet and pulls open the door. It's full of dry goods, and she takes down a bottle. "What else do you need?"

"A big pot, and we'll boil some water, then boil the greens." Kitty takes out a pot and fills it, then puts it on the stove. "This is gai lan," I note, "and it's delicious once it's been cooked for a little while." I go to her fridge and pull open the door, scanning the condiments. I spot the oyster sauce tucked behind a jar of mustard. "It's very simple." I place the oyster sauce on the counter.

"What should we do with the chicken?" Kitty says. "I was thinking some garlic and ginger, maybe a bit of soy sauce. And some hot sauce."

"Sounds delicious. Do you have a wok?"

Kitty blushes, then pulls a nonstick wok from one of the bottom cupboards, along with a lid. "I bought this once I got home from your place. I hope it'll do."

I take it by the handle. Nice weight, and the nonstick is handy. "It'll work perfectly."

"I wasn't sure because it wasn't steel."

"Steel's good, but it has to season and cure, so nonstick is easy. We'll sauté the chopped garlic and ginger, then sauté the chicken and toss it with the soy sauce. Greens on the side."

Kitty pulls out her ginger and the green onions and then a cutting board from a thin cupboard near the fridge. I pull open a drawer and find her cutlery and knives. There's a nice solid knife, and I take it out, testing the feel. It looks brand new.

"This new too?"

Kitty chuckles. "Afraid not. But I've hardly had time to use it."

I take the bundle of green onions, remove the elastic bands, and trim the tips and the ends. Then I start chopping, keeping the onions nearly minced. "How come you don't cook much? Especially since you love it?"

"I work," she says.

"So much there's no time for meals?" I can hardly imagine it. Even after a long day on the farm, I know that I can manage a meal.

Kitty shrugs. "A lot of days, I'm not home until nine, sometimes later."

I stop what I'm doing. I know I must look surprised, maybe even horrified. Kitty seems suddenly shy, looking away, taking the ginger out of its paper bag.

"I want to make partner," she says. "It's expected to have a heavy workload."

I finish with the onions and push them to the side of the cutting board, then set the knife down. Kitty still isn't really looking at me. I reach for her hand, curl my fingers around hers. She looks at me then.

"That's a lot of work," I remark. "I hope you're getting enough rest, and enough free time."

Kitty squeezes my hand. "Cindy makes sure I don't work too hard," she says. With her free hand, she pulls out her phone and brings up her calendar, showing me the dates. The first thing I notice is that her weekdays are packed solid. I doubt she even has a spare moment in there to eat lunch, much less take a break.

"That's a lot."

"My weekends are free, though," she says, and I notice that they are indeed free. Small white blocks of space in that sea of color. I'm relieved to see those spaces. More than I'd expected. Seeing all those colors, all those days full, made me wonder when I'd see Kitty, if at all. She has rearranged her schedule for me. Coming from someone as busy as she is, that sort of step is flattering, and surprising.

"I know how we can fill them," Kitty says. She tugs me closer, and my heartbeat quickens. She brushes her lips over mine.

"I have an idea too," I reply. Then her hand is on my cheek, and my eyes are closing, and her mouth is on mine, and I forget that we're in her kitchen.

CHAPTER FOURTEEN

I want to cook, but with Lucy standing there, looking so delectable, and having missed her so much over the past few days, cooking can wait. Her mouth is mine and she's hot against me. Her arms come around my neck, and I have a feeling we're not going to get to dinner for a while yet.

My knees are weak when we finally part, both of us breathing heavily.

My stomach growls. Then so does Lucy's. She laughs, resting her head on my shoulder. "Rain check for later?" she asks.

My stomach growls again. "I think so." We're still reluctant to part. I take out a second cutting board and knife, and take the chicken thighs out of their packaging. "How do you want these cut?"

"Diced in larger cubes, or pieces, just not too big," Lucy says. "They'll need to cook quickly in the wok."

I get to work. Standing next to her, our elbows brushing now and again, the scent of ginger and onions rising in the air…it feels right. Our time in the kitchen is a bit like a dance as we move around, getting ingredients ready, the oil in the wok, the bamboo wood utensil, turning on the stove burner. I watch as Lucy watches the oil in the wok.

"Once it shimmers, it's hot enough," she says. She takes the cutting board with ginger and onions and scrapes the contents into the oil. There's a sizzle and a pop and the sharp scents rise in the air. It smells amazing.

"Do you have any sesame oil?" Lucy asks. "It'd go great on the chicken before we toss it in."

I go to the pantry and do the bottle shuffle, finding the small bottle of sesame oil I think I've used maybe twice in the last six months. I hope it's still good. I open it and sniff a bit. It doesn't smell rancid.

"How's this?" I hold it out to Lucy. She'd probably know better than I do. I've cooked for years, but I feel out of practice. It's been so long since I've made a proper meal, aside from helping her mother that one night.

"Still good," Lucy says. "Chicken in a bowl and tossed with the oil, then we'll get that in the wok." She stirs the onions and ginger while I do as asked.

"Ready?"

"Let 'er rip," Lucy says, and I dump the chicken into the wok. There's another sizzle, and Lucy stirs a bit, making sure the chicken is well spread out.

The water in the larger pot is boiling.

"Now what?" I ask.

"Slice the ends off the gai lan, and then plop them in the pot," Lucy says. "It won't take too long for them to cook. They'll get nice and tender."

My stomach growls again. "It won't be too soon."

"I know what you mean." Lucy leans over to me, and I meet her with a kiss. "We need to do this way more often."

"Kiss?"

"That. But cook too," Lucy says. "If we're ever going to get the restaurant off the ground, we'll have to do a lot of testing."

Hours in the kitchen with Lucy.

I want that.

I really want that.

❖

Before long, the meal is ready. I plate up the chicken, which has been drizzled with soy sauce, and Lucy drains the gai lan before tossing it back into the now empty pot with some oyster sauce. She tosses it, lightly coating the greens, then places it alongside the chicken.

"We could have done rice too," Lucy says, "but this will be delicious on its own."

I can't help but pluck a piece of chicken from the plate and pop it into my mouth. It is delicious. Better than I've ever had. I close my eyes.

"Let's eat at the bar," Lucy says. "Try not to inhale it all."

I laugh and open my eyes and take the plates to the bar. Lucy grabs cutlery from the drawer and tears off a piece of paper towel for each of us. "For the extra drool."

"Want a glass of wine?" I head to the fridge and pull out a bottle I've had chilling.

"Just a small glass," she says. "I don't drink much."

"It's a good one. French, from Sancerre."

We dig in, and it's quieter than it's been all evening. I'm savoring every bite, that flavorful zing of the ginger and onions, that brief taste of the sesame, and the tender crunch of the stalks of gai lan, with its wilted leaves reminding me a bit of sautéed spinach. I feel like I could eat this forever.

Lucy eats slowly, thoughtfully, and I wonder what she's thinking about. I take a sip of my wine, trying to slow my own eating, but honestly, it's so delicious that I can't be slow. When I'm done, I sit back in my chair, savoring what I've just eaten, taking small sips of wine. I glance at Heimei, sitting there in her metal catlike glory watching over us, then at Lucy. I can't help but feel a bit of wonder at her presence here, loving her being in my apartment, in my kitchen, sitting here with me. I don't know why I feel like this with her. I know my apartment has felt lonely, even a bit sterile. All work. Lucy brings warmth here, just like her sculpture. Her creativity amazes me.

"I've been thinking," she says after she finishes her last bite. She sits back in her chair, shifting to face me.

"About?"

"Names. We can cook and eat, but if we can't get the people in, then what? We need a name that pops, that grabs their attention." She picks up her glass of wine and takes a sip. "But I don't know what the place should be called."

"Brainstorming. Hold on." I hop down from my chair and go to my home office, my second bedroom, grab a yellow legal-sized pad and a couple of pens. I come back and shift my plate to put the notepad down.

"I know you suggested The Cat's Paw, but if we do Cantonese/Canadian fusion stuff, then what about Canasia?" Lucy suggests. I write it down. "Or what about something about the location, or the food itself?" Lucy adds. "There's a small storefront in town that I was thinking might do, and it's just around the corner from the main street."

"Around the Corner?" I suggest. "Around the Bend?"

Lucy rests her chin on her hand. "Maybe. Write those down."

I scribble down both names.

"Cantonese Corner?" Lucy adds.

"Sumo Corner?" I add, thinking of a restaurant a few blocks away.

"Not unless we're doing sushi."

"What if we name it something similar to your farm?" I ask. It makes sense to me—Lucy already has a presence in town, and even here in Calgary, with Country Mouse Farms.

"A restaurant named Mouse would be really weird," Lucy says, though she's smiling. "It'd make for a cute logo and theme, though."

I write it down. We sit in silence, and I find myself struggling to think of something creative, something fun. Something that will draw people in.

"Cantonadian?" I suggest, though just saying it, I feel a cringe at the silliness of it. Like the celebrity gossip rags and their Brangelina nicknames.

Lucy chuckles. "That sounds awkward."

"It really does. The worst kind of celebrity couple."

"Kitlu."

She says it so quickly I'm not even sure what I heard. "Say that again?"

"Kitlu," she says. "Kitty-Lucy shortened."

"Kit-Lu." I write it down, both hyphenated and not.

"We could always use my Chinese name," she says. "Ming Kitty."

That one's catchy. And it brings up something I've been wondering about. "Why do you have a Chinese name and an English one?"

"Easier, mostly. Especially when I was a kid. How many kids at the country school had even met someone named Ming?" Lucy shakes her head. "And I always liked *Lucy*. Mama used to watch *I Love Lucy* on TV when I was really little. She was funny."

"I've only seen clips."

"Why are you called Kitty?" Lucy asks.

"Short for Katherine," I reply. It's automatic, a question I've had so many times.

"I like Katherine," she says. "Like Katharine Hepburn."

"But hard to say when you're two," I quip. "That's why *Kitty*, at least at first. Then it stuck." I shrug. "So, Kitty."

"Do you like it?"

I haven't really thought about it before. But it's me. I've never really thought of myself as a Katherine. "I've always been Kitty. Katherine would be weird."

"There we are, both of us with names we didn't quite intend," Lucy says. She lifts her glass of wine and we clink the rims.

"At least here we can choose," I say. I shift on my chair. "Let's go sit in the living room. It's more comfortable there."

Lucy slides off her chair, taking her glass in one hand and the notepad in the other. I move into the kitchen and grab the bottle of wine from the fridge, scooping up my pens and glass on my way back. Lucy settles on the sofa, propping her stocking feet up on the coffee table.

"I'm really feeling Kit-Lu," she says, holding out her glass for more wine. I oblige, sinking down next to her.

"Or Ming Kitty," I say.

"Ming Kitty. Ming Kitty. You don't think it'd start to sound silly?" Lucy asks.

"Almost anything does if you say it too many times." I pull my phone from my back pocket and google the name. The first hit is a cat looking for a home on one of the pet-finder websites. I keep scrolling. Nothing there that's anywhere near what we'd be doing. I type in the name of a domain provider and try it out. It's not taken yet.

I show Lucy. "That's a real possibility. Should we?"

"Do we want to take that leap?" We look at each other.

"Do we ever."

We have a domain name. And a plan.

CHAPTER FIFTEEN

I'm giddy. Sitting here with Kitty, with our pop-up restaurant name now a registered domain, my stomach full and my head buzzing with the wine, it's the best sort of feeling. I don't want it to end.

"We're doing it, Lucy," she murmurs to me. "We will do it." We clink glasses again. Kitty downs her wine. I follow suit.

"We need to celebrate," Kitty says.

"How?" I ask.

"I can think of a few ways." Kitty takes the glass from my hand and sets both onto the coffee table. I feel a rush of anticipation—the tingles spread through me, from my head to my toes and back again. We meet in a crush of mouths, of bodies together on the small sofa. She tastes of ginger, of wine, of Kitty. I can't get enough of her.

Kitty shifts her thigh between my legs and I rock against her, every movement causing a heady rush of desire. We're not even naked, and already I feel like I'm close to losing it, to losing myself in this need, this want. I've never felt this way, never felt such intensity.

I pull Kitty's shirt from her waistband, slide my hand up under the back, against her hot skin, undoing the clasp of her bra. Her breath is a caress on my cheeks as she pulls back.

"Bedroom," she says breathlessly. We untangle ourselves, and she rises, grasping my hand and pulling me up with her. She leads me to her room. It's sparse like the rest of her place, a queen-sized bed with its plain black headboard against one wall. The window has white blinds, closed against the night. There's a large photograph on one wall, so startling against the starkness. It's green, leaves and trees of an old-growth forest, and in the middle ground, a woman with her back to the camera, a brilliantly red dress swirling around her. It's fanciful yet real, and so different from everything I've seen so far.

"That's beautiful," I say, stilling Kitty as she tries to pull me toward the bed. "Where'd you get it?"

"Online," she says. "A photographer I came across. It's my favorite."

I turn to her, away from the photo.

"I could see you like that. Intense. Beautiful. Determined."

"You could?" Her eyes are wide with surprise.

"Absolutely."

Kitty has an energy to her, a determination that she might not even know she has. I don't really know how to describe it to her.

"I think you're the only one," Kitty says. She seems solemn, suddenly, some of her energy dampened.

"I'm sure others see it too," I say. I hope they do. I don't see how they couldn't.

"I don't know." Kitty sinks down onto the bed, and I go with her, sitting next to her. Our fingers intertwine.

"If they don't, then they're missing out." I reach out, catch her chin with my fingers, gently turn her face toward me. "And if they don't know, they will know soon, just as soon as we open our restaurant. It's going to be incredible."

"It really will, won't it?" Kitty says. Her expression brightens, and she relaxes into my touch. I lean forward, brushing her lips with mine, and her lips part, and the kiss becomes something more. It's desire, need, sex, but it's also trust and partnership and that emotion I feel but cannot identify. It's us.

"Ming Kitty," I say when we break apart. "It's so us."

"We're going to rock this," Kitty says. She takes my hands in hers and squeezes. "We need a menu, and a website, and a logo, and permits, and—"

"Tomorrow. And next week, and the week after that, and the months after that. We have time." I lean in, kissing her again, this time a gentle press of lips. I glance at the alarm clock she has on the bedside table. It's way later than I expected, and I still have to drive back to the farm. "I need to head home."

"Don't go yet," Kitty says. "Stay. I promise you that we can get up early, but you shouldn't be driving at this time of night."

"I have chores in the morning," I add, though my heart thrills at the idea of spending the night with Kitty, curled up in bed together.

"I can set the alarm for whenever you want," Kitty assures me. "I'm always up early for work."

I pull my phone from my back pocket, text Alice. "I'll just give Mama a call," I say. "She'll worry if I'm not home."

"I'll find you some pj's," Kitty says, rising.

I chuckle. "Pj's? We won't need them."

Kitty blushes then, something I don't expect. After what we've done together, she's blushing over pj's?

"We will after. Or I will, anyway. I get cold."

"I'll keep you warm."

"Prove it." Kitty bends to drop a kiss on my lips, then heads away, pulling open the door to her walk-in closet.

I will prove it. She'll never need pj's again while I'm around. I speed-dial Mama.

It's late when we finally turn out the light. I know I'm going to regret this late night in the morning, but right now, I don't care. I'm boneless, relaxed, and for the first time in a long while, I'm warm lying here in bed. Lucy was right. I don't need pj's when she's around. She's on her back and I'm on my side next to her, our legs aligned, her hip pressing against my pelvis, my foot over her ankle, my arm across her chest. Her arm is under my head, and I've never felt so peaceful, so content. Her breathing is slow, steady. I wonder if she's fallen asleep already. I don't want to ask, to make a noise that could wake her.

"Go to sleep, Kitty," she whispers, squeezing my hand that rests at her shoulder. "I'll be here when you wake up."

I can't stop thinking. I can't help it. It's going to be one of those nights where I run everything through my mind, over and over. I'm already thinking ahead to menus and dishes and who to invite. I wonder if Jo will come if I ask her. She's leveraged her love for food into a restaurant critic's job at the local paper, and though they don't do as many features as she'd like, she might be our in to the industry, a good connection.

"You're not asleep yet," Lucy murmurs. "Why is that?"

"I can't help it," I whisper back. "I'm too excited."

"It's not Christmas," Lucy says. "Not yet. Tell me what you're thinking about."

I tell her.

"That's amazing," Lucy says. She yawns and shifts so we're face to face. I can just see the outline of her eyebrow, her eye, the line of her nose, in the dim light from the crack in the blinds. "We'll do it tomorrow. But we don't have to rush. We have time." She strokes my hair, a gentle, delicate touch that is amazingly soothing. It's calming, rhythmic, and my eyes are fluttering shut, and somehow, some way, my mind has quieted.

"Good night, Lucy." Or at least, that's what I think I've said. But I'm not sure, because that's all there is. Then, sleep.

❖

Restaurant critics. The idea makes my stomach roll and flop and clench. Judgy people that I don't know how to handle. It's far different than with the farmers' market. There, people want the fruit and veg, know what they're looking for. Restaurant dishes are a far different animal. Far more complex. Fruit and veg are easy. Someone who likes blackberries buys blackberries. But blackberries in a sauce? Perhaps not. Or perhaps not done the way they'd think best.

Now it's me that has the mind that won't quiet. I know Kitty's finally fallen asleep—her breathing is slow, quiet, and her limbs have relaxed. I take a deep breath, hold it in for a count of eight, then release slowly. I do it again, and again, and feel myself slowly relaxing.

There's always tomorrow. We're on our way.

CHAPTER SIXTEEN

Your next client is due in a few minutes," Cindy says as she pops her head into my office. My previous client just left and I have a pad full of notes that I need to take care of. And a second pad full of ideas for dishes for the restaurant. I really want to work on that, not on these clients and their needs. Just not today.

"Want me to type that up for you?" Cindy asks, coming closer. She knows my style, knows my compulsion to take notes on everything. She comes around my desk and checks out the second pad of paper.

"Honey in a Chinese food dish?" She picks up the notepad, reading closer. "I can't imagine it, yet this might just work."

"I have no idea if it will," I admit. "But there's a shop near Lucy's farm that sells local honey, and we want to make things as local as possible, so…"

"That is so awesome!" Cindy picks up the other notepad, the one with my actual work notes. She tears off the top sheet. "I'll get this typed up while you're with this client. And then we have a few things that need to go to the courthouse for filing, and one lien to Land Titles."

"I don't know what I'd do without you," I say. It's a cliché, but with Cindy, it's utterly true.

"I know." Cindy smiles and gives me a wave as she leaves the office. I check my calendar, refresh my memory on the client to come. He's part of a larger corporation, and they're dealing with a few contractors who say they're owed money. I've dealt with this many times before, in various capacities and volume, and this one seems reasonably simple. The contractors did not complete the jobs and thus were not paid, and as far as I can tell, the client has proof of work not done. It should be easy. The contractors, however, are threatening court action, which though unlikely to succeed, could get expensive. So, that's where I come in. Negotiate, determine next steps, then execute.

Through my open door, I hear Cindy talking with the client. I rise and smooth out my skirt, putting my shoulders back and straightening my posture. I do it even though my shoulders want to slump and my eyes are burning from lack of sleep. Lucy and I did actually sleep last night, but I kept waking up, feeling her next to me. I couldn't get settled. I'm hoping that won't be an every night occurrence, but it's hard to say. We'll have to spend more time together. I feel warm at the thought, and I know I'm smiling. I dial it back a bit to professionally pleasant.

"Ms. Kerr, this is Mr. Barrow from CRL Estate Homes. Mr. Barrow, Ms. Kerr."

I stride forward confidently, my hand held out. "Nice to meet you in person, Mr. Barrow," I say. He gives my hand a firm shake. He's a bit older, late fifties would be my guess, his carefully coiffed hair a mix of salt and pepper, a few laugh lines around his eyes and mouth, and a crease between his brows. He dresses well, his suit possibly off-the-rack but carefully tailored. He reminds me a bit of my father in terms of polish, but my dad wouldn't be caught dead in something off-the-rack, of course.

"Lovely to finally meet you too," he says.

"Shall we get started?" I indicate a chair. "I've been reviewing the file, and I think that if we offer them a partial payment, we can get them to release the lien. It might be less costly than drawing this out in court."

Cindy gives me a wave and disappears, shutting my office door. Mr. Barrow settles himself into one of the visitor's chairs, and I head back behind my desk, pulling his file front and center. I position my notepad and click my pen.

"I would prefer that they not receive one penny for work they didn't do," Mr. Barrow says firmly after a moment. "My father built this company on honesty and hard work, and he would have been loath to capitulate to such men. An honest day's work is what he expected from all his employees, and these two did not do it. I could do better drywalling myself. With my eyes closed," he adds.

I can't quite picture Mr. Barrow in the rough clothes of a drywaller, his hair and hands caked with dust, but I won't doubt his statement. My boss has spoken many times about how Mr. Barrow the elder made his kids work from the ground up.

"What we can do to speed things along is respond to their filed liens," I say. "If we serve them notice, then they must begin court action within a thirty-day period. If they miss the deadlines, we won't have to deal with any sort of court action."

"That would be ideal." Mr. Barrow grins at me. "I am so glad Jack recommended you. I usually do these things over the phone, but I wanted to meet you in person. I think we'll get along swimmingly."

"I think we will too," I reply, feeling pleased and a bit more relaxed. I shuffle through the file, pulling out the information I need. "We have their contact information from the liens, and I'll make sure the notices are sent out via registered mail today."

"Excellent. Thank you, Ms. Kerr. I have no doubt we'll come out ahead. It's not a great deal of money in the scheme of things, but morally, it's rather essential. I would hate for CRL to have any slip in our reputation." He rises to his feet, and I rise with him. I walk him to my door, and he shakes my hand once more.

"I'll keep you updated with our progress," I assure him.

"Thank you."

Cindy looks up from her work. "That was quick, Mr. Barrow," she says.

"The best meetings are," he quips. "Have a good afternoon, ladies." We watch him go, walking down the hall. I know he'll stop in to see Jack. Those two have been fast friends ever since university, according to Jack.

"Anything we need to do?" Cindy asks.

"Notices to take action on the liens for these contractors," I say, heading back into my office. Cindy follows. "I have the forms and will get them sorted out before my next client. Then if you can get to the post office and send them registered mail, that'd be perfect. And we'll start the countdown for when we can file the lapses and other paperwork."

Cindy grins. "Easy as pie. Speaking of, what's for dessert at Ming Kitty?"

I hadn't even thought of that. No idea. Dammit. I hurry back into my office and grab my pad with menu ideas, flipping to a new page. *Desserts*, I write out in big capital letters at the top of the page. "No idea. None."

"Chinese desserts, like the rest of the dishes, or something more Western?" she asks.

I stare at the blank page.

"Blackberries?" Cindy suggests. I know I'm blushing, my cheeks heating as I look up at her. "I know you like those."

"Cheeky." I stick my tongue out at her.

"Of course I am." She laughs.

"They're not in season anymore, though," I note, but I put blackberries on the list anyway. We'll need something. I add *ice cream* beneath.

"You could bring them in, I guess," Cindy says. "Or use another kind of berry. Raspberries, maybe?"

"Could do." I write down *raspberries*. "I should call Lucy, see what she thinks. I don't think she'd be able to grow any more blackberries."

"You'll find something," Cindy says. "Now get to those notices, and I'll run to the post office on my way out to grab coffee this afternoon."

"Fantastic." I write *fruit salad?* on the notepad. Not my favorite, but it'd be a good way to showcase some of the variety of fruits at Country Mouse. *Poached pears*, I write next, the idea popping into my head. It's a bit fancier, something my mother would order at a French restaurant, but still, a possibility. I wonder what sorts of desserts Lucy had growing up. I jot down that question. Hopefully she'll have some good ideas that we can add. I'll also need to take home a few cookbooks from her mother's collection when I'm there this weekend. I flip back to the front page and add that note in, putting a star by it. There are so many things to deal with, and I haven't even started considering the permits.

I text Lucy. *Permits?*

❖

My phone buzzes, but I ignore it, as Alice and I are driving to town in my van. Our chores are done, and I'd mentioned to her that I'd been thinking about finding out who owned the empty storefront along First Street, the small one that used to be a café but had sat empty for so long.

"Beatrice will love you," Alice says confidently. "And I know she'll be delighted to have someone in the shop. After the big box stores opened up in the main shopping area, she's been beside herself trying to find a new tenant." Alice shakes her head, tutting. "The town council should never have allowed those stores in here. They've taken out all the good local shops. If I wanted to buy groceries, clothes, drugs, and garden things at one store, I'd go into the city."

"We won't be a full-time tenant," I tell Alice again. "This is a pop-up thing."

"How can a restaurant just pop up?" Alice asks. "It's not a mushroom or a groundhog."

"It's a limited edition thing," I explain, or try to. I'm not sure how to explain it exactly. Kitty and I haven't quite yet nailed down our concept. We've texted and talked, but there's nothing quite like having time together to brainstorm. I mentally note that we'll need to do that this weekend.

"Limited edition? But how do you make any money?"

"I don't know about that yet. But making it pop-up means we don't have to devote ourselves full-time, like we would otherwise. We both have other jobs."

"But how will people know that you're open?"

"Social media," I reply. "Just like what I do for Country Mouse, to tell people when we're at the farmers' markets."

Alice nods. "I suppose," she says. "But you'll have to do something for the folks in town too, the ones that don't do this social media stuff."

"There's email," I reply, "newsletters, that sort of thing. The newspaper, I guess."

"I bet you could get an ad in the *Eagle*," Alice says. "And that's delivered every week, so you'd get lots of eyes on it."

I turn on to First Street and cruise slowly down the street. We pass the storefront, and I pull into the first open parking spot I see. Alice unbuckles and hops down from the van, surprisingly spry after recovering from the flu. I lock the van and follow her down the sidewalk. An older woman, older than Alice or my mother, greets Alice with a hug and me with a smile as I step up beside them. It's Beatrice.

"Lucy, my dear, so good to see you," she gushes, pulling me into a hug. It's awkward, but I pat her on the back. I'm in clean clothes, but I worry that there's a smudge of dirt somewhere that could mar her immaculate pastel pantsuit.

"Thanks for considering us for your shop," I say.

"Oh my goodness, of course I would," Beatrice says, patting my arm. "Now, come see the space. It's cozy, but Alice says you don't want a big spot."

"It needs to have a kitchen," I note, "and enough space for maybe twenty or thirty guests."

"That we can do," Beatrice says. "We also have tables and chairs stacked in the storage room upstairs. My last tenant"—she makes a moue of disappointment—"slipped town without paying his rent, and he left behind all his furniture. It could be useful. I'd be happy to let you use it if you make sure to invite me to your restaurant on opening night."

"Of course we'll do that." It's an easy promise. We'd have invited her anyway—she's the owner, after all. "We're not sure when that would be. I still have to look into permits and such."

"That shouldn't be too hard," Beatrice says. "Now, what kind of restaurant are you thinking of opening?"

"Chinese and Western food, but more fusion than the old-style cafés."

"Sounds fancy," Beatrice says. "Though I don't know how popular it would be. That's quite a specific style for a small-town place."

"It'll be a pop-up, so we won't be doing it full-time." I repeat my earlier explanation that I gave to Alice.

"Pop-up?" Beatrice looks puzzled still. "I'm not sure how that would work out with this space. I need a longer-term tenant, not someone who rents for a night or two."

"It'd be every weekend," I say quickly, my stomach tensing. If she turns us down, I'm not sure what we'll do. I can't imagine us finding a food truck.

"I'll have to think about it," Beatrice says. "Come look around, though, and see what you think." She unlocks the front door and lets us in. The windows out front are large and let in a lot of light. The floor is hardwood, painted white. I'm trying to recall what sort of look this had in its last incarnation, but I can't remember. It's been several businesses in the last five or six years. At the back is a long counter that runs parallel to the front windows, and behind it is a typical café setup: microwave, drip coffeemaker, stainless steel shelving, and a glass case. There's a swinging door behind it, and Beatrice takes us through, into a small square kitchen. There's a gas grill, a two-burner stove, an almost U-shaped counter, and a rather battered looking industrial oven. One side has doors underneath that are propped open.

"That one's a cooler," Beatrice says, pointing out the doors. "It's not a lot of storage, but you could bring in more if you need it. The oven is on its last legs, and I can't guarantee it. I'd like to, but it's just getting too old." She points into a small hallway. "Dishwashing sinks are down there, and a staff bathroom. There's stairs that go up into the storage. Should show you that before we go on." She takes out her keys again, and Alice and I follow her back. The dishwashing area is small but neat and tidy. It's completely devoid of dishes. We're going to need to supply those too. I pull out my phone to make a note.

Kitty has texted me. I'd forgotten about the buzz earlier during the drive.

Permits?

On that soon, I text back. *Looking at the space now. I think you'll love it.*

No quick reply, but I know Kitty's working hard.

I follow Beatrice up the stairs. It's a snug stairwell, likely because the building is so old. The stairs themselves slump, and the linoleum on the risers is worn. She takes out a key when we reach the top and unlocks the door, flicking a light switch just inside. The light flickers, and she steps inside, moving to allow me in. The place is dim and seems full. There are tables stacked on one side, and chairs in stacks on the other, and a substantial number of storage boxes in between. I mentally count the chairs—there's probably fifty—and the tables. For our needs, they all should work, at least for the first few pop-up events. Beatrice walks forward and runs a hand over one of the chairs.

"They might need slip covers," she says, "but they might not. Some are more worn than others. The tables will need tablecloths, of course."

"I think we can do that." I make another note. We might have to take a trip to the dollar store or find somewhere to rent or buy what we need. I can picture our space, with tables arranged just so, checkered tablecloths in place, a bright space with barn accents. And we need a little something more. Each table needs something as a centerpiece, something small yet quirky, something that helps to emphasize the farm-to-table concept.

My fingers itch for my sketchbook, but I've left it at home, thinking I wouldn't need it. Silly me.

"Will it suit?" Beatrice asks, and I realize I've been quiet for too long.

"It absolutely will," I say, "but I'll need to run it by my business partner first. And to make sure I can get the permits."

"You'll be able to do that easily," Beatrice says. "My cousin works for the town, and I can put a call in next week when she's back from vacation. I think they'll like the idea. It's something new here, something that isn't a food truck. Did you ever think of doing that?"

"I did," I admit. "But it'd be far easier to cook what we need with a traditional space. I suppose if this goes well, we could think about it." I can't quite picture it, Kitty and me stuffed into a truck with cooking materials and serving out the side. But you never know. It might work.

"They're very in," Beatrice says.

"You two done up there?" Alice calls from below.

Beatrice and I glance at each other. Beatrice looks amused. "Let's go. Alice and I should go for coffee and catch up."

"And I'll head to the town office."

We retrace our steps and walk back out into the main area. Yes, I think this place will be incredible with a few personal touches. I can't wait to tell Kitty.

CHAPTER SEVENTEEN

When I get home from work, I finally get a chance to check my phone. My stomach growls, reminding me that I haven't had dinner, and that it's far, far too late. It's dark, which means it's at least ten o'clock. I meant to leave earlier, but one of the other associates needed to leave and someone had to stay to finish up.

There are several texts from Lucy and a missed call from two hours ago. I rub my eyes and open my fridge as I scan the texts. They're excited, bubbly, and I love that Lucy's found our spot. She's attached a few photos, and I stand with the fridge door open, looking at them instead of grabbing food. The space is bright, airy, small but not in a bad way. It'll work perfectly for us, and the kitchen space is useable. That had been one of my biggest fears, having to cook on tiny induction cooktops in a makeshift kitchen, bumping elbows and squeezing into too-small spaces. As it is, I still worry about us getting the menu right and managing the restaurant. What if something happens and it all goes wrong?

I check my fridge. Embarrassingly, there is very little. My goals of cooking every night and figuring out new recipes have been just that: goals. And goals that aren't being met. Not nearly enough for us to have a proper menu in place by opening night.

When will that be? I hope Lucy was able to sort out the permits.

I take a bit of cheese from the fridge and dig out some crackers. I prepare a plate and take it with me into the living room, sinking down onto the sofa. I look at the plate on my lap and the glass of milk that I put on the coffee table.

Something has to change here. I need good, real food. Not this snack food in a pinch. My stomach grumbles again, and I eat a couple of the crackers with slices of cheese. Not nearly enough, but it'll have to do. My feet ache and I feel a deep tiredness. And I'll have to get up and do it all over again early tomorrow morning. I knew making partner would be hard, but these late nights and long days are more of a grind than I had imagined.

I check my voicemail, also from Lucy.

"Hi, Kitty, I'm sure you're still at work, but I wanted to tell you all about the space. It'll work so well for us, and I can't wait for you to see it. I went to the town office too, and I'll update you on that when we talk. I can't wait until we can do this. Give me a call when you get home. Later!"

My heart warms, silly as it sounds. Her voice is the best thing I've heard all day. I set my plate aside and call Lucy.

The phone rings five times before she picks up with a sleepy, "Hello?"

"It's me. Just heard your message."

"Kitty!" Lucy sounds like she's perking up, but I hear a yawn.

"Did I wake you?" It's ten o'clock, but that's not super late. Is it?

"A bit," Lucy says, "but that's okay. I'm glad you called. I thought you might call earlier, though."

"Long day, sick associate, too much work," I say. "That's the short version."

"I hope that doesn't happen every day. You need your rest. This weekend we need to go see the space," Lucy says. "I know you'll love it. Small yet airy, and just right."

"Like Goldilocks?" I joke.

"Not too hot and not too cold," Lucy teases back. "Although the bathroom is a bit drafty."

"Not a bad thing in the summertime."

"No, but in the winter, it'll be awfully brisk."

"Maybe by then we'll have a full-time restaurant." That'd be brilliant.

"Maybe we will. I'll have the permits and licenses in motion once Beatrice gives the town office a call, but it may take a little while. I know we talked about a month, but I think it'll be longer. She says the office won't guarantee a quick turnaround. The town is growing, and there are a lot more businesses starting up."

"We'll do what we can," I say. "Cindy made sure my weekend was clear. Do you want to come here and we can experiment with the menu?" A weekend cooking in my kitchen with Lucy sounds like a perfect, blissful way to spend the time.

"I don't think I can this weekend," she says, but I hear the reluctance immediately. "I have work here and the farmers' market in Calgary. Why don't you come out here next weekend? Mama can show us some more of her magic with the wok, and we can experiment with some of our produce. I also pulled out a few more cookbooks from her stash. I'll have to translate, but they look promising."

A weekend on the farm. We'll have to wait, but I'll manage somehow. I close my eyes, picturing Lucy and the greenhouses and the cozy worn sofas and homey atmosphere. And real food. Full meals. I open my eyes and look at my apartment, its crisp minimalism. It feels cold to me, somehow. It never did before.

"Let's do it. I'll drive out on the Friday night. I think. Hold on." I pull the phone back from my ear and flip to my calendar. Late meeting. Of course. "Make that Saturday morning. I have a late meeting on Friday."

"You work too hard," Lucy chides, but kindly.

"It'll be worth it," I say. "Once I'm partner, I'll be making more money and will be able to dictate my own hours."

"When will that happen?"

"Soon, I hope." I don't really have any idea. It's at the whim of the other partners, not just my boss, if I can impress them enough.

"I hope so," Lucy says. "I miss you when we're not together." My heart clenches, and suddenly I want to get up, to leave all this behind, to drive out to the farm and crawl into bed with her and never leave.

"Me too, Lucy. Me too. Long distance relationships suck."

Lucy chuckles, a musical sound I love to hear. "It's not *that* long distance. We're only an hour or so apart."

"Too long for my taste," I quip back. "I want inches, not miles."

"Saturday morning, next week," Lucy says. "Then we can be joined at the hip."

"It can't come soon enough," I say. The need in me is an ache.

I hear Lucy yawn again. "Sorry," she says.

"I should let you sleep," I say, though I know I'm reluctant. I'd love to talk to her all night, but I have to think of her, not myself. "I'll text you tomorrow."

"Sleep well, Kitty," Lucy says. "I want you rested and happy next weekend."

"I will. You too."

"Miss you," she says.

"Miss you back," I whisper. "Good night."

I hate hanging up the phone. But I do.

An email pings into my inbox, the notification popping up on my phone. It's from my boss.

❖

I'm in the office at what feels like the crack of dawn. My boss's email was a list of things needing doing since Jeff, my associate colleague, is down for the count for another day. Even with Cindy's help, I won't be getting all of this done today, or even tomorrow. I set my coffee down on my desk and check my calendar. It's packed, even without Jeff's action items. I have no idea what I'm going to do, absolutely none. I can't clone myself and meet with my clients and his at the same time.

By the time Cindy arrives at seven thirty, I've made a list of changes to the calendar, which clients need to be seen, and which ones can be moved to tomorrow. Looking at my sketched-out calendar, I feel exhausted already. I will be in meetings from eight thirty this morning until at least eight this evening.

"You look wiped," she says, setting down a tray of coffees. She takes one and hands it to me. "Here, you'll need this. I got an extra shot of espresso."

"You are a lifesaver," I say and take a sip. It's hot and goes down smoothly. Today will be a day for caffeine. All day.

"I know," Cindy says. She glances down at my calendar sketch. "Who died?"

I manage a tired chuckle. "No one, but don't go to get lunch from wherever Jeff got his," I quip. "That's today and tomorrow. I still don't know how I'm going to do it."

Cindy comes around to my side of the desk and takes a closer look at the calendar. "This client here"—she puts a finger on one of Jeff's corporate clients—"will be happy to reschedule. Jeff's assistant always complains about how they don't keep appointments. I'll call them. And this one"—she sets her finger on one of my clients—"would likely be able to move to Friday. That's what she'd asked for originally, but at the time I had a free spot today."

Two short blocks of time. Just enough time to take a bit of a breather. I might even get to eat lunch.

"Did I mention you're a lifesaver?"

Cindy grins. "Only every day. Now, drink your coffee. Did you have breakfast?"

I shake my head.

"I'll grab you a breakfast bar from my stash," she says. "Let's get moving."

CHAPTER EIGHTEEN

Saturday morning at the farm could not come soon enough. That was my thought all this week and last, as I struggled with Jeff's clients and my own, and with too many late nights and early mornings. Right now, driving from the city on the highway, the fields of canola and hay on either side stretching as far as the eye can see, is incredibly peaceful and just what I need. It'll take about an hour to get to Lucy's. My eyes are sore from lack of sleep, but I didn't want to sleep in and miss any time I could get with her. I need her. I need this break from my work.

In the back of my car is a cooler full of groceries—chicken, beef, sauces—and my notebook full of ideas. Like, Cindy ordered in pizza from Una, and it was four cheese with truffled honey drizzled on top. That place makes the best pizza I've ever had, but the truffled honey was something else. So before I went home yesterday, I stopped at one of the specialty grocery stores and bought some truffle oil and I texted Lucy about getting some honey from her friend in town. I'm not sure how I'm going to make it work, but I've been pondering soy sauce and honey coated chicken stir-fry for the last few days. Truffle oil might work, or it might not.

My stomach growls. I stopped for a coffee on my way out but didn't bother to grab anything to eat. Usually a latte does the job, but I'm needing more today. I take a deep drink of my latte, hoping it'll quell some of the hunger.

My phone rings just as I make the turn onto the secondary highway. I push the button on my steering wheel. "Hello?"

"Hi, honey," my mom chirps. We've texted a bit, but it's been a month or more since I've seen them.

"Hi, Mom," I say. "You're up early."

"Just off for a run," she says, sounding far more energetic than anyone should be at this time of morning. "What are you up to? It sounds like you're driving."

"Going out to see Lucy at her farm this weekend." I mentioned Lucy to Mom and Dad but didn't really give them too much detail. Too much information and it gives them the opportunity to criticize or at least speculate why one of my ventures might not work. I noticed the pattern a long time ago, and honestly, these days, eighteen or so years after my realization, I've put my parents on a bit of an information diet. Dad gets updates from my boss, of course, given they've been friends for a million years, but my nonwork life has always been just for me. It's enough that Dad wants to discuss law when we see each other. We don't usually get onto much that's personal.

"All weekend?" Mom says. "That's quite intense."

Intense. Mom's code word for *moving too fast.* She's always been super cautious. Absolute certainty is required at all times before making a decision. It works for her job, being a physician, but in real life, intimate life, not so much.

"Just how I like it." My reply is as upbeat and chirpy as she is.

"All right," she says. "Dad and I were thinking we should get together for dinner on Sunday."

"I'm not sure I'll be home," I say. "It's going to be a busy weekend, and I'll need my sleep. One of the other associates was sick and I've had to take over his clients. Once I get home, I'll be working."

"Oh, dear, poor man," Mom says. "But he's lucky to have you to help. How about we aim for next weekend instead then?"

"Sounds good." I slow down to turn onto the township road. "Mom, I'm going to have to go—I'm starting to lose my signal."

"All right, honey. We'll text later. Have a fun time."

She hangs up, and I take a deep breath as I turn onto the gravel road. It's a bit more rutted than I'd like, and my car's suspension was not made for so many ruts. By the time I turn in to Lucy's driveway, I feel like I've been rattled out of my bones.

I pull in to a spot behind Lucy's Country Mouse van and kill the engine. When I step out, Alice's dog Goldie has dashed down from the porch and comes over, her tongue lolling. I scratch her behind the ears, and her eyes close as she leans against me happily. I'd love to have a dog. Or a cat. Someone to be home when I get home. But I know that right now it wouldn't be good for them, having to wait for hours and hours alone. Once I'm partner, I'll get a pet.

"Goldie!" Alice calls from the porch. "Don't you jump on her."

I chuckle. "She's fine, Alice. No jumping at all."

"Oh, good," Alice calls back. "Come on up to the house. Lucy's just in the shower."

I give Goldie one last scratch and then grab my bags and head up to the house. I come up onto the porch and see Alice and Lucy's mother sitting in chairs with cups of coffee or tea. Goldie bounds up behind me and goes to lie at Alice's feet, panting.

"You'll love the space Lucy found," Alice says. "It's lovely. And they have plenty of tables and chairs to accommodate everyone."

"I'm looking forward to it."

"Go inside," Michelle says. "There's space in the fridge and in the pantry if you need it." She smiles. "And help yourself to some tea. It's on the stove."

My stomach growls again, and Michelle looks knowingly at me. "And there's congee there too."

"Thank you."

Michelle nods and I continue inside. I put all the perishables in the fridge and leave the rest on the counter. I take a cup from the cupboard, find a bowl, and scoop myself out a portion of congee. There's a bowl with green onions and mushrooms and a few other things, and I take some and put it on top. I set the bowl on the kitchen table and pour myself a cup of tea, then sit down. The savory smell of the congee is making my mouth water. I take a bite, and then another. I'm just scraping up the last bit as Lucy comes downstairs, her hair damp, her white T-shirt showing a few wet spots on the shoulders. I might have just eaten, but now I'm hungry, this time for her. It feels like ages since we've been together.

"You're early," Lucy says, and I rise as she comes to my side. There are no more words as she slips into my arms, tilting her face up, her lips inviting me to kiss them. And I do. It's perfect, a deep embrace, and I feel like I've come home.

We're in the midst of that kiss when I hear voices and the slam of the screen door to the porch. We break apart, and when I look over, Lucy's mom is standing there, grinning like the cat that ate the canary.

"Not much work getting done here," she observes, her tone teasing. I glance at Lucy. She's blushing, her entire face going a deep shade of pink. I touch my own cheek and find it hot too. We really should have been working.

"We have all weekend to work," Lucy chides, resting her arm at my waist, holding me close.

"I know, Ming Nhon," Michelle says, waving a hand. "You two are lovely together. I just wish your papa could see you so happy." She comes over to us, and suddenly I'm in the middle of a hug with her and Lucy. Michelle's eyes look damp with unshed tears, and I find myself hugging her back. And I hug Lucy too, and we're all hugging, and then laughing, pulling apart. Lucy wipes at her eyes, and I see Michelle doing the same. I blink hard, twice. I won't cry, but it's so sweet, nothing like my relationship with my own mom. Sure, we hug sometimes, but it's not really the same, not like this. I want this. The feeling is intense, and I know it's too soon to want that, to want that casual intimacy, that family. Lucy and I are just a sexy fling. We haven't talked long-term, and with the restaurant, well, what if something goes wrong? My stomach twinges with anxiety.

And I'm reminded of dinner next Sunday night. Mom and Dad. My stomach twinges again. Lucy's mom heads over to the teapot that's always on the stove and pours herself a cup of tea. She makes her way back to the screen door. "You two cook dinner tonight," she says. "I want to know about this honey dish." Then she's gone, back to her seat on the porch with Alice.

"Soy sauce and honey will be a good glaze," Lucy says, following her mother's suggestion.

"And I think we can add a little bit extra to it. I had a pizza with truffled honey on it, and it was amazing." Food is much better to think about than my parents.

"Truffles?" Lucy asks, sounding skeptical.

"We should try, at least once," I say. "If it works out, it'll be a fancier dish to add to the menu. It'll bring in the people who really want a standout, unique meal."

"I can't picture it," Lucy says, "but we can try. What should we do as a side?"

I consult my list. I hadn't put much there besides the truffle oil note. "Something quite healthy and green, I think. But not standard. Something that will be crisp and not overtake the truffle flavor." I tap my fingers on the page, trying to think of what might suit. "Butter lettuce?"

"Perhaps," Lucy says, "but we might have something a bit more unusual. Have you ever had frisée lettuce?"

I can't even picture it, though I might have had it once or twice before. I must look puzzled. Lucy takes my hand. "Come with me to the greenhouse. I think I have a lesson to teach." We head outside, and it isn't until we're at the greenhouse door that I start.

"I didn't wash my bowl."

Lucy chuckles and opens the greenhouse door. "Don't worry about it. It'll still be there when we get back. Or Mama might wash it if she feels like it."

"But I don't want her to do any extra work."

"If she wants to, she will, and if she doesn't, she won't," Lucy says with a shrug. "It's only one bowl, Kitty."

I know it is, but I still feel bad. But I follow Lucy into the greenhouse. She takes me to one side, where long tables sit with rows of different lettuces.

"We don't do a lot of the specialty lettuce," she says, "because it doesn't always sell that well. But we do have frisée, and mizuna, and a few others." She walks down the aisle and stops at several rows full of a very light, small-leaf lettuce that seems to curl around itself in tendrils. She takes up one small head of it and grabs a tray from beneath the table. "That's the frisée," she says. "And here," she says as we walk farther down and she grabs a slightly similar-looking lettuce, with darker leaves, "is the mizuna. Try a bit of each." She sets the mizuna into the tray, and I pinch off a couple of leaves, one from each.

I try the mizuna first. It has a definite flavor, though it's not harsh or sharp, a gentle crispness, and I'm already in love with it, but somehow, with soy sauce and honey and truffle oil, I just don't know if it would fit. Then I try the frisée. There's not much flavor, just a hint, but it seems fresher somehow, brighter. I could picture it with truffle oil in a light dressing as a side to the soy and honey chicken. I snag another leaf from the head and pop it into my mouth, closing my eyes.

Yes, it's perfect.

❖

Kitty with food is like no one I've ever seen before. She savors and enjoys like every meal is her first after a long fast. And I love her passion for it. I love that she closes her eyes and chews slowly, her lips pursing, that low hum of contentment. And to find her sitting there in my kitchen this morning, devouring the bowl of congee? My heart went pitter-patter, and my whole body vibrated with need. That kiss we had was not nearly enough.

"Which do you like best?" I ask as she opens her eyes.

"Definitely the frisée for the soy sauce and honey chicken," she says. "And we're going to need a name for it. Something catchy yet informative. The frisée would be brilliant on the side with a truffle oil dressing. Toss it lightly, and the smokiness of the truffles will be a great foil for the sweet and salty of the chicken. I'm certain."

"Done and done," I say. "By the time our permits are processed, this whole row should be ready to go."

"How long does it take to grow lettuce?" Kitty asks, sidling closer. "I have no idea."

"Depends on the lettuce. But forty days, give or take a few." I touch the frisée. "I'll have to plant more of this if we're going to keep that dish for every supper."

"We could," Kitty says, "but who knows, maybe we'll want to shake it up every time, do something completely new." She hooks her arm through mine. "What other veggies do we have?"

"So, so many," I assure her. I hold the tray in one hand and we clasp hands as I lead her down the rows. "We really should use bok choy, or Shanghai choy, in one of the dishes. Have we thought about something vegetarian? Maybe tofu?"

"I've never been vegetarian," Kitty admits. "I don't really know where to start."

"Let's see what we have here." I tug at her hand and we head down the aisle. I set down the tray and pick up some bok choy and Shanghai choy, and then I lead Kitty outside, to our other garden. Choosing a row, I take her to the middle, then bend down and pull a few carrots out by their leaves, then walk down the next row to the broccolini. Then we head down another row and I pull out a large daikon radish. Kitty stares at it.

"Daikon," I say when she still looks puzzled. "Never had it before?"

"I don't think so," Kitty says. "How do you cook it?"

"Lots of ways. But let's keep going. We should grab some peppers too, and a few other things. Have to go back into the greenhouse, though."

We gather up some red and green peppers, and some spring onions and a few other things. The tray is groaning with its bounty, and I can't hold Kitty's hand anymore since I need both to hold the tray. I don't mind, though, because she goes ahead of me with the two daikons, and as we walk, I take a moment to admire the view. It's an even better view as she takes the few stairs to the porch. Mama is sitting there still, doing some needlework, her teacup empty.

"What will you cook for dinner?" she asks, looking at the tray. "Are we having company?"

"No company," I say, "but we should definitely invite Alice."

"Alice went out," Mama says. "Her friend called and took her to the mountains." She shrugs. "So just us."

"We won't make it all," Kitty says, holding open the screen door for me. "But there will be a lot."

Mama pats her stomach. "I can eat."

Kitty grins. "Be prepared to be amazed."

I want to kiss her again as I head through the door and into the kitchen. Kitty follows up behind me.

"Soon," she says.

"Soon?"

"I think I need a nap before we start cooking. I'm too tired now." Her eyes twinkle.

"A nap is a good idea." I'm sure we can find something to do in bed.

I set the tray on the kitchen table and Kitty puts down the daikons, and I catch Kitty's hand and take her upstairs. Closing the bedroom door behind us, I glance out the window. The rolling hills stretch for miles, but I've always felt a little bit paranoid. I adjust the curtains, pulling the light lace ones to obscure the view while still leaving the room fairly bright. When I turn back, Kitty is pulling her T-shirt over her head, revealing a snug white bra, her small breasts delicately pushed up. She's more delicious than the greens we just picked. She tosses the T-shirt aside and unbuttons her jeans, pulling down the zipper and pushing them off her hips. Her white bikini underwear is simple and matches her bra. In a moment, I find myself in front of her, my hands going to her waist, fingers tucking inside the elastic waistband of her underwear, over her hipbones. She rests her arms over my shoulders, around my neck, sidling closer, her lips brushing my cheek.

"You're wearing too many clothes," she murmurs, her hot breath causing tingles down my spine.

"I'll change in a minute," I say, "but first..." I drop to my knees in front of her, drawing down her underwear until it reaches her ankles. She lifts one foot and then the other, and I rise on my knees, level with her curls. It's tantalizing to reach out, to caress her between her legs, and I can see and feel her sudden shudder, sudden trembling. I shift forward, pressing her thighs open, spreading her lips with my thumbs, licking her exposed flesh, teasing her clit with a flick of my tongue. I feel her hands come down on my shoulders, but she's not pushing me away. As I tease her, taste her, her grip on me gets tighter, her thigh muscles under my hands tense. My tongue goes farther, and I angle my head so I can lick her slit, tease her opening, taste her unique flavor.

She pants above me and I'm getting more turned on even as I slide a finger into her wetness, into her center. She gasps when I do that, leaning on me even more. I know she won't last long like this.

"Lucy," she gasps out. "I can't..." Her knees tremble and I slow my touch, sit back on my heels. She loosens her grasp, takes a deep breath.

"It might be easier on the bed," I quip, and we shift over. Once there, Kitty spreads her legs, and it's easier now for me to get between her thighs, to taste her and touch her. Two fingers slide easily inside her, and she relaxes back into the quilts, arching her hips into my touch. Her hands fist in the blankets as she quivers under me, and I know she's close. Her insides are clenching and releasing around my fingers, and when I press harder into her, she arches more, rocking her hips against my hand.

I want her more than anything, and I'm soaking through my own underwear. I squeeze my thighs together, looking for a bit of friction as I tease Kitty closer and closer to orgasm. It's not enough, and I unbutton my jeans awkwardly with my free hand, fumbling, feeling desperate. I pull down the zipper and push my hand past the denim, past my briefs until I'm feeling my own wetness, my own throbbing clit. I'm so close, and I know Kitty is too. She's the one who needs to come first. I want her on my tongue when she does. I scrape my teeth gently over her clit and then suck, my tongue pressing against her. She's soaking my hand and she's trembling and gasping, and then suddenly she's moaning and jerking under me, crying out my name before she goes limp, still trembling, her taste on my tongue.

I work my fingers against my clit, hard and fast, slick and soaked, and it takes very little for me to come, feeling the delicious tension building and releasing, traveling from my belly to my toes and to my head. I slump down, resting my head on her thigh, still rocking against my hand as the last few quivers go through me, my fingers sliding from her wetness, my hand dropping to the floor. I close my eyes, trying to steady my breathing. I feel her shift, feel her hands in my hair.

"Lucy," she whispers. "Come to bed."

CHAPTER NINETEEN

We do nap after having fun, and I wake feeling refreshed. I'm not sure if it's the fresh air out here, so much cleaner than what I get in the city, or if it's just being with Lucy that does it. I feel like I could lie here with her for ages, luxuriating in our shared warmth, in the scent of grass and fields coming through the window on a light breeze. But I know we have cooking to do, and I'm impatient to get started.

Lucy yawns and sits up after I move to the edge of the bed and snag my clothes from the floor. My shirt and jeans are wrinkled, but it doesn't matter. I shake out the worst of it and pull everything on, run my fingers through my hair, smoothing the snarls. In my pocket, I have a hair elastic, and I use it to put my hair into a ponytail. Lucy sits up next to me, tugs on the end.

"I wish we could stay here for a while longer," she says, leaning in to press her lips against my neck.

"Me too," I reply, "but that chicken won't make itself." My stomach growls.

"I'm hungry too," Lucy says.

We rush downstairs after Lucy has dressed, and I see her mother puttering about in the kitchen, singing to herself. She's tidied up, washed all the dishes, and all the vegetables are piled neatly on the counter, gleaming with dampness.

"I washed them all," she says, turning to greet us. "It's still a lot for one night."

"We'll have leftovers for days," I quip.

Michelle goes to sit at the kitchen table. "What will you do with the daikon?"

"I was thinking fries," Lucy remarks. I look at the large white bulbous vegetable, and I can't quite see it. Isn't it a radish of sorts?

"Will people want to eat radishes?"

"That's why we make them as fries," Lucy says. She picks up the daikon and takes out a wooden cutting board and a large knife. She chops the top off and then makes quick work of slicing it into fry-sized pieces. "Call it fries and everyone will want some," she says. "But what to put on it? I was thinking a bit of vegetable oil for the baking, then some chilies and sesame oil for flavor."

"Let's do it."

"There's a cookie sheet just there by your foot," Lucy says, pointing, and I bend down to take a sheet from a small cubby at the end of the counter. Lucy finds a bowl and dumps the daikon pieces into it. I set the cookie sheet on the counter. "And there's sesame oil and chilies in the pantry," Lucy adds, and I go to collect what she needs. The scent here is tantalizing, a mix of spices and other things I can't quite identify. I glance about after I turn the light on and finally spot a rack of glass jars. Chilies are in a smaller jar, and I take it down. On a lower shelf are a number of bottles, and I see the sesame oil. I take both back into the kitchen. Lucy takes a spoon to the chilies and sprinkles a good amount over the daikon, tossing it in the bowl. I open the sesame oil. It's stronger than I expected.

"Just a bit of that," Lucy says. "Too much and it's overpowering."

I let a small stream into the bowl and Lucy tosses the daikon some more, coating it evenly. She puts the radish onto the cookie sheet and then turns to the oven. "Still not hot enough," she says. "But soon. We can snack on these while we work."

I turn to the fridge and take out the chicken. Lucy sets out another two bowls, one larger, one smaller. The honey is nearby and the soy sauce is already out on the counter. I can't resist opening the honey and dipping in one finger, bringing it to my lips. The taste is sweet, but not sugary or heavy, almost floral. It melts on my tongue.

"This is so delicious."

"It'll make the dish," Lucy says.

"I hope so."

"Add some ginger," Michelle adds. "Keep it from being too sweet."

I spoon the honey into the larger bowl and add some soy sauce. Lucy chops up a thumb of ginger and puts it into the bowl. I take the chicken thighs and place them in the bowl, tossing and mixing them with the sauce. My stomach growls again. Lucy takes out a square Pyrex pan.

"We can put it in here," she says. I dump the chicken in, making sure that the sauce is evenly spread.

"I think we need some aluminum foil," I say. "I worry that it'll scorch otherwise."

"In the drawer there to your left," Michelle says. I open the drawer and pull out the box. I cover the pan. Lucy checks the oven.

"Almost hot enough."

Once the oven dings, I put the chicken in, noting the time. "Forty-five minutes should do it. How long will it take the daikon to cook?"

"We should put those in right away also. And I'll put on some rice," Lucy says, opening their rice cooker and taking out the metal bowl inside. I grab the cookie sheet of daikon fries and stick them in the oven on the lower rack. "The chicken will go well with some rice underneath, then the frisée on the side." She measures out the rice, then goes to the tap and pours water over top. She swishes the bowl, stirring with her fingers, then drains the water and refills it to the measuring line. I sidle over as she puts the bowl back into the rice cooker.

"Isn't it easier just to use a pot on the stove?"

"This is a set it and forget it method," Lucy says. She lowers the lid and makes sure it is sealed, then plugs in the cooker. "Perfect rice every time." She pushes down the single button. "There are fancier machines, but this one does the trick."

I glance around the kitchen. Until the chicken is done, everything is ready to go. I grab my phone, where I've stored ideas for other recipes.

"I was thinking we could have one chicken recipe, one fish, and then one vegetarian." I scroll through my notes. Lucy pulls down a well-worn cookbook in a black binder.

"It'll be hard to choose."

❖

We sit together on the sofa, and Mama sits down in the easy chair next to us, looking interested.

"Maybe you should do something more traditional," she suggests. "Like your great-grandparents might have made in their café."

"Here in town?" Kitty asks, leaning forward.

"Here," Mama confirms, "but it wasn't their first. The family had one in British Columbia as well, until they wanted to move. Small towns and villages like their restaurants."

I flip open the old cookbook, seeing the recipes in the familiar simple writing that Mama had said belonged to my great-grandmother. "I'm not sure most of these would work," I say. There are so many recipes here that are just too Western—there's sandwiches and soups and side dishes.

"Let's see." Kitty leans over, closer to me, her gaze skimming the pages. "What about chop suey?"

Mama chuckles. "That's not really Chinese, but it is Canadian, for sure. And easy to make. Noodles, bean sprouts, and scraps of leftovers."

"That's it?" Kitty asks, looking surprised. "I always thought there was more to it."

Mama shrugs. "Depends on the café, and what they have around. Ming Nhon, you could make your father's favorite. Pineapple chicken balls."

"That was Dad's favorite?" It's my turn to be surprised. "Those aren't Chinese."

"Canadian Chinese, like the chop suey," Mama says. "And quite delicious on a cold winter day."

"I liked them too, growing up," Kitty remarks. "But we didn't get Chinese food much. My mother didn't really like it."

"Are your parents excited for the new restaurant?" Mama asks. She takes the binder from me and flips through the pages, looking for something.

"I haven't mentioned it to them," Kitty says. She looks down at her hands.

"How come?" I can't imagine not telling Mama about something so important.

"They're busy people," Kitty says, "And I've been busy too. We'll catch up again soon."

I want to ask Kitty more, but I'll do it in private. Here with Mama, she might not feel as inclined to expand on her relationship with them.

"Ginger beef," Mama says, turning the binder back to me. "That is everyone's favorite. Always."

Kitty leans in, looking over the recipe. "You know, I've tried to make ginger beef so many times, but it never turns out the same way as in a Chinese restaurant, no matter how I try."

Mama taps the page. "Here's the secret," she says. "Not too hard. Your father got it from the fellow at the restaurant in Calgary that made it up."

Kitty looks awed. "The Silver Inn. We ate there once when I was a kid, and it was so, so good," she says. She leans back against the sofa, a dreamy smile on her face. "They let me eat as much as I wanted that visit."

"We might be able to make it for the restaurant," I offer.

"We can't make too many things," Kitty says, opening her eyes. "There's only the two of us cooking and serving."

"The storefront has enough chairs for fifty," I add, "but I think we'll do less than that. Thirty, maybe. And if we have as much prepared ahead of time as possible, or at least prepped, we should be fine."

"Thirty plates, plus serving?" Kitty rubs her temples. "I don't know if that will work." She frowns. "We might need to hire a server."

That will complicate things, add more paperwork and tax. Beatrice mentioned it as we were leaving the store. "I don't know if we can afford that. I think we might need to speak to an accountant."

"We can do that," Kitty says. "I think Cindy knows someone. Her brother, maybe, or a cousin. I can't recall. But I'll ask her." She pulls out her phone and texts.

"If you can't, then I can do it," Mama says.

"Mama..." I begin.

"No *Mama* anything," Mama says, holding up a hand. "I've worked hard all my life and one more night or two won't hurt me. I'm not ancient yet." She smiles. "Not quite, anyway. And you can pay me in food." She sniffs the air. "Like your chicken, which is almost done."

The timer on the stove dings, and just then, I hear the click of the rice cooker. Kitty hops to her feet, and I follow. She puts on the oven mitts and opens the door, releasing more of the smell of honey and soy. I inhale deeply. She lifts the glass dish and carefully peels off the foil cover. A rush of steam emerges.

"Almost perfect," Kitty says. "We just need to let the chicken brown." She checks the oven rack, then puts the dish back in, pulling out the daikon fries before she closes the door. "Five more minutes."

"Rice is done," I note. "We should get the salad ready."

"Olive oil, truffle oil, a bit of mustard, and a touch of sherry vinegar, I'm thinking," Kitty says. I take down a metal bowl and hand it to her.

"Sounds perfect."

I grab the ingredients from the fridge and she begins to mix, not measuring any of the ingredients as she goes.

"Make this often?" I ask.

"Not with truffle oil," she says, "but oil and vinegar dressings are my go-to. I never use store-bought." She whisks the mixture expertly, and I tear the frisée into smaller pieces and put it into another bowl. Kitty sets the dressing aside. "We'll drizzle that at the last second. Keep the frisée crisp."

I take a pair of tongs and serve the daikon fries onto each of three plates. They've turned a delicious golden brown and I can't wait to taste them. Kitty peeks into the oven window.

"Chicken looks done," she says, grabbing the oven mitts again. She takes out the dish and the chicken looks and smells mouth-wateringly good.

"How should we do the rice?" I ask. "We can just put a scoop, loose, or we can pack it into a rounded ice cream scoop."

"Let's try each of them," Kitty says, "and see what turns out best."

I place one loose scoop of rice on one plate, then dig out our old ice cream scoop and use it to scoop a second serving, carefully inverting it onto the plate. It mostly sticks to the shape. Kitty takes the tongs and sets pieces of chicken on each plate, either on top of the rice on the loose pile, or beside the molded rice on the second plate. Over each, she drizzles some of the extra sauce, doing a zigzag design on the molded rice.

"The molded version looks more professional to me."

Kitty looks carefully at each. "I agree. I think we should do that for the restaurant." I scoop the rice onto the last plate and she finishes with the chicken and its drizzle of sauce. Then she picks up the small bowl of dressing, whisking it once more. She slowly pours a portion over the frisée and tosses it in the bowl.

I dig out a second pair of tongs and place some of the glistening frisée along the side of each plate.

"It looks delicious," Mama says, coming up beside us. She takes two plates to the table, leaving me with the remaining one.

"Let's eat." Kitty snags the plate from under my hand and sidesteps me, hurrying to the table.

"Trying to beat me?" I laugh and follow Kitty to the table.

"Maybe," Kitty says. She takes a forkful of the rice and chicken, and I swear she inhales it, it's gone so fast.

"You really are hungry," Mama remarks, chuckling.

"Starving," Kitty says after she's swallowed. "Just starving." She looks up at me then, and from the look in her eyes, I'm pretty sure she's not only talking about food.

CHAPTER TWENTY

After lunch, Lucy takes me into town, to the storefront. The owner, Beatrice, has given her a spare set of keys, and we head inside. Our footsteps echo through the empty space, the hardwood floors and the pale walls with their white wainscoting. There's a swinging door, and we push through into a kitchen with pass-through. There's an oven, a gas stove with two burners, and a grill, and a deep fryer. The air is a bit heavy with old oil smell and a bit of mustiness. The oven is one of those ones you could use for pizza—it has a conveyor that runs through.

I'm nervous and excited all at once. Nervous to have to use these industrial-grade appliances, and excited to be able to cook in a real restaurant kitchen.

"I think we can do this." I turn a slow circle, looking at everything. Lucy watches from the side. "I know we can," I add. My stomach flip-flops. Being in here makes it so real.

"Of course we can," Lucy says. "Come up and see the furniture, and we can make some decisions. I don't want to spend too much on refurbishing, but we need to decide on our look."

We go upstairs, through the dingy stairwell, and into the storage room. It's packed, more than I'd expected, but at least we'll have more than enough chairs and tables.

"Tablecloths," I say immediately. "Maybe slipcovers for the chairs, but that could be pricey."

"Too much, maybe," Lucy agrees.

"But if we keep the interest on the tables, and on the food, the chairs won't matter so much." I can see it in my mind now, one of Lucy's creatures on each of the tables, holding court. "What about your cats and mice? Every table, and we can name them all. Or get the customers to name them."

Lucy nods slowly. "I can see it, but do I have enough of them is the question." She does a quick count on her fingers. "I might just. But I might need to make one or two more."

"Can you show me how?" I ask. There's something about Lucy in her leather apron, her forehead damp with perspiration, that gives me an urge I hadn't expected. I sidle up to her, hooking my fingers through her belt loops. Lucy rests her hands on my hips.

"Have you ever welded before?" she asks.

I shake my head.

"It might be better for us to leave that for later," Lucy says. I lean in, my lips close to her ear.

"I just want to see you working in leather," I murmur. Her fingers tighten on my hips.

"You do?"

"But if we can't do that, what about right here?" Lucy grins, tugging me close, our hips colliding, the heat of her soaking through my jeans.

"I'm up for it," she says. "But I'm pretty sure these chairs aren't."

I don't care about the chairs, just Lucy. "There's a wall."

Lucy nudges me until my back hits the wall by the door. "You sure?" She's undoing my jeans, and I feel a zing of desire knowing that she's as into this as I am. There's something about her, and I just can't get enough of her. It's like she's the meal that never ends, the favorite dish, the craving for satisfaction I can't ignore. Her hand slides into my panties, finds my sex, her finger swirling around my clit. I'm sure I drench her hand, even though I'm nowhere near orgasm yet.

"I love that you're so ready," Lucy murmurs, her lips brushing mine. "And now when we're here, I'll remember this moment." I part my lips for her and lose myself in her kiss, in her touch. She tastes of ginger and truffles. Delicious. Then her fingers are inside me, stroking, thrusting. I want to make her feel the same, but I've only just grasped her shirt when she rubs my clit hard, and my orgasm rushes over me so fast that I feel like I'm seeing stars. I'm trembling, panting, my nerves pulsing and dancing, my knees weakening. She holds me up as my head rests on her shoulder, my fingers tangling in her cotton shirt.

"I love that I can do this to you," Lucy murmurs. I nod, still not sure I can find my voice, find my words. I come back to myself as Lucy withdraws her hand, feeling an ache as she does, desire pushing for more. I move my hands to her belt, and she puts hers over mine.

"We should go back to the farm," she says. "I have welding to do, and you need to cook. We need our menu set."

I'm sure I look disappointed.

Lucy leans in and kisses me, this time gently. "Don't worry, it'll be my turn soon."

"I promise it will," I say. I don't want to leave her wanting. "We'll have privacy in the shed."

❖

Lucy sets me up with a stool at the workbench, and I've grabbed one of my legal pads and a pen. I sketch out a diagram of the storefront, trying to figure out the best way to arrange the tables. "Is this crazy?" I ask her, looking up from my sketchpad.

"Which part?" Lucy asks as she putters around the shed.

"It just seems so fast." I'm talking about the restaurant, but I don't really want to admit that *us* seems a bit fast too. Not that it's a bad thing, it's just…fast.

Lucy sets a metal mouse by my pad. "We can do this," she says. "We'll take our time, do it right, no rushing."

I look down at the pad, then up at her. Her dark eyes are warm, and somehow, I feel reassured.

"I've always called this one Bert," she says, patting his little metal head. I'm not sure what he's made out of. I draw a little mouse on top of one of the diagrammed tables. It's horrible. Drawing is not my forte.

Lucy puts down another small creature, this one with wings. "It's a bat," she says, "but not my favorite. What do you think?"

I set down my pen and lift it up. "We could hang it near the door?"

"Or just leave it," Lucy says. She bends and brings up another creature, this one slightly larger. It looks like a Pomeranian.

"That one looks like a Princess, or maybe Queenie."

"Something a bit frou-frou," Lucy agrees. She goes back to a pile of metal and extracts another creature. It's bulkier, but recognizable.

"A cow suits," I say.

"It's a little chubby," Lucy says. "Feels too awkward."

"We could call her Moo," I say.

Lucy shakes her head, but she's smiling.

"That's so predictable."

"But funny," I add.

"We need to think details now," Lucy says, "like dishes. And paying for all this. I covered the costs of the permits, but we need to get the big things in order."

"I'll cover the costs," I say immediately.

Lucy frowns. "We should make this equal."

"I have a lot in savings." I'm not trying to brag, but it's true. That's what happens when I have no time to spend what I make. "All work and no play."

"Even still, we should do this up officially."

"I can ask Cindy to draw up a basic contract," I offer. "We can personalize it."

"I like that." Lucy sets the cow down and pulls out another little mouse. "All the expenses, and then any profit, equally split."

I pull out my phone, check my schedule, and text Cindy. "I'll figure out a time we can meet with an accountant, get everything set up."

"Perfect."

"When should we make this real?" I pull up my calendar.

"After the September long weekend," Lucy says. "If we do it on the long weekend, we risk people being out of town. The weekend after that."

"A month and a half, then," I say, calculating the days. "I think we can do it."

"The permits will be in by then, and we can get the space all set up."

"Lucy, we're really going to do this, aren't we?"

She grins, pulls me toward her. "We really are."

Chapter Twenty-one

I have a surprise for you!"
Cindy opens my door and nudges it with her hip—she's carrying two coffees. She plunks one down on my desk in front of me and drops into a chair.

I lift the coffee. "Latte?"

"Of course," Cindy says, "but that's not my surprise." She's excited and can't sit still, her feet tapping.

"You found out how I can be independently wealthy?" It's an ongoing joke.

"Pfft. No. Better than that."

"What can be better?"

"I've set you up on Facebook and Instagram and set up a basic website with the domain name you bought. You needed an online presence, stat."

"What?"

"For Ming Kitty, of course," Cindy says. "Kitty, you can't have a pop-up restaurant with no social media. That's how we're gonna get the word out." She sets down her coffee and takes out her phone, bringing up her browser. She types something in the search bar, then passes her phone over. Loading is a curled-up cat with brilliant orange text over top: *Ming Kitty.*

"Cindy, you are…" I hardly have the words. "Amazing. Incredible. Unbelievable. And so, so smart."

Cindy grins. "I know. And you can pay me back by letting me attend the first night, and every night thereafter. Or most of them."

"Done and done, and you'll get free meals besides." I'm in awe.

"You just need to give me the menu and the address and I'll put it in," she says. "And if you give me all your domain details, I'll get it transferred over. It's super easy. And give me whatever else you want on there. Pics, bios for you and Lucy, the works."

"I should be the one bringing you coffee."

"Caramel macchiato, extra caramel," Cindy says immediately.

"Noted."

"Have you and Lucy thought about a date for the first dinner?" Cindy asks, leaning forward and grabbing her coffee again.

"It'll be just after the September long weekend," I say. "We think we can get everything sorted by then."

"Do you have an invite list?" Cindy asks.

"Not yet, but we have some idea."

"And what about critics? You can't have an opening without a restaurant critic or two. It's publicity."

My stomach churns with nervousness. The idea of being judged wanting for my cooking is terrifying. I don't want to admit it, but there's so much riding on this, so much I want to accomplish. And I want it to be a success for Lucy and for her farm. If the critics end up hating us... that could be the end of everything.

"Your friend Jo Raj is a freelancer, isn't she?" Cindy asks.

Jo. She's taller than me—not that that's saying much—a bit crazy, super energetic, dresses with incredible individual style that I've always envied, and is one of my favorite people that I haven't seen in too long. Freelancer extraordinaire. "She works for one of the local free papers," I say. "I'll email her."

"There. Perfect. And the sooner you get the guest list, the sooner we can send out real invites. I've been looking online and this printer has fabulous templates that we can customize with the logo and everything."

"You are way too good at this. Why are you working in a law firm? You need to be in promotions."

"One day," Cindy says. "One day. I just need to get a bit more seed money so I can manage it. Event planning is so much fun. So much better than arranging meetings and lunches for the partners."

I hand Cindy back her phone. "What do I owe you for the website and Facebook page?"

"Nothing for the page," she says, "and I'll make you an admin there, and the web space right now is free, until you move it to your own. I'll update the DNS and stuff when you want to do that."

"You are incredible."

"I know." Cindy rises from her seat. "Your nine o'clock will be here soon. And I hope you brought me some delicious leftovers for lunch."

I didn't forget her when I packed up rice and chop suey yesterday before heading home from Lucy's. "Check the fridge. I have a few containers in there. A bit of everything we made yesterday. Let me know what you think."

"Yes!" Cindy pumps her fist. "Brilliant."

She heads to the door, giving me a wave as she exits.

I text Lucy, bringing her up to date. Then I open my email, searching through for Jo's address. I swallow another gulp of coffee, trying to ignore my anxious, fluttering stomach.

Jo, I have a new project, and I think it'll be right up your alley. Do you like Chinese food? I can only hope she does.

When I'm done with the email, I pull out my legal pad from my bag, the one with all the sketches and notes from the weekend. I flip to a clean page and start a list.

Cindy
Jo
Alice
Mom & Dad?
My boss?
No, probably not Jack.

And there, my brain stalls. Who else can we invite? We can't have tons of people, especially not for a first time, but we need a few more. I think again about inviting my boss, but my stomach does a flip-flop at that, a big one. No, that's one pressure too many.

I text Lucy. *Who should we invite? People in town?* We did discuss this a bit, but I feel like there should be more invitees. Should we ask the town mayor? Or is that too much?

I set the pad aside as I hear Cindy's voice just outside the door. The door opens, and it's my nine o'clock. I rise to my feet.

❖

At lunchtime, I meet Cindy in the firm's break room. She's already taken out the containers and is starting to put the contents onto a couple of plates.

"I can't wait to try these," she says, spooning out some rice next to a small heap of the honey and soy chicken. "My stomach is growling just at the scent."

"I hope they microwave well."

Cindy takes a fork and pops a piece of chicken into her mouth. "Fabulous cold. Is that a bit of truffle I taste?"

"It is. But we had it on the frisée, not in the chicken. Some of it must have transferred."

"It's good in the chicken too," Cindy says. She takes a large spoonful of the chop suey and puts her plate into the microwave. Another full plate is there, and my mouth waters even though I was eating all this food over the weekend. I have plans to make it again this week, each and every dish. I need to be able to do it quickly, and get my timing down. I want it to be like second nature by opening night.

The microwave dings, and Cindy takes out her plate and puts the second one in. She takes her plate to one of the three small round tables, then comes back for a glass of water. "I'm not going to wait for you," she says. "It smells too good."

"I won't hold it against you," I quip.

"Mm-hmm," is her reply as she takes a full forkful of rice and chicken. She gives me a thumbs-up as she chews, nodding.

The nervousness I've felt subsides, and there's a feeling of accomplishment instead. This will work. We can do it. I know we can.

When my plate is ready, I take it over to the table across from Cindy. She's devouring her meal, and I'm glad I brought a lot of extras. I take a forkful of my chicken, and she's right, it *is* delicious. Even better the next day, although I don't know that our customers would think so. I can imagine coming out to say "Thanks for coming everyone, enjoy your leftovers!" I try not to cringe. But if we could do that, it would keep the work of the evening down a bit. I'm going to have to practice the dishes, get them down pat. Figure out the quick methods. It's been a long time since I've cooked in a commercial kitchen.

God, I'm nervous again. I need to stop worrying, but I can't help it. I want everything to be perfect.

Cindy scrapes her plate clean with her fork, gathering the remaining rice. "You two are going to rock this pop-up," she says. "Have you figured out who to invite? A friend of a friend works for *Avenue* magazine, and his take might help. And maybe Jack knows a few people."

"I don't know that I want work people involved in this. At least, not until we've figured this out and are making a bit of money."

"Your dad will probably tell Jack, though, don't you think?" Cindy says. "They chat often."

"I hope he doesn't," I say. "I don't want more pressure. But I haven't told them yet, either."

"Are you inviting them?"

"I don't know."

"You should," Cindy says. "I know you've got them on the info diet, but this is something you want to trumpet. Brag a little."

"I guess so. They just get so judgy. They hated that I worked at a restaurant during my degree."

"Their loss. Want more food?" Cindy asks, rising. I shake my head. I have plenty for lunch, and I know I'll be eating more tonight, working on the steamed fish. "Oh, good, more for me." She grins and empties the container of chop suey onto her plate.

I pick at my own food. I should be inhaling it, but talk of my parents has put me off.

"Don't invite them if you don't want to," Cindy says. I look up from my plate.

"How is it that you know me so well?"

"I just do. But seriously, if it's going to upset you to have them there, then don't have them there."

"I want them to see what I'm doing," I reply, "but it's just…what if they don't like Lucy? Or don't like that I'm with her? Not to mention that if they meet her, they'll assume it's serious."

"Isn't it? Serious, that is?"

I shrug. "We're having fun. Lots of fun."

"Then keep having fun. Don't worry so much. Things will work out."

Easier said than done, but I'll try.

I text Kitty late in the afternoon. Over the past couple of weeks, things have started to come together, but I'm starting to worry, starting to wonder if this really was a good idea. It was, wasn't it? A restaurant, a pop-up restaurant? But what if we mess up? What if we burn the food? Or what if no one comes?

It's silly to worry, I know. My dad would have told me as much, told me to worry about things when they happen, not before.

We should do a test evening in the kitchen, Kitty texts back. *I've been worried too.*

Can you come out? I reply, texting quickly.

Maybe. This weekend for sure, but maybe earlier. Let me check my schedule.

I take my phone with me to the greenhouse, going through my regular walk, checking the hoses and trays, that the lettuce is growing and not wilting. Another batch will be ready soon.

Kitty texts me back about ten minutes later. *I'm done as of half an hour from now. I can drive out. Can we get into the storefront?*

Absolutely.

Let's make the steamed fish, and the chicken again, Kitty replies. *Do you know anyone who wants a free meal?*

I chuckle to myself. No one turns down a free meal.

I'll find someone.

My anxiety is slightly dampened, and I continue along my usual route. Tomorrow is farmers' market day in Airdrie, and I have to be ready bright and early.

❖

"I'm liking this," Alice says as she walks around the tables we've set up in the store. I'm so glad Beatrice isn't fussy about what we do, and that she hasn't found a new tenant. There aren't any tablecloths yet, but I ordered some on one of my quick breaks from work, and they should be here in time for the first night. Lucy's in the back puttering about, making sure we have enough stock for this evening's almost soft launch. I'm holding a bag, and Alice has been eyeing it since she came in. I know she's curious, but it's a surprise for Lucy.

"It'll be even better with the tablecloths," I reply. "It's just three of you tonight, right?"

"Beatrice will be here shortly," Alice says. "I think inviting her helps to soften her up, you know? You can get her more interested in the restaurant. And maybe she'll give you a good deal."

Beatrice has already given us a good deal, but she also confided in us that she was having a hard time getting anyone to lease the store.

"I'm sure she will." I glance back, toward the kitchen. "I'd better go find Lucy."

Alice waves me away. "I'll get the chairs set up and set the table."

I head back into the kitchen. Lucy has turned on the oven and the hood vents, and there's a rushing sound of air that wasn't there when we were first looking at the place. It brings me back to my days working in restaurants, and I'm not sure if that's good or bad. Those jobs were hard work, real hard work, not just paperwork. I sniff, and I can pick out the scents of the oven heating up, and of the food Lucy has set on the stainless-steel counter, the green onions and ginger and greens.

Michelle walks in with a grocery bag, and Lucy follows her. They take out chicken and fish and a package of tofu. Michelle smiles at me. "You two will be the best cooks," she says.

"We will," I agree, and Lucy nods.

"Now we need some time to work," Lucy says. She pulls out her phone and reads off our working menu. "You can choose from the soy sauce honey chicken with frisée, or the steamed fish fillet with rice and vegetables, or the tofu with the broccolini."

"I'll tell Beatrice and Alice," Michelle says. "We are more than ready." She leaves the kitchen, and Lucy turns to me.

"This is so real now," she confides. "Even though it's just the three of them. What if we mess this up?"

"We won't," I promise, sliding my arm around her back. She leans on me. "Besides, I have something that should make you feel a bit more professional."

I give her side a gentle squeeze before I withdraw and open the bag. I pull out a substantial folded square of white cloth and hand it to her.

"What's this?" she asks.

I had something similar when I worked as a cook, and I stopped at one of the kitchen supply stores in the city a few days back, knowing that we'd need real uniforms. Lucy unfolds the chef's whites, holding them up against herself.

"Do I look like a chef?" she teases, turning from side to side, looking down at the uniform.

"Of course you do." I pull out a second set of whites for myself, and then I pull out a chef's hat, a toque blanche, for her. "And with the hat, you can't be mistaken for anything else." I set a second toque on my whites on the counter. "We're professionals."

Lucy sets the toque on her head. "What do you think?" It presses down her dark hair, and it's not the most flattering of hats, but she's grinning and happy, and she looks amazing. I scoop up my whites.

"You look fabulous. Let's go change—then it's time to get cracking."

We head back to the storage room upstairs for a bit of privacy, and

I'm holding back my desire as I watch Lucy slip into the whites. We have a job to do. But the euphoria is there, and I'm hopeful that later we'll be able to celebrate properly, the two of us.

Once dressed, our street clothes folded up and in my bag, we head back to the kitchen. I take a small pad of paper and a pen from the pocket of my whites. "Shall I go take their orders?" I ask.

"Absolutely." Lucy's grinning ear to ear as she sorts out the food and pulls out a cutting board. Then she opens the bag of rice, and I notice that she brought her rice cooker from home.

"That will save us so much work." Thank goodness.

"Of course," Lucy says. She heads to the prep sink and runs the water as I go out to the front of house.

Alice, Michelle, and Beatrice are sitting around one of the tables in the middle of the restaurant, their place settings all ready and set for dinner.

"I brought a bottle of wine," Beatrice says, lifting a bottle and a corkscrew from a bag by her chair. "I hope you don't mind."

"Not at all," I assure her. "What a nice treat to have with your meals. Now, what can I get everyone?"

Alice starts. "I have a hankering for that tofu dish you have," she says. "I'm trying to eat healthier, so I think I need the veggies."

I write down her order.

"And you?" I ask Michelle.

"The steamed fish," she says immediately. "It's my favorite."

I turn to Beatrice, who smiles. "I've heard such great things about the honey and soy sauce chicken that I can't turn that one down. You'll have one of each to make."

I write down her order. "That'll be perfect," I say. "Please, enjoy yourselves and we will bring your meals out soon."

I check my watch. We should have everything out within fifteen minutes or less if we want to make it in this business. It's not fast food, or fast casual, so we do have a bit of leeway, but not that much time. Hungry customers are never that patient.

I hurry back into the kitchen.

"One of each," I tell Lucy, and we whip into action. I grab the chicken and everything I need for the soy sauce and honey marinade, then collect a metal bowl and a cutting board. Lucy checks on her wok, turns on the burner. She takes out all the ingredients for the vegetarian dish, the crisp tofu with broccolini. She marinated the tofu the night before, and it's in a large plastic container, ready to go. The red light signals the rice cooker is on, and we are on our way.

"Chop some green onions and ginger for the steamed fish," Lucy says when I finish mixing the marinade and chopping up the chicken, tossing it in the bowl before putting it into a baking dish. I pull out the second cutting board and chef's knife, prepping enough for the single dish. When I've done that, I get the frying pan and its lid ready.

"Eight minutes for the fish?" I confirm with Lucy.

She nods as she brings the vegetables over to the now heated wok. I pass her the vegetable oil, and she readies her chopsticks. I'd love to watch her cook with the wok—it always amazes me the way the vegetables cook in the wok, the way things are sautéed, crisp yet soft, flavorful with the sesame oil. I turn on the burner under the frying pan, my heart beating a little faster, feeling that anticipation, that excitement about cooking for others. And this time, it's cooking professionally, not just in my own kitchen. In a real commercial kitchen. I look over at Lucy, and she looks back at me, and she's grinning as much as I am.

A pair of grinning fools, my father would say. But it's brilliant, and I don't want to be anywhere else. I put the ginger and onions into the heated pan, listen to the sizzle, smell the delicious, sharp scent of the ginger, the freshness of the onions. I stir briefly, watching the pan closely to make sure I don't scorch the onions. This is the dish's flavor, right here. When it's done, I empty the pan into a small bowl, leaving the hot ginger and onions to steam on the counter. Then I put the pan on the burner once more, putting in a touch more oil. I toss the fish fillets onto the pan and hear them pop in the oil. I set up a mental count, knowing that I only need about a minute and a half before I can flip the fillets.

I flip them. Another minute or so, and they're ready for the ginger and onions. I take up the soy sauce and the sake, and I eyeball the amount. There's a whoosh of steam, and I grab up the lid and put it over the pan. I turn off the burner and set my watch for eight minutes.

Lucy's got the vegetables under control. I lean in and kiss her cheek. "Looks delicious."

"Go check the chicken," Lucy says. "That oven is so hot—we have to be careful."

I take a cloth and pull open the oven door's handle. The chicken is merrily bubbling away and looks like it's cooking quickly. We will make our time goal after all. I think.

I find the frisée and pull down another bowl. There's going to be a lot of dishes to wash, even though we're only making three meals.

"Truffle oil?" I ask Lucy, not spotting the tiny glass bottle.

Lucy points with her chopsticks. "In the bag there." There's a small plastic bag by the entrance to the kitchen. I hurry over and find the truffle oil. Perfect. Along with a bit of olive oil, also in the bag, I mix together a basic dressing for the frisée. Then I set it aside. The frisée is already cleaned, but I make sure it's free of its roots and trimmed.

I toss the frisée into a large bowl and go check on the chicken one more time. From behind me, I hear the rice cooker click.

"Rice is done," Lucy says. "Chicken should be shortly too. The tofu dish is nearly there."

I take three plates and head to the rice cooker, scooping out rice for each of the dishes. The ice-cream scoop works well; the rice is just sticky enough to hold together. Then I'm back to the counter, and I toss the dressing with the frisée and plate it for the chicken dish. The pale, gleaming leaves look appealing on the plate, and my mouth waters.

Lucy takes one plate and brings it to the wok. She pulls out pieces of tofu and vegetables and arranges them just so. And then my timer goes for the steamed fish. I lift the pan from the stove and bring it to the plate, carefully arranging the fish on the scoop of rice, now slightly flattened.

"Use a bit of the sauce over it," Lucy suggests. "And we can put some frisée with it tonight as well as the leftover veggies from the tofu. I'm not sure yet if I want to cook more veggies for this dish for our opening or not. We'll have to figure out what works."

"We could, but it might be more work," I say. Not that I mind.

"We'll see what I have ready at the farm," Lucy replies. She takes the oven mitts, opens the oven door, and pulls out the pan of chicken. It's bubbling away and smells amazing. Something about the savory of the soy sauce and the sweetness of the honey makes for an appetizing combination. Now my stomach growls. Lucy chuckles.

"We will have leftovers," she says. "We can eat while we do all the dishes."

"And we'll have a lot," I remark, looking at the range of bowls, utensils, and other dishes spread over the kitchen.

I take a pair of tongs and arrange the chicken on the plate next to the rice. "Should we put some sauce on the side?"

"That'll work. Let me see what I have." Lucy finds a small white ramekin on a shelf and rinses it out and dries it hastily. I take the pan and pour some of the sauce into it. It steams and bubbles a bit as I place it on the plate.

Lucy straightens her chef's whites and apron. "Ready?"

"Totally." Lucy grins at me, and I know I'm grinning back at her. We pick up the plates and, with great ceremony, take them out into the restaurant.

Alice, Michelle, and Beatrice are chatting animatedly when we appear, but they go silent, watching us approach, gazes eager as they take in the plates heaped with food.

"This looks amazing," Beatrice gushes as I put down her soy sauce and honey chicken. Alice doesn't even wait on ceremony; she lifts her fork and takes a bite only a second after Lucy sets down her plate.

"Soooo delicious," she says through her mouthful. "O-M-G, as the kids would say."

Michelle tastes the dish, taking a bite of tofu with vegetables. She nods as she savors it. "This is just right, crisp and the right flavor," she says. Then she looks at her daughter. "Your father would be very proud."

I can see Lucy starting to tear up, and I hook my arm around her waist. "We'll let you eat," I say, and Lucy nods. We leave them to their meals, and once we're back in the kitchen, Lucy wipes at her eyes.

"I wish he was here," she says. "It'd make everything that much more perfect."

"We could put out some photos on the walls, including him," I suggest. "And if we do this more often, we could have a special family wall."

"And maybe a little shrine," Lucy says. "Every Chinese restaurant has one, and we could have a bit of incense and photos of family."

She wraps her arms around me and I hug her back, feeling snug and safe and content, more than I ever felt possible.

But it only lasts a moment or two. We break apart.

"Dishes," we say in unison.

The work isn't yet done.

CHAPTER TWENTY-TWO

Kitty texts me a confirmed list of invitees as I'm just finishing up the loading of produce for the day, and my stomach flip-flops at the names of two food critics on the list. I've read their work, and I know they are tough customers. I know we need them to get the word out, to gain us some market share, but it still makes me nervous to know we're going to be carefully judged. The day of the opening is getting so close. My mind goes to the what-ifs, but I try to push them out. We can only do the best we can do. After the other night, I really think we can do it. We'll just have larger amounts of food. I would think that'd even be easier.

"Ready to go?" Alice asks as she pops into the house. I grab my binder and point-of-sale terminal. Today is the farmers' market down in inner-city Calgary, and I know we'll do a brisk business. It's an area with a lot of affluent customers, ones who are quite particular about their food and about where it comes from. I love that we have such success there, but I wonder about making the food more accessible. If we could do a discount day, or make more donations. I make a note in my phone. We've helped out charities before, but I'm starting to wonder about being more consistent. And what if we attached some of that work to the pop-up restaurant? There are so many possibilities, but right now, Alice and I need to get moving. I head out with her to the van, and we get on the road.

"You two are really going to make it," Alice says as we turn on to the highway. "The meal was right about perfect."

"Right about?" I tease.

Alice chuckles. "More people would give the place some ambiance," she says. "It was pretty echoey with just the three of us in there."

"We have a good list happening," I reply. I hand her my phone. "Check out Kitty's text." Alice flips to the message.

"Wowzers. We're going to have a full house, aren't we? She's so organized."

"I sure hope so. Cindy has a Facebook event scheduled and started up a page for us. Between the two of them, everything is sorted. It blows me away how much they get done. I feel like I don't do near as much."

"Oh, you do plenty, Lucy. It's just different." Alice pats my arm. "Just think—you might have to turn people away."

"If only," I say. "But we'll see. I think we'll be able to manage it. I'm so glad you're helping us with the opening night. I don't think we could cook and be servers at the same time."

Alice nods. "It'd be like a chicken with its head cut off. Running around all over the place, all panicky. I've seen it before. My first job was working at a little café in the town where I was raised in northern Alberta. Lunchtime rush with all the rig workers..." She shakes her head. "Insanity. Even as a hostess, and with a server and two cooks, we couldn't keep up. Those guys eat big, all the time." She looks at the list again. "What's Kitty's parents' names?"

Kitty told me once, but I'm having trouble remembering. "Last name is Kerr," I say. Alice skims the list.

"There are no other Kerr folks on here," she says. "Are Kitty's parents still alive?"

"They are. Are you sure there's no one there with that name?"

"Positive," Alice says. "That's a bit odd, don't you think?"

I frown. I thought Kitty had planned to invite her parents. Heck, I'm inviting Mama and several other townsfolk on top of that.

"You should talk to Kitty," Alice says. "We don't want to forget them." She pauses. "Have you met them?"

I haven't. And Kitty's never offered. That is a bit odd, but I didn't really want to pry after what Kitty had explained about her parents. But I really should ask.

❖

The farmers' market does a brisk business, and I barely have time to talk in between ringing up orders and packaging up vegetables and fruit for our clients. But Alice chats up everyone, and instead of her usual casual banter, she's all about the restaurant, gushing and hyping it. She's a one-woman advertisement, and we couldn't have better.

"When's the next pop-up?" one woman asks me. "This sounds so brilliant—I know my husband and I would love to go."

I find a piece of paper and write up a quick heading. "If you want a notification, give me your name and email, and I'll put you on our list."

"Fantastic!"

Soon I have a small but growing list of names, and I know we'll have to have more and more nights. Maybe every weekend, at this rate.

When the afternoon ends, and we pack up our empty boxes and bins, Alice is grinning. "You and Kitty are going to have the best restaurant ever," she says. "I can't believe we've had so much interest." She holds up the list of emails. "There's over fifty here."

"I should tell Kitty."

"I'll drive us home," Alice says. "You call Kitty."

❖

I've just closed the door on my last client of the afternoon when my cell phone rings. I hurry over to my desk to grab it, feeling the twinge in my feet as I do. I wish I could wear flats at work. I pick up the phone.

"Lucy, hey."

"We have so much interest!" Lucy sounds almost breathless with excitement. "At the farmers' market today, we collected emails, and we have over fifty people interested in the next evening for Ming Kitty."

"Fifty? Really? That's amazing." I hadn't even considered marketing the restaurant at a farmers' market. But we should have. It's exactly the sort that would be our customer base. I feel like an idiot but try to push those feelings away. "We really should figure out our next dates after the opening."

"What if we did it every Saturday?" Lucy suggests. "One night a week, and then if we keep having steady interest, we can expand. Beatrice says she hasn't had much interest in the storefront, and she'd rather we pay her for each use rather than have it always sit empty."

"I don't know how often I could do it," I say. Cindy's been a godsend with my schedule, making sure I have free time, but she's not a miracle worker.

"We'll figure it out," Lucy says. "But I wanted to ask you about the list for the opening—are your parents coming? I didn't see them on the list."

I pause. I don't know what to answer, or how to explain. Lucy's mom is so involved with her life, but mine...? Well, I see them, but we've always had our own lives. I decided not to invite them to the opening. Knowing them, they'd be busy or out of town.

"Kitty?" Lucy asks.

"I wasn't sure they'd be able to make it, so I didn't ask." It's a half-truth, kind of.

"Ask them," Lucy says immediately. "I want to meet them. And I'm sure Mama would love to as well. And Alice."

"All right," I say, though I'm dragging my feet.

"If they can't make it to this one, there's always another," Lucy reasons.

"I know." I just don't want them to turn me down. The shadow of too many school events with just a nanny loom in my mind, dredged up from the depths.

"They'll be so impressed," Lucy says. "Their little girl, running her own business."

"They might." Or they might not. *Lawyer* is impressive. *Chef*, not so much. Mom made it pretty clear when I was working during my degree that being in a restaurant was a temporary thing.

"Of course they will," Lucy says. "Call them."

"I will. I promise."

I hear a knock on my door, and I rise to get it. Cindy's outside. "I have to go—looks like I have more work."

"Call me tonight," Lucy says. "Tell me what your mom and dad say."

"I will."

Cindy comes into the office as I hang up. "Jack has socked us with another client," she says.

I drop back into my chair behind my desk. Suddenly I feel tired. So tired.

Cindy sets a file on my desk. It's not gigantic, but it's definitely bulging. "I've pushed back the meeting until tomorrow morning," she says, "but there's background information for review." She pats the file. "If you take it home, you can put your feet up and read it while you eat dinner."

Putting my feet up. Dinner. That sounds brilliant. And it might be the last time I get to do it before our big night.

"I'll get everything else sorted here for tomorrow," Cindy says. "And I'm so, so looking forward to the opening." She does a funny little excited hop. "It's almost time. And I want those delicious, delicious meals. I'm thinking of ordering one of each."

I can't help but laugh. "I don't think we do combos."

"That's your next market," Cindy says. "Trust me on that."

CHAPTER TWENTY-THREE

I feel like I hardly slept last night, the last night before our big day. Even with Kitty beside me, her warmth and breathing a comfort, I still couldn't sleep. I kept picturing all the things that could go wrong. Not enough rice. Scorching the fish. Burning the tofu. Tofu crumbling into bits. Spilling the rice. Serving raw chicken. Breaking the bottle of truffle oil. Running out of dishes. Heck, breaking dishes.

I rub my eyes and stretch, trying not to wake Kitty as I carefully move to the edge of the bed and sit up. The bed rocks a bit anyway, and Kitty's eyes flutter open.

"Morning already?" She looks a bit tired too, but nowhere near what I'm feeling. I didn't know I could feel so anxious. Even when Alice and I were first starting out with the farmers' markets, I still slept fine.

"It is. How'd you sleep?"

Kitty shrugs. "I've had better. But I've had worse." She smiles and wraps a hand around my forearm. "Don't get up, Lucy." She glances at the alarm clock on the bedside table. "We have a bit of time yet."

I glance over. It's not quite seven.

"All right." I pull the blankets back and slide in next to Kitty, who lays a leg over mine possessively. We face each other, and she rests her hand against my cheek.

"You look tired," she says.

"I am." I try to stifle my yawn.

"Worried?" Kitty asks. "We can do this, Luce. We've got it. It'll be a little rough as we smooth out the edges, but we've got this. You are an ace cook. I'm an ace cook. Alice and your mom are the sweetest ever, and all the customers will love them. I know we'll be fine."

I take a deep breath. We'll be fine. I repeat this to myself mentally, once and then again. Breathe in. Breathe out. Now, if only I could get more sleep.

Kitty snuggles closer, her hand sliding up under my tank top, cupping my breast, her thumb brushing over the nipple. A frisson of desire goes through me, right down to my toes. My tiredness is still there, but it's muted slightly. Kitty nudges me to my back and then rises over me, pushing the blankets down, and my tank top up over my breasts to rest just below my chin. I reach for her, but she moves away from my hand.

"Just for you," she says, then dips her head, her tongue teasing my nipples, one, then the other. She sucks them into her mouth, letting her teeth gently scrape the tips, and I shudder. This isn't enough—my need for her grows. I lift my hands, and she lets me put them through her hair, stroking as she works her way down my chest, over my belly, pausing at the waistband of my flowery bikini briefs. She kisses the skin just there above the band and looks up at me, her gaze hot with desire. She inches the briefs down, bit by bit, pressing kisses all the way. I lift my hips and she tugs harder, moving them down to my knees, then farther, and off. I'm not sure where they end up, but I don't care. I part my legs and her mouth comes down on me, nibbling at me, her tongue flicking my clit, tasting me, teasing me. Her touches are light, then firm, then light again, never consistent.

"Spread your legs," she murmurs, and I follow her direction, letting my legs fall open. She bends, lifting my buttocks in her hands, her mouth covering my sex, and there's no more teasing. She's on me and in me, licking and sucking, and I struggle to stay still, but I can't. I've never been able to. My hips arch against her, and she murmurs against me, the vibration another delicious sensation. I'm getting closer already.

Kitty shifts her grip and a finger slides into me, curling up, stroking my G-spot, and I can feel the orgasm fluttering, hesitating, waiting for that one touch to take me over. And she does, her mouth on my clit, her finger pressing into me. The shiver, the shuddering, the full-body sensation, takes over, and I lose every thought but her, her touch, her feel, and the orgasm.

She takes her mouth off me as I come down gasping, dropping kisses on my belly as she makes her way back up to my mouth.

"Better?" she asks, her satisfied grin looking impish.

I pause. The tiredness is still there, but it's like it's been quieted, almost fully muted. I'll probably notice it later in a bad way, but right now…I feel like I could climb mountains.

"How'd you know?"

"Serotonin," she says, surprisingly serious. "And I'll keep it up later if you need another shot." She laughs. "You look gorgeous in your chef's whites, you know. And there's a staff bathroom that needs christening."

I can feel my cheeks heating, but I can totally imagine us in there, blowing off steam. "Maybe once the evening's over," I say.

"Maybe," Kitty says. "Or maybe before it starts." She kicks the blankets the rest of the way off the bed and goes to get up.

"Not yet." I catch her, pull her down to me, my hands sliding into the back of the cute boy shorts she likes to wear to bed. "I'm not awake enough yet."

"No?" Kitty chuckles. "If you say so." Her hand slides between my legs.

❖

Everything feels like a rush, a blur, but I have my list on my phone, and we're on our way. All our food is in Lucy's van, and though my stomach's roiling with nerves, I know we've got this.

We've got this.

I keep repeating it to myself, but it's not stopping that roiling.

"Kitty," Lucy says, reaching over to take my hand. I've been fiddling with a loose thread on my jeans, and just having her hand on mine starts to calm me down. "We've got this." She winks at me, and I smile back.

"I said it aloud?"

"Yeah, you did."

"Oh."

"We'll be fine," Lucy assures me. "We have enough food for thirty plus a bit, which is all the space can hold, and we know what we're doing. We're awesome chefs. And if for some reason something bad happens, we'll handle it. It's not like we're going to burn the place down."

Just the thought of that happening makes my stomach roil even more, and I'm sure my face has gone pale.

Lucy squeezes my hand, hard. "Forget I said that. Everyone is going to be happy, we're going to make a bit of money, and we're going to ace this."

"We are going to ace this," I repeat. I mentally shove all my worrying thoughts away. We are both fully capable, fully sensible adults who can cook, and do it well.

Fortunately, I don't have too long to ruminate, as we hit the first set of lights in town, and from there it's not long until we're behind the shop, our restaurant for the day. Everything is quiet. There were a few people walking along the main street, but not many. We'll have a bit of peace in which to prepare.

I get out on my side and Lucy on hers, and she opens the back of the van. She hands me several boxes of produce, then accompanies me to the door, unlocking it with her key. She props it open with a rock that was left nearby, likely for that very purpose.

"I'll be right behind you," she says as I head inside.

The restaurant is silent, dark but for the light streaming in through the open door. I walk through into the kitchen, my sneakers barely making a sound on the standard red tile. I place the boxes on one side of the kitchen on the counter and head back to the door. Lucy has the boxes of chicken she ordered from the local Hutterite colony, and I take them from her.

"Thanks," she says. "I'll get the fish too."

I put the chicken in the fridge under the counter, though I know we'll be sorting it out soon. I run into Lucy on my way back out, and she slips past me with the fish, purposely bumping my hip with hers as she goes.

"Sauces and oils are in the box labeled *moving*," Lucy says. "And the tofu and rice are in another box."

"Got it." I pick up my pace, jogging back out to the van. I grab both boxes, carefully stacking them. They're heavy, but doable. I head back in and pass Lucy one more time. Once I put down these boxes, I find the light switch and turn on the overhead fluorescents. I blink into the sudden glare, the gleam of the light on the stainless steel.

"Beatrice told me there are some Cambros upstairs," Lucy says as she joins me in the kitchen. "We can run those through the dishwasher and use them for storage." She pushes her hair back from her forehead. "We have a lot to do."

I check the time on my phone. It's eleven in the morning, and the restaurant opens at five thirty.

"We've got this," I say, yet again. "Six and a half hours for prep."

"And food for us," Lucy adds.

"Want to make a doughnut run while I set up?" I ask.

Lucy's stomach growls. "I guess that answers that question."

"I'll find the Cambros if you get the doughnuts. Chocolate with chocolate icing for me."

"You'll have a sugar crash," Lucy teases, "but all right. Coffee too?"

"Black," I reply.

"No double-double?"

"Then I'd really crash."

"I'll be back." Lucy blows me a kiss as she leaves. I look at all the food, mentally plotting our day. I have a list, but seeing it all in front of me, I know what to do.

❖

I'm back from the doughnut run, coffees in a tray in one hand, a box of doughnuts in the other, and when I walk into the kitchen, I'm blown away by how much Kitty's done already. I glance at my watch, double-checking the time. I wasn't gone that long at all. But from the looks of things, I might as well have been away for an hour or more.

"I thought we were doing this together," I tease as I come in and set down the coffee in a clear spot.

"Oh, we are," Kitty says, laughing. "This one mine?" I nod and she grabs the coffee cup and takes a long drink. "That totally hits the spot," she says when she puts it back down. She looks utterly professional in her chef's whites, even more at home than seeing her in her lawyer's office and her skirt suits. She's more vibrant somehow, cheerier, and even though we have a lot of work to do, her energy level is off the charts.

"Go get changed," she says, "and stop ogling me." She comes over from where she has been chopping green onions and leans in to me. I loop an arm around her waist, and my lips meet hers. She tastes of coffee, lots of coffee, and when we part, I take a long drink from my own cup. I'm going to need the caffeine and sugar to keep going today. I'm nervous—in a good way—but I know that once I get started, I won't have time to worry about anything.

I change in the bathroom. Before I leave, I glance in the mirror. There I am, midforties, my rounded face under the toque, my hair looking even blacker than usual, my cheeks tinged with pink against the tan yellowish undertone. My eyes are animated, and I grin. I'm here, I'm cooking, and Country Mouse will move into a new era. It's not just about produce anymore. I can share my family's recipes, and in some ways, I'm carrying on the family business.

I hurry out to the kitchen, where Kitty is putting a huge pile of chopped green onions into a Cambro.

"The chicken's out. Want to get started on the marinade?" she asks as she sweeps the onions into the plastic container.

"Absolutely." I take up my knife and a nice big cutting board and get myself set up with a large Cambro, nearly a foot square, and open the box of chicken. The Hutterites have given us a box of chicken thighs, and while they did piece them out, they're not skinned or deboned. It's going to be a bit of work to get these ready, but I can do it. It brings me back to cooking with Mama when I was younger, when she taught me how to peel off chicken skin and to make the quick cuts to part the flesh from the bone. We used to save the remains for Alice's dogs, but today I'll just be putting them into the compost bin.

Kitty starts humming, and I can't quite make out what song it is. Something familiar, yet not. "What are you humming?"

"'Born This Way,'" Kitty says. "Apparently, a really crappy attempt at it."

"Why hum when you can sing?" Kitty grins and I want to tackle her. Instead I turn back to my chicken and picture Lady Gaga when I saw her in concert. Kitty hums again and I recognize the first bars. In a few moments, we both break into song. There's nothing quite like deboning chicken, tapping your foot, and singing along to Lady Gaga with your lover on a Saturday morning.

Until, that is, our memories falter.

"What other songs do you know?" Kitty asks when we both run out of lyrics.

"Madonna?" I grew up the geekiest Chinese Madonna fan ever.

"'Into the Groove'?" Kitty suggests. She's cleaning the frisée now, and I stop with the chicken, watching her dance in place as she hums the chorus. I chime in with the lyrics and then we're off. When I'm done with the chicken, I mix the marinade and shake it up in the Cambro before putting it into one of the fridges below the counter.

Time flies when you've got a lifetime's worth of Madonna songs in your memory and a companion who knows almost every one of them.

"Next time we do this, we need to bring in a radio."

"But it wouldn't be as much fun," Kitty says with a laugh. "Next song, your turn."

❖

"We're here," Alice calls out from the front of the restaurant. Lucy comes around the corner from the kitchen, wiping her hands on her apron. I have a bin of clean cutlery in front of me and I'm rolling it into paper napkins like I used to do during my previous job. Back then, it was a hostess's job to roll cutlery, but I used to help out when things were slow. It was a good chance to sit down without taking a real break, and that's a bit of what I'm doing right now. All our food is prepped and ready to go, and I feel like I've been on my feet for way too long. By the end of tonight, I'm going to be exhausted. Somehow this work is harder than being a lawyer, although it's also a lot more fun. I've never been able to sing Madonna's greatest hits during a deposition.

"This looks great," Alice says, coming to hug me and then hug Lucy. Michelle is carrying a large bundle in her arms, wrapped in paper.

"We stopped at the florist," she says, "because I wanted to give you both a little something to help brighten up the restaurant." She sets down the bundle and unwraps it, revealing two beautiful summer bouquets in slim glass vases. They are brilliantly colored, bright with daisies, baby's breath, carnations, and other flowers I've never learned the names for.

"Mama, that's perfect." Lucy hugs her mom, and I wish suddenly that I had that sort of relationship with my mother too. They're coming tonight after all, if they can make it. They said they would, but they've often missed engagements due to emergencies or last minute work things. More often than not, Mom's got an emergency at the hospital. I don't begrudge her, but every now and again, I wonder if she could just find a night off. I take a deep breath, pushing those thoughts aside. Whether or not they come, tonight will be amazing.

Michelle comes to hug me too, and I stand, hugging her right back, enjoying the sensation of being loved. Michelle is petite and getting older, but her hugs are strong, her arms wiry. In the last few months, she's become like a second mother to me. A more attentive, more present mother.

"I'm so proud of you both," Michelle says. "And tonight, it will be amazing. I know it will. And Alice and I will run around like crazy ladies."

Lucy laughs. "As long as no one drops any plates, we're good."

"It'll be perfect," Alice says. "We're confident." She pulls out a small notepad and pen from her back pocket. "And I'm set to go."

Lucy checks her watch. "We open in one hour." She glances at me and looks a bit panicked suddenly. "One hour," she repeats. I rise from my chair with the finished wrapped cutlery. Alice takes it from me.

"Go get ready," she says. "We'll finish up with the decorating."

I come up to Lucy and hold out my hand, and she takes it, gripping mine tighter than expected. As we walk back into the kitchen, I can hear her breaths in and out. Her hand is clammy.

I can remember crazy, chaotic nights in the restaurant biz, the running about and occasional panic as something burned or spilled or was missed. But with the two of us together, I know that we'll avoid that. Most of it, anyway.

"What if we mess this up?" Lucy says in a low voice as we step back into the kitchen. "Maybe we should have had another soft opening, but with more people."

"We'll do fine," I say, taking her in a hug. She clings to me, or rather, we cling to each other. It's not a sinking ship, but my stomach roils a bit. "There are seats for thirty and we can handle that many. It'll be the cleanup that gets us, all those dishes."

"Dishes I can do," Lucy says. "That's easy."

"We'll get all the chicken in first, and get the rice going, and then we can tackle all the rest. I'm hoping we won't just get orders for one dish, though."

Lucy leans back, though we're still embracing. "We don't have enough chicken if everyone orders it," she says worriedly.

"If we run out, we run out." I shrug. "We have as much as we can manage, and if we're short, then we'll substitute one of the other dishes. People will understand."

"I hope so." Lucy takes a deep breath, drops a kiss on my lips. "Let's get this party started, Kitty."

"Yes, let's." I kiss Lucy back, longer this time, no mere peck on the lips.

"People are lined up," Michelle says, coming back into the kitchen. "No more kissing, not until after." She chuckles. "Should I let them in?"

Lucy and I part. "Let them in," Lucy says. "And we'll get rocking."

❖

I never thought a restaurant kitchen would be so insane. I mean, I've seen the shows, *MasterChef* and a few others, but still…this is something else entirely. Maybe it's because I'm right in the middle of it, in the middle of the heat and smells and seeing a couple dozen orders up on the rack, Alice's white notepaper fluttering in the breeze created by the hood fans. The busiest day at the farmers' market has nothing on this.

Kitty's got four plates on what I've started considering her side of the kitchen, and she has everything set up and ready to go. On my side, I've got the rice cooking in the rice cooker, but a second pot on the stove, because I just know the rice in the cooker is not going to be enough. The majority of the dishes have rice, and the rice in the pot is just about done. I have the tofu happening, but I'm worried it's not going to be good enough. Fortunately, though, there haven't been as many orders for that one. The big seller so far is the soy and honey chicken. The fish is a close second, and I check my timer. Only a few more minutes on that steaming, and the fillets will be done. I check the time again and count back in my head. The rice should be done now too.

I take up a spoon and lift the lid on the rice. There's a lot of steam, which is good, but when I look at it, I see that there's still too much moisture. Damn. I give the rice a good stir and put the lid back on. Just a couple more minutes on that. I hope. I will admit that it's been a long while since I've cooked rice without using the rice cooker. It's not hard, but it's not quite so easy, either.

"Fish up?" Kitty asks, turning toward me.

I check the timer. "One more minute."

"And rice?"

The rice cooker clicks off. Thank goodness. "Yes!" I take up my dish towel and open the rice cooker's lid, lift out the inner pot. I take it and the scoop over to Kitty's side. She's checking on the chicken. And there are daikon fries coming out of the conveyor part of the oven. Everything at once. This is nuts, but it's exhilarating at the same time.

"Rice on those four plates," Kitty says, pointing, "then I'll get the fries on the plates for the fish"—she waves a hand to a stack of plates sitting nearby—"and then the chicken." I plate the rice in its molded scoops.

Not bad if I say so myself.

"Frisée," Kitty squeaks, and I turn to look at her. She grabs a metal bowl and takes the frisée out of the fridge below the counter. I turn to grab the truffle oil and olive oil, and when Kitty holds out the bowl of frisée, I hold the open bottles above it.

"How much of each?" I ask.

"Five drops of the truffle, maybe six," Kitty says, "then a couple tablespoons of the olive oil." Once I do that, my hands suddenly slick with truffle oil, she tosses the frisée with a pair of tongs and then plates it with the rice.

My timer goes for the fish, and I rush back over, taking the stack of plates with me. Alice is waiting at the pass-through, and Kitty says "Two fish, two chicken."

I rush back with the fish, and she plates the daikon fries with both dishes and puts them on the pass-through. Then she grabs the chicken from the oven and starts plating those. I check the next order. Three fish and one tofu. I take up the rice, scooping enough for each, then grab the fish, and then take my scoop to the wok and scoop out a healthy portion of the tofu and broccolini over the rice. Then back to the pass-through. And again.

And then I realize the rice is still on the stove. Shit.

I rush back and turn off the burner, and lift the lid.

There's definitely no moisture there. I take a sniff, and to my relief, there isn't that horrible smell of burned rice. A bit of scorch, maybe, at the bottom, but the majority is just fine. Thank goodness.

"Rice," Kitty squawks, and I take the empty cooker pot from her and move the pot from the stove to a spot on the counter. We scoop and prepare plates, trying our damnedest not to make things look like a mess. I make more stir-fry, and Kitty puts more daikon fries in the oven.

And then, about as suddenly as it started, all the orders are done.

They're done.

We've done it.

I look at Kitty. She looks at me. Her hair is coming loose from its ponytail, and her face is flushed, and her toque is askew, and I have no doubt that I look similarly ruffled.

"I think we did it," she says, and we lean against each other and against the counter. My hand is in hers, and she squeezes my fingers. "We should go look."

"In case anyone's getting sick from the food?" I joke.

Kitty nudges me. "Don't jinx us," she quips. We tiptoe out of the kitchen and poke our heads around the corner to look out at the dining room. Alice and Mama and Cindy are moving around the tables, taking dishes, talking to the customers, and everything is running as smoothly as I could have imagined. The murmur of voices and conversation is louder here, the clink of cutlery occasionally heard over the chatter.

"Should we say something?" I ask. I'd thought about it a little bit but could never settle on anything specific. Kitty nods.

"We really should. Just a brief *thank you for coming* and all that?"

"You or me?"

"Both of us," Kitty says. "I'll talk restaurant, you talk food?"

I nod. She smiles, and I lean into her for a kiss. "We've got this."

I step out into the dining room, Kitty just beside me.

Everyone is talking and eating and having fun, and I'm amazed to see everyone enjoying the food we made. You'd think it should be a given, should be obvious, but until you see it with your own eyes... well, until then it's just a hope, a wish.

Cindy spots us and she stands from her table, ringing a spoon against her glass. I glance at Kitty, and she glances back at me, and Kitty gives me a quirky grin. Then she faces our customers.

"Thank you so much for coming to the first evening for Ming Kitty," she says, her skilled lawyer's voice going out over the crowd, projecting to every corner of the dining room. "It means a lot to us that you've come and tried our food, and from the looks of the plates, enjoyed it right to the very end." There's a slight tinkle of laughter.

"This is a dream come true for us," I add, "and it's one that I've always wished for. And I'm so proud to announce that the majority of the food you've enjoyed tonight is very, very local. The produce is all from Country Mouse Farms, the honey is from the shop down the road, the Verandah, and the proteins are from the Hutterites."

"The only bits that aren't local are the truffle oil and sauces," Kitty quips, "so if you know a local source for those, our next pop-up will be even more local than it already is."

"Our next dinner evening will be posted on our social media," I add, "and we'll put the word out locally too. As a thank you for being our first ever customers, we have two kinds of dessert for you: a homemade red bean soup and locally made ice cream."

"Thank you so much for coming," Kitty says. "You guys are the best."

There is applause, loud enough that I feel like my ears are ringing.

Kitty squeezes my hand. Mama waves at me from their table in the back. Next to her, I notice an older couple, and the woman looks an awful lot like Kitty.

"Did your parents come?" I ask her, leaning over, my voice quiet. Kitty scans the room. "There, by Mama."

"They did." Kitty sounds shocked, surprised. But we don't get a chance to go over there. A woman approaches us.

"Hi, Kitty! Oh my God, you've done something amazing, you two." She turns to me. "I'm Kitty's friend Jo Raj, freelance food critic extraordinaire. Can I chat to you about your pop-up?"

Kitty nods. "Why don't you come back into the kitchen while we prepare the desserts? Then you can ask us whatever you'd like."

"Plus we'll give you an early taste of the red bean soup," I add. Jo looks delighted.

"It's been so long since I've had any," she says, "and that was only once at a restaurant in Chinatown. I wish I knew how to make it."

"I might tell you while we're plating it up," I say, "but I hope you'll come back to our next pop-up for more."

"Of course," she gushes.

Once we're in the kitchen, I set to organizing thirty bowls, and Kitty goes to bring out the ice cream from the walk-in freezer. Earlier we had figured on ten bowls of the red bean soup and twenty of the ice cream, with room for refills. We saved a bit of money by buying the ice cream in bulk, but it's a definite investment, offering it free. But I'm glad we're able to do something to thank our customers, even if most of them were direct invites. I don't want this to be our first and last evening.

"Where did you come up with the idea?" Jo asks.

Kitty and I look at each other.

"I met Lucy at her stall at the farmers' market," she begins, "and I tasted her blackberries."

"Do we get blackberries tonight?" Jo asks.

"Unfortunately we're out of them right now," I reply, "but in future evenings, we definitely will have some. Tonight, though, we have some fresh raspberries for the ice cream."

"How did you go from blackberries to Ming Kitty?" she asks. "And how did you come up with the name?"

I feel suddenly shy. I didn't think that a reporter would want the full details of our story. I go to pick up the pot of red bean soup and let Kitty answer that one.

I carefully fill each bowl and listen to Kitty as she tells our story. She is so confident and steady that it's easy for me to fall into the story, to listen like it isn't our own.

"And the name of course," Kitty says, bringing me back to full focus, "is for both of us, right, Lucy?"

Jo turns to me. "It's part of both of us," I say. "Ming Nhon is my Chinese name, and of course, Kitty for Kitty. It's both Western and Chinese, like our menu, and us."

"That is so great," Jo gushes, scribbling in her notebook. "I have enough to make an article, and then some."

"Fantastic," Kitty says. "We really appreciate you coming. I hope the publicity will help us on our way."

"I think you have a great concept," Jo says. "And you'll have a full-time restaurant in no time at all." She finishes scribbling in her notebook and then tucks it away into her purse. "I'll get out of your way, and of course, I'm looking forward to that red bean soup."

"I'll make sure you get a bowl," I promise.

Mama and Alice appear in the doorway. "Are you ready for us?" Alice asks. They are both carrying trays, and I see Mama has a second one.

"We are," Kitty says. Alice comes in and holds out her tray, and Kitty places bowls of ice cream, each decorated with half a dozen raspberries. Mama comes over to me, and I fill her tray with bowls of red bean soup. Then I fill the second tray and lift it up.

"Ready?" I ask Kitty. She has laden herself with bowls even though she doesn't have a tray.

We head out into the dining room. The chatter is still there, a dim roar, but there's a slight quieting as our customers take in their dessert. To my surprise, I run out of red bean soup and have to go back for more. Mama does too, and Alice has to come back for more ice cream as well.

After we've made the rounds and everyone is eating, Kitty and I start helping Mama and Alice clear the dinner dishes. It's a lot of trips back and forth from the dining room to the dish area with the three trays, but it's more elegant than hauling in a big plastic tub like it's an old-time diner. I scrape the minimal leftovers into the organics bin and stack the dirty plates on the counter, and Kitty finds a spot for all the wineglasses. Alice comes back.

"You two should get out there and talk to people," she says. "Let me organize this. Go talk to your adoring public."

Kitty sets down her tray. "Yes, ma'am," she says, and Alice laughs. "I'm not old enough to be a ma'am. Go on, you." She waves us out.

In the dining room, our customers are lingering at their tables, empty dessert bowls in front of them. We start at the nearest table, where Cindy and a few of her friends have set up camp.

"So delicious," one of Cindy's friends gushes. "You have to tell me when your next night is, because I want to bring all my friends."

"We're not all here already?" jokes another of the women at the table.

"Other friends," the first woman replies, sticking her tongue out. It's hard not to laugh.

"You'll be full every night," Cindy says, "and deservedly so."

"Thanks, Cindy," Kitty says, bending to give her a hug. Then we move on. I keep looking at the table where Kitty's older almost-lookalike is sitting, and eventually we come around to that table. The woman smiles and rises to her feet.

"You did so well, honey," she says, giving Kitty a hug. "And so did your...friend."

"Girlfriend, Mom," Kitty corrects, but gently. "This is Lucy."

"It's so good to meet you, Lucy," Kitty's mom says, shaking my hand. It's very formal, but then, Mrs. Kerr seems like a formal kind of lady. She's wearing a similar type of skirt suit to the ones Kitty wears to work, but somehow it seems stiffer, less comfortable. The man with her rises as well and gives Kitty a kiss on the cheek.

"I always thought you might become a chef," he says to Kitty.

"Really?"

"You were always trying out new recipes," he says. "It was bound to happen." He smiles at me. "I'm Clarence, Kitty's dad."

"Nice to meet you," I say. "Glad to hear you liked the food."

"We wouldn't have missed it," Kitty's mom says. I notice Kitty stiffen, but it's subtle and I doubt anyone else has noticed. "Can we take you two for a celebratory drink?"

"We have a lot to do," Kitty says. "Those dishes won't wash themselves. But how about we have dinner next weekend?" She turns to me. "Would that work for you?"

"Friday?" I suggest. "I'll be in the city for the farmers' market."

"Sounds perfect," Kitty's mom says. She gathers her light jacket from the back of the chair. "I'll text you," she says to Kitty, "and we'll leave you to your fans." She gives Kitty another hug, and Kitty's dad does the same. I want to ask Kitty more about her parents, but we're beset by Beatrice, and then by some of the other townspeople. By the time we get back to the kitchen to start tidying up, I feel like I'm floating on air.

CHAPTER TWENTY-FOUR

Washing dishes is soothing. There's something about how methodical it is, how repetitive, that helps me come back to a less anxious side of myself. I'm still on edge from seeing my parents, and from having them compliment me on our venture. I never thought they'd be proud of this, of my being a chef, a restaurateur. The expectation of having an important job—lawyer, doctor, investment banker, that sort of thing—was always high, always pushed as the best and only option. Cooking, well, that was just for fun at home, if that.

I glance behind me. Lucy's cleaning up the kitchen, turning off the oven, wiping down the stove and the counters, and gathering up all the leftover food, which isn't much, thankfully. We'd guessed right. Or mostly right. There's still enough produce left over, which means we'll be eating frisée for a few more days at home. Or I'll be taking it for lunch.

My stomach grumbles.

"Anything left for us?" I call out to Lucy.

"Oh yes," she calls back. "Which do you want? I can make some more fish, or we can have the stir-fry."

"Fish sounds great," I call back. "With frisée, though, not the daikon?" I've been craving that truffle dressing all night.

"Of course." Lucy sets the pan up on the stove and goes to chop some more ginger and green onions. I turn back to my work, sending another full tray through the dishwashing machine, and pulling out the clean tray. I gingerly grab the hot plates one after the other and stack them at the end of the counter, piles for the plates and for the bowls. Once they've cooled a bit more, I'll put them back into their places.

I grab one of the trays for glasses and fill it, then stack another tray on top, filling it as well. By the time Lucy calls me for dinner, the dish area is nearly clear. I'm glad once again that we were able to find this space. It's worth every dollar we're paying Beatrice for the rental. I almost can't wait to sit down with the books and figure out if we've made any money, or if we've broken even.

We take our plates into the now empty dining room and sit down at one of the vacated tables. Alice and Mama are sitting at a table near the door, chatting with Cindy.

"There you two are," Cindy says. "Did you want any help with anything?"

I look at Lucy, who looks at me. "I think we're good," I say. "Just need to eat before I starve to death." I rise from my chair and give her a hug. "You've been amazing. You don't need to do anything else."

Cindy grins and hugs me back. "I'll head out then. See you on Monday at work."

Work. Right. In the fuss of the last day or so, I completely put the firm out of my mind. "I'll see you Monday."

"We'll head back to the farm," Michelle says. "Leave you two to it for now. I'll keep the porch light on."

"Thanks, Mama," Lucy says. After another round of hugs, Michelle and Alice leave. Lucy locks the door behind them and pulls the venetian blinds on the storefront windows. I look around at all the tables, the bits left over from the evening that we haven't cleaned, and all the tablecloths. There's still a lot of work to be done.

Lucy catches my gaze. "After dinner," she says. "If I don't eat, I'm going to fall over."

We scarf down our food in a rather unladylike way—good thing there's no one around to see us be so undignified. I push back my plate, setting my cutlery on top, and lean back in my chair.

"I could sleep for a week."

"Me too," Lucy says. "But this was brilliant. It went so well."

"It really did." We look at each other, the silence stretching, warm and comfortable. I've never felt so happy. And it's all due to her. To us. "I love you, Lucy."

Lucy's cheeks flush. She clasps my hand. "I love you too, Kitty."

The rush in my body, in my heart, warms me all over. This is how it was meant to be. Cindy was right.

❖

We pull up outside home a fair while later than I'd planned, but Mama has indeed left the porch light on for us. Kitty and I stagger up the stairs, and I can feel the burn in my legs, the exhaustion filling me. I've worked long days, but there's something about cooking and then all the cleaning that has taken it out of me more than a long day in the greenhouse. We kick off our shoes and tiptoe up the stairs in our sock feet. I'm pretty sure Mama is long asleep. She sleeps more soundly than anyone I've ever known.

"I need a shower," Kitty whispers.

"Me too."

"We won't wake anyone?" Kitty asks.

"Unlikely," I say, "and Mama wouldn't mind even if she did wake up. She knows what it's like to work in a hot, smelly kitchen."

"Oh, good." Kitty lets out a relieved sigh. "I could not stand going to bed. I must reek."

"If you do, then so do I."

I lead Kitty into the bathroom, grabbing fresh towels for both of us. Kitty shuts the door and we strip down, piling our chef's whites on the floor. I lean in and turn on the hot water, testing it. The heavy splash of cold water on my arm raises goose bumps. Kitty rubs my back, chuckling.

"It's warm in here," she says.

"Not with the water," I reply. I take my cold hand and cup her breast, and she lets out a gasp of shock.

"Lucy!" She sounds breathless, yet trying not to laugh. I take the moment to squeeze her nipple. She shifts so we're touching from knee to chest, and I slide my arms around her, this time cupping her ass. Kitty chuckles. "Not much junk in the trunk," she says.

"Doesn't matter." I squeeze her there too. "You're just right."

"Like Goldilocks?"

"Better. Way better." I lean over to check the water. It's hot, finally.

We shuffle into the tub and under the spray, and there's almost nothing that feels better on sore muscles. The smell of cooking and food rises from us and I wrinkle my nose. Kitty bends to grab a bottle of body wash and a washcloth.

Unsurprisingly, we're too tired to do much but wash. My dreams of another celebration will have to wait until morning.

CHAPTER TWENTY-FIVE

When I come into work this Monday morning, feeling like it is too, too early, all I can think about is Lucy's face, the crinkling around her eyes when she laughs, the way her cheeks go a bit pink, the way she feels next to me in bed, and the way we worked hard together on Saturday night. In short, I'm dragging, because lawyering is starting to pale against being with Lucy and the hectic, yet fun environment of Ming Kitty. Seeing all those faces, all those people eating our food, enjoying each other's company…that was so satisfying.

I push open my office door, turn on the light, and head to my desk. The piles of paper I left there on Friday are still there, and I'm pretty sure that new paper has joined them. Does paper multiply like fruit flies? I haven't been able to prove it yet, but I'm pretty sure that it does. I set down my bag and take off my sneakers, changing into a pair of low heels I keep specially at the office. My feet protest, but I'll have to ignore them. I settle into my chair and pull the closest file toward me. There's going to be a lot of catching up to do, and I know my schedule is solid today and tomorrow. My first meeting is at nine, at least, so I have a couple of hours to get sorted.

As I'm reviewing a contract for a new client, I hear Cindy come into the assistants' area outside of the office, talking to one of the other paralegals. I look up as she comes into my office, carrying coffee— thank goodness—and a newspaper under her arm.

"I didn't know that you read the newspaper in paper," I remark as she sets the coffee down in front of me. "Thank you so much." I take a deep drink. "I need this so badly today."

Cindy grins, setting down her own cup and taking the newspaper out from under her arm. She spreads the broadsheet over my desk, draping it over the files, and flips to the food and entertainment section.

Then she points at an article. The headline, though small, reads: *Perfect Pop-up for Your Chinese and Western Cravings.*

"Jo just *loved* Ming Kitty," Cindy gushes. "You need to get out the word for another evening really soon. This will bring in the interest."

"It's in the paper already?" I turn my attention to the article, amazed that we could have gotten such a good review so quickly.

"Country charm and good taste," Cindy quotes. "I won't say that you and Lucy will be millionaires, but holy cow, this is a great start."

"I wonder if we can do another one this Saturday." I pull up my calendar. Somehow Cindy has managed to keep all my appointments to the regular workweek, with a few later evenings, and my weekend is free. "I'll call Lucy and give her the news."

"You should do every weekend," Cindy says, "and take advantage of the publicity. Not to mention the great weather. More people will drive out of town."

I reread the article. I can't help but focus on the compliments: *crisp yet roasted finish, elegant frisée with the indulgence of truffles, a carefully curated mix of Chinese and Western cuisine.*

"I'll leave you to it," Cindy says, "and I'll get prepped for the meeting at nine. Mr. Pegau always likes coffee, doesn't he?"

I nod. "He's not fussy, though. Black coffee, no fancy stuff."

Cindy smiles. "The easiest way."

I go back to my files, making notes and setting things aside to send to the court and to other lawyers. I feel like I'm making some progress.

My phone rings around eight thirty. I answer it without thinking. "Kitty Kerr."

"Kitty, it's Jack," my boss says. "My office, please. Now." He hangs up.

Jack's never been that blunt, that short. Suddenly my day doesn't feel so good. It reminds me of when I was a kid, when I messed up and my dad would call me into his office and give me a dressing-down. It didn't happen often, but when it did, I never forgot it. Just the thought makes me tense, and I know my breathing is increasing, my hands clammy. Cindy comes in.

"Jack just said we need to be in his office," she says. She looks puzzled. "I'm not sure why—there's nothing on your schedule."

I shake my head and rise, willing my stomach to quiet, willing my anxiety, my attack of nervousness to subside. It doesn't, but I have to pretend it has.

"Let's go."

"You all right?" Cindy asks in a low tone as we leave my office and head down the hallway.

I shake my head again. Cindy stays quiet; she knows just as well as I do that this isn't a pleasantry for Jack. If he's going to do that sort of thing, he comes to his associate's office, not the other way around. Each footstep feels like a mile.

We reach the desk of Jack's assistant, who waves us in. "He's waiting for you," she says. To me, she sounds pitying, and that makes me even more nervous.

"Come in, Kitty, Cindy," Jack says as we reach his open door. "Close the door behind you." Cindy closes the door once we've entered, and we take the seats that he indicates in front of his desk.

"I had a call from Mr. Anderson on Friday evening," he says, "and it seems that the companies who liened his property filed in the courts and at the Land Titles office. He was very concerned and thought you had filed all the paperwork to have that lien removed." His voice is even, but firm. My heart's in my throat. I remember that paperwork, the notices sent. I think back to the dates, mentally counting, and realize that I forgot the filing.

"I am so sorry," I say. Words can't even express what I'm feeling, that mix of embarrassment, horror, and worry that has no name. "It is absolutely my fault."

"I should have known too," Cindy says.

"Regardless of whose fault it was, it lies with you, Ms. Kerr," he continues, "and that means that our client is now having to defend a lawsuit to pay fees to companies that never completed the work they were ordered to, and who he shouldn't have to pay. As such, you will be taking his defense in this lawsuit, and you will be doing it pro bono. This is a junior mistake, one that I thought you'd be better than to make."

I want to sink through my chair and into the floor. His tone is cold, his gaze icy, his lips thinned. He really is angry.

"Sir, Kitty's schedule is packed solid," Cindy says, bravely defending me. I love her for it, though I wish she wouldn't. That's not going to make things any easier.

"She has evenings and weekends open," Jack says, looking at me pointedly. "And I'm quite sure she can do it. Right, Kitty?"

"Yes, sir," I say, knowing I sound just as I feel, ashamed and at a loss.

"But…"

"Ms. Torres, please be silent." Jack focuses on me. "I appreciate that you are spending a lot of time at work already, Ms. Kerr, but I am also aware of your side project and how it has taken your attention from the firm." He slides a copy of today's paper onto the blotter in front of him. "While I'm impressed with your moxie, I can't help but think that if you really wanted to be a partner, you would have held off on your pop-up, or found someone else to run it while you did your real job."

I swallow hard.

"In fact, your billable hours have dropped recently," he says. "You're in the lower third of associates at the moment, and you used to be at the top." He shrugs. "Mr. Anderson wanted you fired and threatened to pull his business from our firm. You know that he does hundreds of thousands of dollars' business with us every year. I'm not sure that I'm right to keep you on, quite honestly. It's only my long-standing friendship with your father that has me giving you this opportunity to make things right."

"Please give me another chance." The words are out before I can even think about them. Desperation twists inside me, and I can't bear the thought of losing this job, of losing the partnership. I've worked so hard for this for so long. I was impressing Jack, impressing my parents, impressing the other associates…I had been doing so well.

"I will," Jack says, "but on one condition. Mr. Anderson has to win his suit. If he doesn't, our corporate reputation will be sullied, and neither I nor the other partners can tolerate that, or that our insurer will have to pay his costs. I'll expect regular daily reports from you and Cindy in regard to this file, and I will be speaking regularly with Mr. Anderson about how he feels the case is progressing. He's very influential, and he is one of our best clients. Understood?"

"Yes, sir," I reply.

Jack checks his watch. "Your meeting starts soon. You'd best be on your way."

It's a dismissal, and a curt one. I rise to my feet, trying to hide my shakiness. Cindy rises too, and we don't look at each other until we're back in my office. The walk back seemed interminable, as if every associate, every paralegal was staring at us, knowing that we'd messed up.

I feel like I'm going to be sick, but I can't be.

"I'm so sorry, Kitty," Cindy says as I shut my office door. "It completely slipped my mind, and I must not have added it to the calendar."

"It's my fault. I wasn't paying proper attention. I knew better. I should have done better. I should have been focused on what counts." I pace back to my desk, then turn, pacing back to the door. "Dammit. If only I hadn't been so involved with the pop-up. It was stupid of me. Cooking isn't important. I could have had the partnership, and this sets me back." My stomach clenches. I'd let my emotions take over, let Lucy's charm and attention take away my focus.

"But you love the pop-up," Cindy points out. "This weekend was amazing. It was totally worth it."

"Not if I don't make partner, it isn't," I say. "I've wanted that for even longer. Longer than anything."

Cindy purses her lips, nods. I don't need to be a mind reader to know that she doesn't agree with me. We've been friends that long, but I don't know how I could explain it in a way that she'd understand how important being partner is to me. She's a romantic, through and through. I love romance, and Lucy's amazing, but our pop-up can't come before my job. Nothing can.

"I'll make sure your nine o'clock comes in on time," she says. "And I'll schedule in Mr. Anderson's work too. You should have time between meetings this morning to give him a call." She turns and leaves. I know she's disappointed in me, but that'll have to be dealt with later. I can feel the weight of Jack's expectations, and the weight of my own.

I'm not even sure what time I get in to my condo—all I know is that it's late. Too late. My feet hurt from the heels, even though I changed back into my sneakers before I left the office. I have files in my bag, but I'm not going to be able to get to them. All I want is a hot bath and my bed. And I need to call Lucy. I check the clock. Eleven.

It's too late to call, I think. It must be. Lucy's up with the birds. She'll be asleep by now. We texted briefly today, but I didn't mention anything about the restaurant or about work, just that I was busy.

I set my bag down by the kitchen bar and pull out my phone. Heimei looks at me from her perch. I've never been particularly fanciful, but it does seem that she too is disapproving. I text Lucy, a quick *Just got home from work*. I set my phone down and go to the fridge, pull out a bottle of water. I down half of it. The office is so dry, and I didn't have much time to stop for hydration. Cindy did manage to convince me to eat a sandwich at lunch and a salad at dinner, so at least I'm not starving. My stomach growls. Well, I'm a bit hungry. I pull open my fridge again and scan the contents. Not much there. A plastic container that I'd brought home yesterday from the farm. I grab it, pry open the lid. Lucy's mother made me some extra congee yesterday morning and insisted I take a container home. Right now, I am incredibly thankful. It will be the perfect snack to have before I go to bed.

My phone buzzes on the counter. I pick it up. Lucy's calling. I thought she'd be asleep.

"Hey," I answer.

"You sound tired," Lucy says. "Work busy today?"

"Unbelievably. So much so that I'm just about to eat and then crawl right into bed. It's another long day tomorrow." So long. With the preparation for Mr. Anderson's file as well as my other work, I know it's going to be another late night. I feel overwhelmed with all I need to do.

"Thanks for sending the link to the review," Lucy says. "We really did well, didn't we?"

"We sure did." A surge of love, of accomplishment surges through me, a feeling I thought I'd almost forgotten after today's woes, but it fades quickly.

"Alice thinks we should do another one this Saturday," Lucy says, "and capitalize on the review. We definitely have enough produce to stock the place again. And I think we can afford the chicken and fish. Unless we should try some new dishes? I don't know."

"I can't do it this weekend," I admit after a long pause. "My boss has given me a ton of work this week." I try to keep my voice strong, keep it from shaking. I don't want to admit to my screwup, even to Lucy.

"Can he do that?" Lucy asks. "That's not fair. You have a life outside work."

"Work's not fair," I agree, "but there's not much I can do about it. I'm *thisclose* to making partner, and it's what's expected."

"What about the weekend after?" Lucy asks. "We can't let this go too long. Or what if we do a quickie pop-up booth at the farmers' market here in town? I can talk to the woman who does the bookings, and I'm sure she'll be able to squeeze us in. It's Saturday morning from ten o'clock until two in the afternoon."

"I can't." My heart is sinking, but I have no idea if I can even carve out the four or five hours that Lucy is asking for. I don't want to be unemployed. I want that partnership.

"We need to keep doing this," Lucy says.

"I know we do." I try to hold back a yawn but fail. "I'm sorry, Luce. I can't do this. Ming Kitty is taking away from my real job. I need a break."

There's silence on the line. Then I hear a deep breath.

"All right," Lucy says, though her voice is tight. "But we need to figure out when we can do another evening, so we can start advertising it."

"I can't. I'm sorry, Lucy, but I can't. I need a break from this."

More silence. My stomach churns.

"What kind of break?" This time Lucy's voice is quiet, barely heard.

I don't want to say the words, but I know that I can't focus on work and her at the same time, can't take any time for a personal life. It feels like there's a vise around my chest. "A break from everything."

"Right." The word is sudden, sharp. "Don't let me keep you up." There's a click, and then empty space. Lucy's gone.

I set my phone down with shaking hands and look at the congee on the counter, waiting to be warmed up. The last thing I want now is to eat, especially not Michelle's congee. It reminds me too much of Lucy, too much of the farm. I need to focus, and it's late. Bedtime.

I dump the congee into the compost bin and go to bed.

CHAPTER TWENTY-SIX

I don't know what to do. I'm in the greenhouse, but I'm not really focusing on my work. I keep hoping to feel my phone buzz in my pocket, to hear Kitty's voice, but she meant it when she said *a break*. My deadline for arranging the farmers' market is coming right up. I know Betty, the organizer, and I need to call her and tell her the plan is off.

Every time I've gone into town this week, people have been stopping me to ask when our next pop-up night is, and I haven't been able to tell them, just to direct them to our website or to our Facebook page. I wanted to be able to say *Next Saturday, be sure to come!* or something similar.

And I worry about Kitty. Monday night she sounded utterly exhausted, more than I've ever heard her sound before. More exhausted than after cooking Saturday night, or even after any usual work night for her. I shake my head. I shouldn't even be thinking about her. I should have known a city girl would choose her city life over me. They always do. And with her job, with it being so all-encompassing, I really should have known better. I let our casual thing become a lot more, got swept up in the excitement of Kitty, of the pop-up, of finding a real partner and a real passion.

❖

Alice and I get into Calgary early, early enough that I can deal with the traffic downtown, find a spot outside Kitty's building, and grab two punnets of raspberries to take up to her. I had thought about it and decided not to bring her anything, but Alice encouraged me to do so anyway. "If you let her know you still care, then maybe she'll figure out what's truly important." Typical Alice. I'm not so certain, and once I pull up outside the building, I sit back in my seat. I shouldn't be going up there. I should leave Kitty alone, let her work. Get her out of my mind and my heart. But Alice waves me on when I continue to sit there.

"I'll just relax here—you go on. Remember what I said. She'll come around."

"I don't think she will." But I undo my seat belt and take the punnets with me.

I'm wearing my nicest jeans and a clean shirt, but I feel utterly out of place next to all the executives and lawyers in the elevator and then in Kitty's law firm as the receptionist calls back to let her know I'm here. In a few minutes, I spot Cindy coming out from the depths of the office. She smiles at me, but her smile doesn't stick. She looks a bit harried, a bit overtired. Like she's been burning the candle at both ends.

"Hi, Lucy," she says, giving me a brief, gentle hug. I hug her back.

"I thought I'd surprise you two," I say. I hold up the raspberries. "Just a little something to help you through the day."

Cindy smiles again, this time a little more widely, a little longer.

"You are a lifesaver," she says. "I feel like I haven't seen real food since Saturday. And Kitty is stuck in meetings. I'm sure she'll be disappointed to miss you."

"I don't know that she'd want to see me at all."

"What do you mean?" Cindy looks shocked. She takes my arm and we walk out into the hallway, then into a stairwell. "What's going on?"

I swallow back the lump in my throat, blink back the tears. "She wanted a break. From everything. I don't know what's with her. It's hot and cold. I thought…well, I'm sure you can guess what I thought. I don't know why."

Cindy shakes her head. "I had no idea. But at work, it's a long story," she says. "Kitty's under a lot of stress, a lot to handle to make things right."

I wish Kitty had confided in me more. I feel unimportant, unwanted. "I see. I guess I'll be on my way. We're at the farmers' market today and need to go get set up."

We move back into the hallway. "Maybe the berries will bring her back to her senses," she says. I shake my head.

"You can keep them. I have to go."

❖

When we get to our spot at the market, Alice puts out a framed copy of Monday's article from the local paper, proudly displaying it for all to see.

"When did you do that?" I ask.

"When you were in the greenhouse yesterday," she says. "Your mom found the frame." She adjusts it slightly on our table. "You and Kitty should be proud."

"We are," I say, "but I don't know when we'll be able to do it again. If ever." I bite my lip.

"You'll figure it out," Alice says confidently. "Maybe the rarity will add to Ming Kitty's cachet?"

"Maybe." I hadn't thought of that. But I doubt it will happen at all.

After that, I don't have much time to think of anything but getting Country Mouse's produce into the hands of our customers. It seems that the review has brought more attention than I'd expected, and we quickly sell out of raspberries and strawberries, and our stock of vegetables is quickly depleting. I feel my phone buzzing, but my hands are full with two bags of salad for my latest customer, a woman with two young kids who fuss as she pays with her debit card. It's late in the afternoon, and I'm sure they are about ready for their naps.

I come out from behind my table, blueberries in hand. I signal to the mother what I'm about to do, and she nods approval. "Do you like berries?" I ask the kids. They both go surprisingly quiet, eyes wide. They look up at their mother, who nods.

"Brett, Sherri, what do you say?" she asks.

"Yes, please," Sherri says. "And thank you," Brett adds.

I hold out the punnet, and they each take a small handful of blueberries. Sherri stuffs hers into her mouth, eyes closing. At that moment, she reminds me of Kitty, of the first time she had one of my blackberries. Brett slowly eats each berry, savoring every bite.

"Thank you," their mother says. "Add that to my bill."

I wave it off. "Tasters are free," I say.

"*Mom*," Sherri says, hooking her arm around her mom's leg. "Can we have more blueberries?"

"Next week," she says. "We have all we need today." She gives me a smile and leads her kids away. Another customer takes her place, and it's a good half an hour before I get a chance to check my phone.

There's a missed call from home. That's not usual—Mama knows when we're busy, and she wouldn't call to chat if she didn't need to. I notice there's a voicemail icon flashing, so I dial in. The reception isn't very good, and the market is loud, so I move a few paces away, putting my finger into my free ear to block out some of the noise.

It's not Mama's voice on the message. It ends, and I hit the button to repeat it. This time, I catch more of the words.

"This is Tony, I'm one of the paramedics here. Your mother has had a fall, and it seems that she may have broken her ankle. We're taking her into the hospital in south Calgary. You can meet us there. We'll be in the emergency department." The paramedic rattles off the phone number for the hospital. I grab a pen and find a scrap of cardboard, scribbling down the number. When I hang up, I feel queasy, lightheaded.

"What's wrong?" Alice is ever perceptive.

"Mama's going to the hospital. That was a message from a paramedic."

"Let's go," Alice says immediately. "We're almost sold out—there's no harm in leaving now. This is way more important."

We pack up in a rush, and when we're in the van, I pull out my phone and look up the route to the hospital. My hands are shaking, and Alice takes the phone from me, tapping in the information.

"She'll be fine," Alice says. Her calm voice is soothing somehow, but I can't wait to get moving. Alice passes the phone back over. "We can get out to Deerfoot Trail, and it's the Seton exit," she says. "Easy."

The drive passes in a blur, though I know I'm being careful. My knuckles are white from clutching the steering wheel, and I feel like we're going far too slow. Once we get to the hospital, it's hard to find parking. The surface lots are full and once in the underground parkade, it feels like we've driven kilometers before I find a spot.

Alice unbuckles her seat belt and we meet at the hood. I hit the button on my fob to lock the van, and we find the nearest elevator. Alice is leading the way and I have never been more thankful for her presence. We follow the signs to the emergency department, and after Alice inquires with the triage nurse, we're led into the back to a bed. Mama's lying there, her face pinched and pale. She smiles wanly at us.

"I was clumsy," she says before we can say anything. She waves a hand at her foot, carefully braced. "Tripped on the stairs and fell."

"Can you come home soon?" I ask.

A nurse sticks her head in. "Are you Mrs. Shen's daughter?" she asks. I nod. "Your mother has to have surgery on her ankle, so she'll be in for a long while yet. We are still waiting for the surgery to be scheduled."

Alice frowns. "How long will it be?"

The nurse shrugs. "When we know, we'll let you know. Hopefully by tomorrow, if not earlier."

"Tomorrow?"

"We're a busy hospital. She's stable, and we just had two people from a collision come in, so she's not the highest priority. But I can promise you we'll get her in as soon as we can."

The nurse leaves. I sink down into the chair next to Mama's bed. Alice perches on the side of the bed opposite Mama's broken ankle.

"I can take the van back to the farm if you want to stay here," Alice suggests. "And I can come back in the morning and spell you." She shakes her head. "I sure hope we're not going to be here too long. Are you doing all right, Michelle?"

"Been better," Mama says. She indicates the IV in her arm. "They gave me something for the pain. It helps, somewhat."

"Are you sure?"

Alice bends to hug Mama and then pats my arm before she leaves, van keys in her hand. I move to take her place on the edge of the bed.

"I will be fine, Ming Nhon," Mama says. "The doctors have assured me I will be."

"I should have been there," I fret.

"You would have caught me from falling?" Mama asks. "No, these things just happen. I made it to the phone and called. I am fine," she repeats.

"But what if it had been worse?"

"It wasn't," Mama points out. "And I have always managed. Just like how I came from China to marry your father. If I could come that far, what's a broken ankle?" She takes hold of my hand. "I will be fine. But you can't blame yourself."

I nod, though I'm not sure I can make myself blameless. I should have been there.

"How is Kitty?" Mama asks after a short time of quiet, as we listen to all the bustle of the emergency department around us.

"Busy," I say and relate my earlier visit. "But that's typical."

"She will come to her senses," Mama says.

"I'm not going to wait on her to do that," I retort, more sharply than I intend.

"She needs to find her way. I know she will." Mama is a lot more confident than I am, but then, I've kept the worst from her. She wasn't the one who had to hear Kitty's words over the phone, the finality of them.

"You should text her," Mama says. "She will be worried if you don't."

I don't know that she would be, since we didn't even see each other today, but I pull out my phone and send Kitty a long text, letting her know what's happened to Mama. If nothing else, Kitty has been kind to Mama, and I know she'd want to know.

I set my phone on the bed beside me, though it doesn't sit there long. It buzzes, and I see that it's Kitty calling.

"Will your mom be okay?" she asks as soon as I pick up. "I can come help."

"We're just waiting for her to be cleared for surgery," I say, "And it might be a while. They're busy here."

"Do you need anything to eat?" Kitty asks. "It's dinnertime, and I'm almost finished here and can come down."

"Whatever you want to bring," I say. "I'm not picky." I look at Mama. "You?"

Mama shakes her head. "The doctor told me I can't eat until after the surgery."

"I'll pick up some takeout and then be down as soon as I can. Hang in there, Lucy."

"Thank you," I say.

"I'll be there in a bit."

"She's the best girl for you, even still," Mama says after I hang up. She squeezes my hand. "Maybe we can give Cindy some free fruit every month for bringing her along that day to meet you."

I chuckle. "I'm sure she wouldn't say no to fruit, but she might not take it. I don't think that was a setup."

"Don't be so sure," Mama says. She lies back and closes her eyes. "Wake me when Kitty gets here."

I move back to the chair. If Cindy really did set us up, I sure owe her. Although with what's happened, I'm not sure if it's a good thing or not, no matter what Mama says.

❖

I'm exhausted when I walk into the hospital, peering at signs, trying to find the emergency department. I've picked up some Chinese takeout—perhaps not the best choice, but the restaurant was close and I was craving. I just hope Lucy likes chop suey Chinese food. Until I met her, I had no real idea how different the Chinese restaurant food was from what she and Michelle made at home, from what was in all those cookbooks that Michelle had collected over the years. In some ways, the food is completely different, yet in others, close to the same.

I have chow mein, almond soo-gai, ginger beef, and a mixed vegetables selection in my bag. I'm not sure how we'll eat all this, but I picked up some paper plates and made sure the restaurant threw in a few pairs of wooden chopsticks. I may have overdone things. I hope she wasn't expecting a sandwich and a can of Coke. I take a deep breath. It's silly to be worrying about this, of all things. There's work and Michelle to worry about. Real things, not this silly thing about food. Lucy and I might have taken a break, but Michelle's still one of the best people I've ever met.

I take another deep breath as I come to the entrance of the emergency department. The triage nurse eyes me; her glance is at once skeptical yet welcoming.

"I'm here to see Michelle Shen," I say. The nurse looks at her computer, then presses a button that opens the door next to her. I walk through.

"Mrs. Shen is just through there," she says, pointing at a long hallway with curtained beds.

"Thank you." I walk slowly down the hallway, glancing back and forth, not seeing them yet. When I've nearly reached the end, I hear Lucy's voice. She must be on the phone, because I don't hear Michelle replying.

"We're still waiting. I don't know when the surgery will be." I hear Lucy sigh. "I'll be here as long as I need to be. We can skip the market tomorrow." She pauses, and I take that moment to pull back the curtain and slip inside.

Michelle is asleep, and Lucy is turned away, her cell phone to her ear. "Alice," she says, "Mama is more important, and it's too hard for one person to work the market alone."

Alice must say something forceful, because Lucy sighs again. "All right, you can do it. And I'll come home as soon as I can." She hangs up the phone and turns back to the bed.

"Hey," I say. "How's your mom?" I lower my voice. "I've brought Chinese."

"She's all right, but we're still waiting for the surgery time. I think I'll end up being here all night. And Chinese sounds great. I'll take anything. The vending machines are lacking."

We maneuver the tray over Michelle's bed. Lucy perches on the edge of the bed, carefully avoiding jostling her mother. I perch on the edge of the chair, sliding it as close as I can. We lay out the containers on the tray, and I hand Lucy a plate and a pair of chopsticks.

"Serve yourself. I'm not sure we can eat all this."

Lucy gives a low chuckle. "Probably not, but it looks delicious."

I try not to overload my plate; the paper is flimsier than I expected. We eat slowly, trying to stay quiet and let Michelle sleep without interruption. When we finally finish all we can manage, I package everything back up in the bag and find a garbage can for our plates and chopsticks.

"Do you want to come home with me and rest for a while?" I ask quietly. "I can have you back here first thing in the morning."

Lucy shakes her head. "I'd like to, but I should stay. I don't want to leave Mama alone."

Michelle shifts on the bed, opening her eyes. "You should go home with Kitty," she says. "You need your rest. They aren't going to do anything bad to me." She smiles tiredly.

"It could be anytime," Lucy objects. Michelle shakes her head.

"Go ask the nurse," she says. "If they don't know about surgery yet, then you should go and rest. It's getting late."

Lucy rises and leaves. The curtain falls back into place.

"Thank you for coming," Michelle says to me. "And for taking care of my girl. She works too hard sometimes."

"Don't we all." I shake my head. As if on cue, my phone buzzes. I check it and see a new email from a client.

"You work too hard too," Michelle observes. "You'd be better working at the restaurant, or even the farm." She smiles. "You look happier there than looking at your phone."

"I'm close to making partner," I tell her. "So close. But I have some work to do to make up for a big error."

"Partner," Michelle echoes. "Isn't that just another way to get you to work even harder?" She pats my hand. "I know it's hard to establish yourself. Even when you're close to forty. Younger than Lucy, though."

"Not by much," I say.

Michelle smiles again. "It's like having a second daughter," she says. "I couldn't have more than one. But Lucy's father never minded." She shakes her head. "I'm getting old, though. Never would have fallen like that if I'd been younger."

"It could happen to anyone," I say. "A friend of mine fell and broke hers, and she was in her early twenties then."

"Bad luck," Michelle agrees.

Lucy comes back around the curtain. "It won't be until morning at the very earliest," she says. "They'll keep you here until then, though, because there aren't any beds available in the ward yet."

"So you go home with Kitty and come back tomorrow," Michelle says. "I will sleep and the nurses can keep an eye on me."

Lucy glances at me, then back at her mother. "Are you sure?"

"Yes." Michelle's tone is final, yet kind.

"All right." Lucy sounds uncertain, but she gathers up her hoodie, then bends to kiss her mother. After, Michelle waves me over and I come close. She tugs me down and gives me a kiss on the cheek.

"See you two tomorrow," she says.

"See you then," I reply.

"Bye, Mama," Lucy says. We slip out from the curtained alcove and into the hallway.

"It's a bit of a drive to my place from here," I say, "but not too bad. Are you tired?"

Lucy nods. "It's been a long day."

I lead her out of the hospital to where I've parked in the underground parkade. I pay, and then we're off, driving back down the freeway toward the inner city. When I pull in to my space at my condo, Lucy is dozing in the passenger seat. She wakes when I lay my hand over hers.

"We're home," I say. We head upstairs, Lucy leaning against the wall in the elevator. I'm feeling tired too, and I know that I can't go to bed yet. That email still needs to be read and possibly answered. And I'll have to make sure to set my alarm bright and early, earlier than usual. Driving Lucy to and from the hospital will eat up a good hour or more of my morning. I'm calculating it in my head as the elevator makes its way up to my floor. I should text Cindy, let her know what's going on.

We reach my floor, and I lead Lucy down the hallway. Once inside, she settles on a chair at the breakfast bar.

"Heimei looks just right here," she says.

"She scolds me for working too hard," I say.

Lucy turns to me. "You have been working a lot more lately. How come?"

I sigh. I didn't tell her yet about Jack, about the client, about what happened. I'm embarrassed that I made such a mistake, but I know I shouldn't be hiding it, not from Lucy. I give her the rundown, though I step into the kitchen and put the kettle on for tea just to keep myself doing something, trying not to feel as utterly useless as I did when Jack reprimanded me.

"Oh, Kitty, I wish you'd said something to me," Lucy says. I take down two mugs from the cupboard as the kettle heats.

"Green tea or something else?"

"Earl Grey," Lucy says. "Or whatever you're having."

"Earl Grey too," I reply.

"Why didn't you tell me about work?" Lucy asks.

I shake my head. "Felt like an idiot. I should have known better. And now I have so much work that there's nothing I can do but work my ass off. And what I really want to be doing is making Ming Kitty awesome." I pause. Did I really just say that?

Lucy pauses. "We all have to do what we have to do." She sounds a bit resigned. "With Mama and her broken ankle, I won't be able to do much for the next while. I know I have Alice, but with the farmers' markets and all that entails, along with Mama out of commission, I'm not going to have much time either."

I pour the boiling water over the tea bags in our cups and then bring the cups over and sit in the chair next to Lucy. It's hard not to sigh.

"We're going to have to talk to Beatrice about backing out. And it'll cost us some money to do that," Lucy says.

"I can cover it," I say immediately. It'll help with the guilt I feel for not being there for Lucy, for the pop-up.

"We should split it," Lucy says. "It's both of ours, after all."

"But it's my fault," I argue.

"Things happen. Life happens," Lucy replies.

I know she's making sense, yet I still think that it is my fault. I totally screwed up at work. Lucy's mom didn't purposely break her ankle. There's a major difference. I absolutely could have kept this mess from happening.

Lucy nudges me. "Don't get so down," she says. "I can tell from your expression, you know."

I shake my head. "I hope my boss can't tell."

"I doubt it," Lucy says. "It's subtle, but it's there, at least for me. I know you, remember?"

She does. She knows me better than anyone.

"You don't have to be perfect at everything," Lucy says. "No one is."

"I know I'm not perfect, but I could have done a lot better."

Lucy picks up her mug, and mine, now empty, and takes them around to the sink, rinsing them out. Then she comes back to my side. "We both need to rest," she says. "Things will seem better in the morning."

"My grandmother used to say that," I say as I follow Lucy down the hall to the bedrooms.

"So did my grandmother," she says. "And Mama says it now and again too."

"Do you want pj's?" I ask.

Lucy nods. "I probably should. I guess I should be in your spare room, shouldn't I?"

I waver. I want her in bed with me, wish she could be next to me, but it wouldn't be fair to either of us to pretend that we're together. I nod. "There's clean sheets on the bed. And I have an extra toothbrush, a new one, in the bathroom that you can use."

We get ready for bed, and there's something comforting about having Lucy here, even if she's in the spare room. Too many things to worry about, too much to do. I try not to toss and turn, but it's midnight before I finally manage to fall asleep.

CHAPTER TWENTY-SEVEN

K itty lends me her car in the morning, since Alice is taking the van into the farmers' market today. I drop her at work before I head to the hospital. She looks exhausted, definitely not fit for a full day's work, but I know she can't stay at home and rest.

"Text me when you know what's happening with your mom," Kitty says before she gets out of the car. "We can figure out what to do next after that. I can take a taxi home tonight if you need the car longer, so don't worry about it."

"You're sure?"

"Positive. And if your mom's stuck here overnight again, come back to my place."

"I will." She slides out of the car and shuts the door. I take a moment to breathe, and then I carefully signal and move the car into traffic.

I get to the hospital in record time, since my trip is against the flow of rush hour traffic, heading away from the downtown core. It's a blessing, and I don't have to white-knuckle it through gridlock after all. When I get to the hospital, I find that Mama has just gone in to be prepped for surgery. The nurse leads me to a waiting room.

"It'll be a few hours," she says. "You can stay here, or there are coffee shops and such downstairs. But make sure you're back here by ten, and I'll come find you when your mother is in recovery."

"Thanks." I wander over to the window, looking out over the stretch of prairie as far as the eye can see, except for the new low-rise condominiums going in a couple of streets over. This used to be bald prairie only a few years ago, yet now it's not even the outermost edge of the city. I feel a pang of sadness for all that wildlife displaced. Then I turn, look around the bare, quiet room, and decide to go downstairs for a coffee. I check my watch. I'll have time to call Betty, let her know we can't be there for the Saturday market, and then to call Beatrice. They'll both be disappointed, but hopefully they'll understand. I have no doubt that the entire area knows of Mama's fall by now, and word will get around about Ming Kitty. It's a blessing and a curse of living in a rural area.

I get my coffee and a muffin, find a seat, and make my calls. Then I text Kitty. Afterward, I put down my phone and focus on my muffin, letting my gaze wander out the window once more, though this time my view isn't as pleasant. It's cars and a parking lot.

After a couple of hours, I am completely and utterly bored. Even the dog-eared magazines and a copy of the local paper haven't been enough to keep me interested. It's a bit early yet, but I head back up to the waiting room, hoping the nurse will have some news for me.

I'm not waiting long before the nurse pops in. "Your mother is out of surgery and doing well," she says. "The doctor will want to keep her overnight just to make sure, and then you can take her home. If you'll come with me, I'll take you to her room."

I follow the nurse out and down the corridor, passing a dozen or more doors. She takes me into a ward of four beds, and I see Mama tucked in a bed at the far end near the window. Her eyes are closed and her chest rises and falls regularly. Her expression is relaxed.

"She's still pretty dozy from the anesthetic," the nurse says, "but she should come round fairly soon. If you need anything, use the buzzer here." She places her hand on the bed rail, where there is a set of glowing buttons.

"Thank you." I take the chair next to Mama's bed and settle in to wait.

❖

I take a taxi home from work, and a little after that, Lucy arrives from the hospital. Between the two of us, I'm not sure who is more tired. I meet her at the door, and she yawns, which triggers my yawn. We both chuckle. The anxiety from my day begins to finally ebb. I'm not sure if Lucy feels the same, but she seems to relax a bit. For the first time all day, I feel content, right.

"It's been a long day. You too?" she asks.

"Has it ever. How's your mom doing?"

"All right. She should be able to go home tomorrow."

Lucy toes off her shoes and I kick off my low heels and move into the kitchen. I pull a bottle of wine from the fridge. "Want a glass?" I ask.

"That would be amazing," Lucy says, taking her seat at the bar. "At least tonight I can rest and not have to worry. It'll just be getting Mama home tomorrow that'll be the trouble. Alice will have to drive in from the farm to pick us up."

"Tomorrow's Saturday, at least," I remark. "Finally. I could drive you two home."

"You don't have work?"

I do, but the urge to be at the farm and away from here is intense.

"I can skip it until Sunday," I say.

"Only if you're sure," Lucy says. "I know you've been so busy, and if you need to work, we'll manage."

I bring two glasses of wine and slide into my seat next to Lucy, placing a glass in front of her. "I'll work on Sunday. And Saturday night if I have to."

"You're the best," Lucy says. She lifts her glass and we clink the rims. It's a light pinot grigio, and it goes down way too easily.

"I still care about you," I say, "and your mom. So of course I would do it."

Lucy is quiet for a long moment. "That means a lot to me," she says finally. "That you do." She takes a sip of her wine, looking thoughtful. "And since I'm feeling a bit emotional"—she lifts the wineglass—"I will say that even though we're not together, I've always appreciated that you've always liked me as I am. It means a lot."

I hadn't even thought of that. Lucy is perfect exactly as she is, and I tell her as much.

"You've never asked me to move, or to stop doing what I'm doing," she explains. "Others have. It's a relief."

"And you've never asked that of me, either," I realize.

"You're you," Lucy says. "All I want is for you to be happy."

I don't know what to say to that, but my sense of contentment grows. My stomach growls, breaking the moment. Lucy chuckles.

"I think we need takeout," she says.

"Delivery," I agree. "I don't want to go anywhere. Pajamas, wine, and takeout."

"Pizza?" Lucy suggests.

"Sushi?" I add.

"Both?"

Conveniently there are both sushi restaurants and pizza joints nearby, and all of them deliver. We decide on a medium pepperoni with mushrooms, and a variety of rolls and nigiri sushi. I know we're going to have food for days, but it doesn't matter. It's me and Lucy, and I've missed being with her.

❖

We pick up Mama from the hospital midmorning, after a fuss and confusion over discharge papers. She's wobbly on her rented crutches, so they give us a wheelchair to get her out to the car. Kitty helps me lift Mama, and we get her comfortably situated in the back seat, her leg propped up along the length of the bench seat.

"You all right?" Kitty asks as she slips into the driver's seat.

I carefully close the passenger side back door, making sure not to jostle Mama's ankle in its boot.

"Just fine," Mama says. "They gave me something for the pain. I might just sleep all the way home." She chuckles as I settle into the passenger seat. "Thank you for driving us."

"It's the least I can do for my two favorite women," Kitty says, smiling. She glances at me before she turns her focus to the road. "It's going to be a bit of a drive."

Mama wasn't joking. It only takes a few minutes before she's dozing in the back seat. Kitty turns the radio down low, quieting the voices on CBC's *Day 6* program. Once we're on the highway, we drive in a comfortable silence until we get to the turnoff to the range road that leads to the farm. Kitty's phone rings, the display on her car flashing the number. It's Cindy.

Kitty declines the call.

"You should answer that," I say. "It might be important."

Kitty shakes her head. "I don't want to wake your mom. I'll call her back once we're stopped and we have your mom in the house and settled."

We take the short drive up the range road. Kitty seems tense, her brow furrowed, but I don't mention it. I don't want to add to her concern over work. She doesn't need more stress. Once we get home, it's awkward to help Mama up the stairs with her crutches, but we manage, getting her settled on the couch in the living room. I go to put on some tea, and Kitty checks her messages, walking back down the hallway to the front door. In a few minutes, she's back, just as I pour the hot water over the tea bags in the pot.

"I can't stay," she says. Her shoulders are slumped, her voice flat. "There's an emergency of some sort at the office, and I'm expected to be there to assist." She shakes her head. "I'm sorry."

"Don't be sorry," Mama says. She gestures to Kitty to come over to her. Kitty does, perching on the couch next to her. Mama puts a hand on her shoulder. "You drove us, and you took care of my girl. Now go take care of you. We'll be here when you are done working." Kitty smiles and squeezes Mama's hand as she rises. I'm glad that they have become close.

"Thank you," she says, then sighs. "It didn't sound good." I walk her back outside to her car.

"Will you always have to work weekends?" I ask. I've worked weekends too, but this seems more intense than farm life. At least I get breaks, and the stress isn't anywhere near what Kitty seems to be facing on a daily basis.

"I don't know," she says. "After my fuckup with that client, and this lawsuit I have to win, I feel like Jack has it in for me, or at the very least he's going to make sure I learn from my mistakes."

"You made a mistake—you didn't kill someone." It's hard not to bristle, even though I've never met her boss. "And you're working to fix it."

"I am, but if I can't, our insurance company will pay out the client," she says. "And Jack hates that."

"Text me when you get home?"

"I will," she promises. "It might be late, though."

"Whatever time it is, call me," I say. "I just want to know you're safe at home."

Kitty smiles, but it seems wobbly. "I wish I could stay."

"Me too."

There's an ache in my chest watching her walk to her car, open the door, and then drive away.

CHAPTER TWENTY-EIGHT

Never have I been so exhausted. Not even cooking for hours in a hot kitchen gave me this kind of bone-weary tiredness. And yet, the work isn't done. Not even close. In quieter moments, I envy the pair of associates that gave their notice, one of them leaving law altogether, the other moving to a smaller firm that does family law. But then I remind myself that I'm ever closer to becoming partner and succeeding in my goal.

That's the only thing keeping me going. That and talking to Lucy every so often. But this lawsuit is coming to a close tomorrow, and while I think we have a good case, I'm not fully confident that we'll win.

As if I don't have enough to worry about, I get an email from the food writer, Jo Raj: *Hi, Kitty, I keep hoping to hear about another night for the pop-up! What's happening? I have so many people interested, but your website and Facebook page haven't been updated.*

I sigh. If only I could tell her that we'll be doing another one this weekend, or next weekend. Or ever. We paid out Beatrice, and I convinced Lucy to let me pay most of the fee, given that it's my fault this has happened. Beatrice has said we can use the space again when we get back up and running, but I have no idea when that will happen.

If that will happen.

I hate to say it, even think it, but some days it feels like Ming Kitty was a one-off. A one and done.

I let Jo's email sit while I make myself a quick dinner. As much as I love the ease of takeout, a home-cooked meal is so much better, and I need something good before going into court tomorrow. Tonight, it's easy—pasta with pesto and garlic pan-fried shrimp. I even stopped by the store to get fresh basil and pine nuts and cheese for the pesto. No pesto from a jar here. In the interest of time, though, I did use a food processor instead of a mortar and pestle.

My kitchen smells delicious once I'm done, and my stomach growls. I ate lunch, but that was hours ago. I'd planned on eating daintily, savoring my meal, but I'm too hungry and my plate is clear and clean within minutes.

I push it aside and take up my phone, typing out a reply to Jo: *Hi, Jo, your email means a lot to us! We've had a few personal setbacks. I'll definitely keep you in the loop. Promise.* Details, but not enough to give everything away.

Jo emails me back surprisingly quickly: *Aw, too bad! I hope you're back to normal soon. Let me know, and I can spread the word.*

A fan. We have a fan.

I go to bed heartened, yet exhausted. I'll need to let Lucy know in the morning. I wish I was there with her, curled up in bed together, smelling the fresh-cut grass, the slight scent of the cows from her neighbor's place, hearing the crickets.

It's hard to fall asleep.

❖

The sun is bright, and though it's early, it's already getting warm. I was up with the dawn, knowing that I'd regret it if I wasn't. The greenhouse bakes in the summertime and through early fall, which is great for the produce, but not so great for me, or for Alice. Even though I've been up for a while, coffee in me, my ass is dragging. Usually these mornings are the best mornings, but today—all this week, if I'm honest—it's been tough to get motivated. Everything gets done, but there just isn't the spark there used to be. Something is missing.

Mama's moving around a lot better now, having gotten the hang of her crutches. I still stick close to home, though, in case she needs me. She scolded me the other day for hovering too much.

"Shoo." She waved her hands at me. "Go call Kitty, do whatever you two do."

"Kitty's working." She texted that morning as she was on her way to court, telling me about Jo's burgeoning fandom.

Mama sighed. "That girl works too hard, and she's not happy."

"She has to do what she has to do," I said.

"She'll learn," Mama replied.

I keep hoping she will. But I know the drive, the need to succeed, the need to prove yourself. Country Mouse Farms is testament to that. And I still feel it, but the farm is established now, and it's not as urgent there.

My hands are itching to create. I double-check the greenhouse, set the watering, monitor the growth, note what needs to be harvested, and then I go over to my studio, the large outbuilding with all my welding gear. The little mice and cats and bats and creatures all seem to eyeball me as I enter, but it's the shape in the middle that keeps my attention. My dragon. She's been neglected in the last while, waiting patiently in the dim barn. There's a slight tingle of energy in the air somehow, and I think she knows I'm here. Fanciful, but true.

I roll up my sleeves, wishing I could just leave on the tank top underneath, and put on my leather apron. There's a pile of old plowshares and scythes in one corner, and I know they'll need a lot of work to get ready. They're rusted, worn, but polishing will bring them back to life, or at least to better than they are. I can still easily envision the spread of the wings from the dragon's back. But before I weld them on, I'm going to need to figure out where to put this dragon. Her body is in pieces, and if I construct everything in here, she'll never go anywhere. She'll be huge and heavy.

I start with the plowshares, piling them onto my workbench and getting my gloves and gear ready. They'll need to be ground down, the rust removed, then polished. They will form the shortest ribs of the wings, where they jut out from the dragon's back. And then, I'll weld the scythes onto them. I can see it in my mind. I wonder if I should sharpen the scythes, or leave them blunt? Blunt might be safer for construction, but a dragon with shining and sharp scythes for wings would be gorgeous and dangerous.

The image of the dragon in the middle of a field of wheat, her wings flashing in the sunlight, hovers in my mind's eye. Somehow though, I feel like the sculpture should go somewhere else, somewhere with more traffic, somewhere that it won't be forgotten, rusting out in the rain. I'll have to consider it carefully. I doubt the town would be all that keen, but perhaps one of their parks could use some decoration.

I set up my grinder and place the first plowshare into the vise on my workbench. Safety glasses are next and then a mask, and before I pull on my gloves, I take a moment to turn on the small box fan I have, getting the air moving. It'll save me from the heat once the sun is high in the sky, beating down on the barn. I also check the barrel of water I keep in the corner. Grinding can throw off a lot of sparks, and though there isn't much here that's flammable, I wouldn't want to take the chance. Then I pull on my gloves and pick up the grinder.

Kitty would love to see this. I'd love to see her trying out the grinder and the welder, her hair up, her arms bare, intensity in her gaze. She's been intrigued by the sculpture, but I don't know if she'd be a builder. But I'd love to teach her, love to see her try.

I need to stop thinking about her. We're over.

Then I start to grind and the noise and sparks make it difficult to focus on anything else.

❖

The judge enters the courtroom, and my heart is pounding. We settle into our seats after he takes a seat behind the bench. We presented our closing arguments a few days back, and now we find out whether or not I've managed to save Mr. Anderson's money, the firm's business, and my job in one fell swoop.

I look up at the judge and realize that he's begun to speak, and I've missed what he was saying. "Given the evidence presented by both sides, and the contracts signed and agreed upon, it is my decision that the plaintiffs' application for payment is denied." He turns his gaze on the plaintiffs and their lawyer. "It is apparent from documented evidence provided that work was not completed and that the filing of the liens was inappropriate at best."

I don't hear what he says next, but I know what it will be. We've won. I've won. The rest of his statement is a buzz in my ears, my heart pounding. Finally, we rise, and Mr. Anderson shakes my hand.

"Well done," he says, looking pleased and almost a bit smug. "Those men didn't deserve to be paid for nothing." I nod. "I'll be meeting with Jack this afternoon, to let him know that you've met my expectations."

"Thank you."

Outside the courthouse, my knees feel weak. I watch Mr. Anderson walk to a waiting taxi, and I turn toward the office. As I walk, I wonder why I'm going back. Every step feels like I'm wading through molasses, the exhaustion I've been suppressing coming to the surface. I take out my phone and dial Cindy.

"Well? Well?" she asks when she answers.

"We did it," I say.

"That's the best news I've had all day," she says. "We should go out for lunch to celebrate. I'm pretty sure I can sneak out."

"I'm wiped," I say. "I need to go home. Do I have any meetings this afternoon?"

"Nothing I can't reschedule," she says. "I'll just say you had a bad oyster."

"Thanks, Cindy. You're a lifesaver."

"Take care of yourself, Kitty," she says.

"I will."

I head to my car. My stomach growls, and I know I'll need to eat, but that'll wait until I get home.

❖

I don't know why I'm coming out here. Taking time off was sensible, and my lunch of leftover pasta somewhat revived me, but I have a ton of work piled up at home on my coffee table and on the sofa next to my laptop, and I should be there instead, using the time to catch up. At times, I wonder if Jack has decided to make me his whipping boy. Whipping girl. Whatever. I'm not the prodigy anymore, even though I've kept Mr. Anderson and his business with the firm. One screwup, and I'm doing everything I can to make it better and then some.

I really shouldn't be thinking about work at all. My chest feels tight, and I try to consciously slow my breathing, breathing from the diaphragm like the online list—"13 Things to Help Anxiety"—suggested.

Breathing helps. Sort of. It doesn't quite help the tightness in my chest, but it keeps me from hyperventilating. I push my gaze beyond my windshield, taking a greater interest in my surroundings: the long stretch of road, the Rockies on the horizon, the rolling foothills. I roll down my window partway, letting in the fresh country air. The noise of the wind keeps me from thinking too much, drowning out all the other noise. All that remains is the need to see Lucy. To be on the farm with her, whether we're walking down the road, or in the house, or tending to the produce. I won't stay long—the work won't let me—but even just a few hours might quiet the longing.

At least, I hope it will.

Cindy's been after me to schedule a break for once the court case was done, some days being pushier about it than others. I think she thinks that Jack is overworking me, and her too. He'd hinted at the partnership the other day, and that put a bit of spring in my step, as my father would say. But it didn't last long.

"He's taking advantage," Cindy said in a low, low whisper after she'd closed my office door. "You need to set boundaries."

"He's my boss," I'd said. "It's his firm."

Cindy shook her head. "Make sure you take some time this weekend, then. Even you can't work 24/7."

No, I sure can't. I worked last night until late, probably eleven, nearly midnight. And I was up not quite with the dawn, but almost. Coffee and a piece of toast fueled me for court. Sort of. What I really need now is a nap. A long, long nap.

Finally, I turn onto the range road leading to Country Mouse Farm. But in a moment of hesitation, I slow, turning into a small pullout partway down the road. There's a house nearby, but it isn't Lucy's. I turn off the car and step out, my sandal-clad feet getting scratched by the long dry grass as I wade away from the car and onto a path through the field. There's a little gully nearby, a large gangly tree overhanging. Just the spot to sit and take in the light breeze, the smell of the fields. And it's quiet here too, no cars to be heard, no honking, no screech of brakes, none of the city noise that fills my days and nights.

There's a log resting near the edge of the tiny pool of murky water. Not exactly a beautiful scene, and I'm sure there will be mosquitos, but I don't care. I lower myself onto the log, adjusting my jeans. A bird chirps nearby, and I look up, spotting a small pair of wrens in the branches of the tree.

Somehow, right this moment, this place is a slice of heaven. I've left my phone in the car, and not having it feels strange, but right. I lean forward, propping my chin on my hands. A water bug skitters across the surface of the pond, and I watch it go, tracking its movement to the other shore. I can hear the slight buzz of flies or bees or both, and the wrens making their noises in the tree. There's a bit of a breeze, but not enough to make it cool. As I sit there, my body seems to lose some of its tension, as if it's draining out through my feet and into the soil. I take a deep breath, and another, closing my eyes. If I could have this every day, my life would be so much easier.

I'm not sure how long I sit there, only that I've lost track of time when I open my eyes, hearing the sound of footsteps through the grass. I blink against the brightness and look up.

Alice is there, looking concerned, glancing between me and my car.

"What are you doing out here?" she asks. "Did you break down?"

I shake my head. "The car's fine. I just needed a moment or two."

"Tough week?" Alice lowers herself slowly to the other side of the log, takes off her hat, and wipes her brow.

"Yeah." My stomach churns just thinking of it, and I have to take another deep breath.

Alice nods. "Michelle mentioned it, said that Lucy was worried about you. That you work too hard."

"I have to," I blurt out, trying not to make it sound like a snarky retort.

Alice nods again. "High stakes jobs are like that," she agrees. "It's good to have a retreat." She indicates the farmhouse that's barely in sight over the hill, its blue roof poking over the grass. "That's my retreat." She smiles. "Absolutely worth it too."

"Have you lived here long?" We've spent time together, but I realize that I don't know much about Alice, not really.

"Since I was about your age," she says. "I bought it off an elderly widow who had to move into the city to be nearer her kids and grandkids, in a home. She wanted to stay but couldn't. I've made a few changes in decor, but it's mostly the same otherwise."

"Where did you live before?"

"In Calgary," she says. "Much like you do now. Working for an oil company, being part of the rat race." She glances back to her house, and her expression softens. "Got laid off in the 80s, part of the recession. I was just glad I had some savings and could move. And Adam was young enough that he came with me part of the time. Being a divorced single mom wasn't easy."

"That'd be rough," I say. My parents were lucky during the recession, or so they tell me. Doctors and lawyers are always in demand.

"It was. I was pretty aimless for a while. Then I met Michelle and her husband, and little Lucy. She was about eight then, I think. Cute as a button, already following her dad around, loving it when he'd let her hold the grinder or try to weld something." Alice chuckles. "Not a girl's girl, by any means. And Adam loved it out here, though he spent more time with his dad, in Calgary."

"I'd love to be here more often." As I say the words, the need rises in me, feeling almost like a panic attack, my chest tightening. But my eyes prickle, and I blink back the emotion and take a deep breath, trying to convince my body to relax.

"You could," Alice says.

"Not if I want to be partner." The reply is automatic, almost.

Alice regards me thoughtfully. "Do you?"

I want to say yes, but something stops me. I look down at my hands, at the nails carefully manicured, and then to my toes, also manicured but now smudged with dirt in my sandals.

Do I?

CHAPTER TWENTY-NINE

Welding the plowshare and the old scythe together is fussy work. My dad's portable welder is loud, and I keep telling myself that I should replace it, get a stick welder or flux core, something easier to handle. But they're expensive, and this one still works. Daddy's girl to the core, that statement. I shake my head and push the welding mask up, inspect my work. Not the cleanest line, but it'll do.

I take off the mask, hang it at the end of the workbench where it usually goes. And then I pick up the scythe and plowshare, meant to be one of the ribs of the wing. I take it over to where I have the abdomen of the dragon and try to position it where I think it will go.

It's heavy. It's awkward as hell, and right then, I realize that it won't work. All those plowshares there in that pile, all for nothing. The only saving grace is that I only polished up one before I gave it a shot. The scythes might still work, but I need something lighter for them to be attached to, something more malleable. I set down the rib and go back to my pile of scrap, outside in a little lean-to of the outbuilding. This stuff is mostly sheet metal, taken off old tractors, combines, and the like. Most of it has ugly paint of varying shades of orange, green, red. It'll need cleaning up before I can do anything with it. Adam used to know a guy who did sandblasting. That may be what I have to do.

I dig through the pile, find a piece of sheet metal that is surprisingly clear of paint. I'm not sure where it came from, maybe a replacement fender, but it'll be perfect to experiment on. I take it back into the barn. I set it on the workbench and grab the scythe and plowshare. I grind down the weld, and the scythe falls to the floor with a clang. I toss the plowshare back into the pile and take up the scythe, bringing it over to the workbench. The sheet metal is slim, and I try to picture how it might go with the scythe, how I can attach the two. I take the sheet over to the jigsaw in the corner, eyeing the sheet. If I cut it in half, then I can bend both pieces to form basic spokes, giving it more strength to hold the scythe. I grab my safety glasses from my pocket, slip them on, and turn on the jigsaw.

The cuts are quick, careful, and when I'm done, I file the edges to remove any sharpness, then take the pieces back to the workbench. There, I shape the sheet with my tools and some clamps, then hold up the scythe to the rounded piece.

Not quite.

I use a thick mallet to bend the sheet almost double, then retry with the scythe piece. It slips into place, and I hold up both pieces, turning them around, careful to keep the pieces together. If I weld the two together, I can turn it to whichever angle I need on the body. I take the piece to the welder and slip the mask back on. I follow the line of the metal with my gaze and then with my gloved finger, memorizing its shape, its length. Then I get to work.

When I have it ready, I take the new rib back to the body. This time, I can see how it would work, and it's not going to increase the weight of the wings as much as the plowshare would have. I prop it against the abdomen and go back to my stack of scythes. There's a lot more to clean up and polish, and I'll need to call Adam soon. There's a lot of sheet metal to deal with.

❖

I go back and forth in my mind—job or no job? Lawyer or not? What could I do instead? How could I make money, keep my condo, keep the lights on? The thought of being broke makes my stomach churn once more, and that vise around my chest pinches. I feel breathless. Alice's touch breaks into my distress, grabs my attention.

"You're utterly white," she says. "This isn't life or death." She rubs my back, shifting closer on the log.

I try to steady my breathing, imagine the tension running down my legs and away. A therapist I had once as a kid had suggested that, and it sometimes works. It's not working very well right now, though. I need to calm down. Somehow.

"Have you ever considered taking a leave of absence?" Alice asks. "Even a short one, just to figure out what you want to do?"

I shake my head. As if Jack would ever accept that. You leave, you're leaving for good. None of this silly snowflake stuff like stress leave or sabbatical. Only if you have a line on an amazing client or an amazing job. And I have neither of those.

"I can't. That'd be the end of my chance at partner."

Alice's hand on my back is warm, reassuring. "Is that all you've ever wanted?"

My immediate answer is yes, but I don't blurt that out. I lean forward, chin on my hands, staring at the water. Being partner means security. Real security. I could pay off my condo, take trips, choose my own clients, make my parents proud. I'd be making as much or more as my mother does as a doctor.

The silence stretches between us, but Alice doesn't seem bothered, doesn't demand an answer. How different from my parents she is. They'd want an immediate decision. No sitting calmly, no waiting. No patience.

"Imagine what your new life would look like," Alice says. "Imagine how it might be, from the smallest detail to the largest. Don't think about what your life is now, or what things weigh you down. Think about what it could be, what it will be when you make the decision." She rises from the log. "I'm no psychic, or even a counselor, so I can't say how your life will turn out or what decisions you should make. But I will encourage you to imagine yourself at your absolute happiest."

I glance up at her, not sure what to say except "Thank you."

"Come up to the house later if you want. Goldie always loves company."

I'm on my own again, but this time my thoughts slide to positive things, dreamy things, things I've never dared really let myself want. I've spent so much time trying to please everyone else: my parents, my teachers, my boss. What if I tried to please myself instead?

My perfect day would be to wake up next to Lucy, whether we're on the farm or in my condo—although if I'm honest with myself, my thoughts go right to Lucy's bed, with its quilts piled high, the slanted ceiling, the gabled window. The condo doesn't even register. It'd be cozy, warm, a fresh breeze tickling my nose with the scent of grass.

We'd get up and go to work, tending the greenhouse and the gardens outside. If Lucy went to a market, I'd go into the kitchen, try out new dishes, figure out new combinations. And then I'd go to Ming Kitty. My imagination first takes me to the storefront in Cochrane, but the kitchen in my imagination is more up to date, shiny and clean and ready. I'd prep for the evening's opening, and then we would open the doors, let in people who want to eat my food, to eat produce from Lucy's farm.

I open my eyes. Peeking around the corner that night of the pop-up, seeing people eating and laughing, savoring the food and the atmosphere…it was just about perfect. And then afterward, we'd clean up and go home, and spend more time together, and crawl into bed together.

I can't imagine a happy life without Lucy.

I try to imagine being at the firm, being a partner with a corner office, in meetings with clients, with Jack, winning cases for my clients, making sure they get the best deals, the best agreements, the best everything.

I can imagine it.

Except it's gray, all of it.

Where life with Lucy is brilliant and energetic, my other life—then and now—has lost all appeal.

I sag on the log, crossing my arms on my knees, resting my forehead on top.

I know what I want. But I don't know if I have the courage. And I have to do this for me. If I were Lucy, I wouldn't take me back. I wouldn't be trustworthy after what I'd done.

But I need to know. I'll need to ask. And hope.

I'm not sure how much time passes, but when I lift my head, I know what I need to do. Even if it scares me half to death. I rise to my feet and head back to the car. Once there, I turn on the engine and the air conditioning to cool myself off. And stall for time. I'll admit it to myself right now. My phone sits in the cup holder, and I know I need to pick it up, need to call Jack.

I swallow hard.

Then the phone is in my hand and I scroll through my contacts until I reach Jack's cell phone number. I rarely use this one, though I've had it since I started. *For emergencies*, he said.

This feels like an emergency to me. It might be to him too, but not for the same reason. I press on the number and put the phone to my ear.

My stomach clenches and I taste a sour flavor in my mouth. My hands shake. The line rings, and rings.

Finally, when I'm about to hang up, Jack answers.

"Hi, Jack." I try not to stutter, not to panic. My chest is tight.

"Kitty," he says. "What do you need? I'm at the golf course and we're coming to the next tee."

I take a deep breath.

"I'm giving you my notice," I say, before I lose my last bit of nerve. "I'll have a letter on your desk on Monday morning."

"What?" The word is loud, loud enough that I take the phone away from my ear, flinching. "This is ridiculous. You have too many clients, too many files to just quit now. And you made Mr. Anderson very happy. I saw him for lunch, and he sang your praises."

"I'll stay on to help my replacement get up to speed," I say, finding my equilibrium somehow. I'm still shaking, but now that I've said the most important words, some of my anxiety is lessening. Only a bit, but it is. "But after my notice period is up, that's it."

"Is this about that restaurant? You'll never make as much there as you will with the firm. And you are so close to being a partner. C'mon, Kitty, you're the reliable one. You're the one I know I can depend on. You can't do this to me."

I swallow. *So close to being a partner.*

The need is still there, that desire to prove myself worthy. And I hate letting Jack down. In some ways, he's been like a second father, looking out for me. But I remember how many times Jack's kept me going over the past year, telling me about how close I was to being a partner, and how I still haven't moved any farther along that path, how he's never given me any indication that my struggle would soon end. I'd like to believe him, but I don't think I can.

"When would that be?"

There's silence on the line.

"Soon," Jack says, hedging. "But not yet."

"I won't do it anymore, Jack. This is my two weeks' notice."

He blusters. "You need to give me more than that. Two weeks is nothing."

"I don't," I counter. I know the rules. "Two weeks is all you're legally entitled to. More than that is by the employee's grace, and I have another job lined up."

I don't yet, but I hope that Lucy won't be too mad at me, won't have given up on me entirely. If not, well, I can figure something out, somehow.

Jack sighs.

"I see. I'm very disappointed in you, Kitty. We'll talk on Monday about how you'll transition the other staff."

The line goes dead while I'm waiting for him to say something more. I pull my phone away from my ear and see the screen light up, showing the call has ended. I drop it back into the cup holder. My chest is still tight, but my hands aren't shaking anymore. I put my seat belt on and put the car into gear.

❖

The grinder is heavy. Not right away, but after an hour of removing rust from the scythes, my arms tremble. I set it down, shake out my arms and shoulders, walk around the dragon, pull off my dust mask and safety glasses, wipe my forehead with my arm. There's a smear of rust there. No doubt I just smeared my face too. I pull up my shirt, blot my forehead, and it comes away brown. Figures.

I check my phone, text Adam about sandblasting the sheet metal. Then I go back to the couple of sheets I have, putting my safety glasses and mask back on. I get down to business, cutting the sheets, shaping them. The vision of the dragon is clear in my mind. So clear.

❖

I pull up to Country Mouse Farms, parking just in the driveway, close to the sign. Once I'm out of the car, I can hear Michelle on the porch, speaking in Chinese to someone on the phone, though she's just out of eyesight. I could go say hello, and she'd be happy to see me, but I'm not here to see her.

I check the greenhouse, but Lucy's not there. Her van is parked where it usually is, so she should be on the farm. The vast outdoor garden is empty too. I spot the open door of the outbuilding where she has her sculptures. There's a hum in the air, and I make my way to the door.

Lucy's inside, a dark red mask obscuring her face, her hands covered by thick gloves, her clothes by a leather apron. There's sparks and I squint, looking away. Clouds of some sort of gas or smoke hover in the air above her. A motor revs and there's a bright light. I keep my gaze directed away from it, skimming along the edge of the workbench. The pile of scythes that Lucy had are arranged there, some of them far less rusty than they had been. She's working hard.

The light from the welding has subsided, so I glance back at Lucy. Her arms are covered with a snug shirt, and she takes off her mask, wiping her forehead with her arm. There are smears of dust or dirt on her face, and she's perspiring.

She's beautiful.

Her sculpting wasn't part of my earlier imaginings, but standing here now, watching her, they slot themselves in—me helping her with the work, maybe even learning how to weld. How crazy would that be? Manual labor, real manual labor. My mother would be horrified. All my degrees going to waste.

I step into the building, and Lucy starts at the movement.

"You're here." She gives me a long look, one that I'm not sure what to think of. Is this good or bad?

She strides over to me and pauses only a second before she drops her mask to the floor and pulls off her gloves, taking me in her arms. This feels so right. So real. She's warm against me, the scent of dirt and metal and sweat making me feel at home. Why did I ever think otherwise?

I don't even know how to say it. I bury my face in her shoulder, breathing in her scent, letting her warmth radiate through me. We stay like this for several minutes, I'm not even sure how long. But then, we finally part, just enough to see each other. Lucy's still holding me, and I'm still holding her.

"What's wrong?"

It's all so much to tell, yet it's not. It could be so simple. I know my lips are trembling, and my eyes start to water. I haven't cried since I was a teenager, but here I am, welling up.

Lucy waits. Her calm, her patience, much like Alice's patience, are a true comfort. That makes me even more weepy, and the tears spill down my cheeks. I bite my lip, bowing my head and trying not to sob. I shouldn't be crying—I don't need to be crying. But I am.

She pulls me close once more, and this time I'm clinging to her; it feels like being a little kid again in some ways, not that my parents ever really had time for hugs and tears. A few of the nannies did, sometimes. And then I do sob. It's ugly, it's messy, it's immense, the feelings spilling out of me through my tears.

Lucy's rubbing my back, making soothing sounds, slowly rocking her weight from foot to foot, a rhythmic movement that is surprisingly calming.

I sniffle in a very unladylike sort of way, wiping my eyes. Lucy takes me over to the workbench and pulls a box of tissues from a drawer.

I sit down, perching on the edge of the workbench, take a handful of tissues, blot my face, no doubt now red and blotchy and swollen. I blow my nose and breathe more deeply. Lucy rests next to me, still patient. I toss the sodden tissues into the garbage, then wipe my cheeks with my hands.

"Are you all right?" Lucy asks, her arm over my shoulder. I lean against her, compelling my breathing to slow, focusing on her touch, on the dirt floor, on the smell of metal and chemicals from her welding. Bringing myself back down, like my therapist once suggested. The emotions are still there, the anxiety still simmering, but I'm much closer to tranquility.

"I—" I start, then sniffle, then take another deep breath. "I'm quitting my job."

Lucy squeezes my shoulder, but she's quiet, surprisingly so. I shift my gaze to her, see her looking at me.

"You're certain?"

"I can't do it anymore. I'm not happy. I thought I was—thought I would be, but I'm not. I won the lawsuit, but it doesn't matter." A couple of leftover tears leak from the corners of my eyes and I swipe them away. "I'm happy here. Happy with you. Happy on the farm. Happy making food, getting run off my feet, and then seeing all our customers happy and eating."

"What about your goals?"

"I can't do it. I thought I wanted it, to make partner. But then I thought harder and I was going to keep doing what I was doing, and I just…I just couldn't do it anymore."

"What will you do instead?"

I might be overstepping, assuming, but I can't not take that chance. "I want to make Ming Kitty a reality. Not just an occasional pop-up, but a real, every day restaurant. And I hope, I really hope, that we can do that. That we can make it a reality, and that I can help you out here on the farm too. And…I'm sorry I broke things off. I know you likely won't be able to trust me, but…" I swallow hard. "If you can find a way to give me another chance…"

My heart thunders in my chest, the anxiety rising once more. What if she says no? What if I've put it all on the line for nothing?

Lucy's solemn face moves, changes, and she's smiling. Grinning.

"We will have the most incredible restaurant ever." She takes my face in her hands, and then we're kissing, through tears and glee and giggles, and the anxiety drains from me, leaving a lightness I've never felt before. I'm giddy, trembling under her touch.

Desire rises and our kisses deepen. I grasp the ties of her apron, pulling them free, and we break apart so she can pull it over her head.

Then I'm tugging up the hem of her shirt and she's working on mine, and I don't care that we're in a cluttered outbuilding, the door partly open, practically in public. We're stripped down, and Lucy lays her apron on the floor, and then we're there. She's pushing me onto my back, bringing my legs up, my feet on her shoulders as she licks me, flicking my clit, then sucking it, then drawing back. And again. It's been so long that I'm starved for her touch, the press of her tongue inside me enough to undo me, shuddering, gasping on the floor. She doesn't stop until I'm limp and panting, then reclines beside me, stroking my breast, then down to my hip.

"We get to do this every day," she murmurs into my ear. The thought makes me shudder again, shiver as she strokes me. I cup her cheek, bring her mouth to mine, kiss her, tasting our mixed flavors. Then I stroke down her body, moving lower, taking a nipple into my mouth, my hand going between her legs, finding her damp center. She takes my hand, presses my fingers inside her, a moan coming from her. I thrust three fingers into her, my thumb brushing her clit, her fingers clutching at my shoulder.

Her head has fallen back, her mouth open, her chest flushed, her hips lifting against my hand, grinding into me as she clenches around my fingers.

I've missed this, needed this. Needed her.

I suck on her nipples, one after the other, scraping them with my teeth, still penetrating her, stroking her clit, until finally her legs squeeze together, trapping my hand, and I feel the flutter of her muscles as she comes hard.

When she relaxes, I withdraw, and we end up on the apron, our legs stretched out on the dirt floor. I'm perspiring and so is she, and there are smudges of grime on her face and likely on mine. We're a mess.

"Your mother is going to wonder what we've been doing," I mutter to her.

"Oh, she'll know," Lucy assures me. "She'll know."

I bury my face against her shoulder.

"She'll be glad to see you," Lucy says, stroking my hair. "And trust me when I tell you that she won't be shocked at our state. At least as long as we don't walk starkers into the house." Her shoulders shake with her laughter.

"I can handle that." My cheeks heat. "Maybe."

"She loves you," Lucy says. "And I know she'll be even more

delighted when she hears the news. All the news. She's been wanting me to settle down for years."

"Years?" I echo.

"Years. She wants grandkids, if you're up for that. I think I'm getting a bit long in the tooth myself."

"I hadn't even thought that far."

"There's always later," Lucy says, kissing me again. "Let's go have a shower. Then we can plot the return of Ming Kitty."

EPILOGUE

Six months later

"I'm starting to think we should have chosen a slightly less ambitious date." I poke my head out from the kitchen, peer at the packed dining room for Ming Kitty. Ming Kitty, the restaurant. No more pop-ups.

"Valentine's Day is so romantic, though," Lucy says, coming up behind me, her voice a whisper. "Now come on back. Ella and Jessie are great servers, and they'll keep things running. We need to be in that kitchen."

My stomach is in knots, but this anxiety is something different. There's nervousness there, sure, but there's also excitement. Finally. Not the worry that I wouldn't work hard enough to become partner, or impress my boss, but that tingling excitement that says we're doing something amazing. And we are.

Ming Kitty graduated from pop-up to the real thing. The pop-ups were packed, the demand crazily high, enough that we were able to negotiate a real lease with Beatrice and talk her into replacing the old oven. And now, on our real grand opening, we have two servers, two cooks, a host, and a dishwasher. I can hardly believe it.

Lucy grabs my hand, tugs me back into the kitchen. "We can rest later. That food won't cook itself." The servers have brought back their first orders, and we get started. We've upgraded the menu a bit, added a couple of appetizers and a salad, but the mains are the same, with some flexibility. Until we can make enough money to hire another cook, that's how it'll have to be. For now. I have dreams of a more substantial menu, with a dozen mains, another dozen appetizers, and a selection of desserts and wines. But I'll take what I can get. My head buzzes with ideas, but I push them aside to focus on cooking.

And cooking. And cooking.

Valentine's Day is insane. But you know what? I wouldn't have it any other way. All those lovey couples out there, having their intimate dinners? It's exactly what we both want.

Lucy bumps my hip with hers. "I think we're going to run out of ginger beef. Genius putting it on the menu, but oh my God, it is nuts."

My stomach growls. "I hope there's some left for us."

Lucy grins. "I got Mama to make us some at home, so it'll be there later."

"You are a genius."

"You know it!" Lucy sets down her plates and goes back to her side of the kitchen. I plate up the frisée, portion out the spicy daikon fries, and put the plates up on the pass-through. Then, my favorite part, I ring the little bell. Jessie comes hurrying back, grabs the order, and takes it out to her table.

The evening proceeds in a blur, a rush of plates, food, desserts, and hauling clean plates back to the kitchen.

I pop out into the dining room briefly, spotting Cindy and one of her friends at a table for two. "Hey, Cindy, where's Roy?" We've kept in touch since I quit the firm, but we haven't been quite as good at confiding in each other. We're both working insanely hard, and it's not leaving much time for rest lately.

"Oh, him." Cindy sighs. "Jerk broke it off a few weeks ago, said he just didn't see himself getting into a really serious thing."

"Damn. I'm sorry, Cindy."

She waves off my concern. "I'm better off. Besides, Jen here wanted to finally experience Ming Kitty, so who better to be my date?" Jen holds out her hand, and we shake. She's a gorgeous, curvy woman, her dark hair shining in the light from the chandelier we had installed. And from how she smiles at Cindy, I wonder if there's a little something more between them.

"I'm glad you could make it, even if things didn't work out with Roy."

"I'd never miss your grand opening." Cindy stands and gives me a big hug. "One day I'll be just like you, running my own business."

"I know you will," I say. "And we need to do coffee so you can tell me all about it."

"I'll text you," she says. "And you'd better get back in there before you get overrun."

"See you later!" I hurry back, finding dessert orders waiting. It's a rush to fill those, everyone seeming to finish their dinners at once, but the rush is exhilarating.

But then finally, oh so finally, we see the last satisfied customers walk out the door into the snowy February evening.

Jessie and Ella take care of their cash-out, and Lucy and I clean the kitchen while our dishwasher, Jessie's younger brother Ethan, takes care of all the dishes. I'm just sweeping the floor when Jessie comes to me with her cash-out and Ella's. "We're going to take off," she says. "Ethan's just finished too."

"That's great." I set the cash-outs on the counter. "Thanks for all your hard work tonight."

"I'm so glad you guys opened up," she says. "This sure beats working in the local pub." She grins. "See you tomorrow!"

Now it's just me and Lucy. She comes back from the dining room, having wiped all the tables and straightened all the chairs. She has a bag full of tablecloths which we'll toss into the washing machine at home and bring back tomorrow.

"I am beat," she says, hefting the bag to the back door. "And I'm starving."

I scoop up the cash-outs. "Let's go home." I hook my arm around her waist, and we head out to the van, locking up behind us. It'll be another long evening tomorrow, but I'm hoping it'll be a bit quieter post V-Day. The drive back to the farm is quiet, the radio tuned to CKUA's *Friday Night Blues Party*. Lucy reaches out over the stick shift, and I twine my fingers through hers.

Once home, we head straight to the kitchen. Michelle has left food warming in the oven, and we take it out. Lucy tears off the foil, and steam rises from the ginger beef, fried rice, and chop suey. We don't even go for chopsticks, digging in with forks and standing at the counter. Once my immediate urge has been sated, I straighten. She looks at me, and I look at her, and she's smiling. I know I'm smiling too. My face hurts from all the laughing we did during the dinner rush.

"Happy Valentine's Day," Lucy says. She leans against me, and then we're embracing, food forgotten. The mood shifts.

"Shower?" I ask.

"Only if you're in there with me," Lucy says.

"Consider it done."

Our food is forgotten on the counter. Showers with Lucy are too good to pass up.

About the Author

Alyssa Linn Palmer is a Canadian writer and freelance editor. She splits her time between a full-time day job and her part-time loves, writing and editing. Her book *Midnight at the Orpheus* won a Rainbow Award in 2016, and her book *Betting on Love* was a Rainbow Award honorable mention in 2015. Find out more about her and her books at alyssalinnpalmer.com.

Books Available From Bold Strokes Books

Brooklyn Summer by Maggie Cummings. When opposites attract, can a summer of passion and adventure lead to a lifetime of love? (978-1-63555-578-3)

City Kitty and Country Mouse by Alyssa Linn Palmer. Pulled in two different directions, can a city kitty and a country mouse fall in love and make it work? (978-1-63555-553-0)

Elimination by Jackie D. When a dangerous homegrown terrorist seeks refuge with the Russian mafia, the team will be put to the ultimate test. (978-1-63555-570-7)

In the Shadow of Darkness by Nicole Stiling. Angeline Vallencourt is a reluctant vampire who must decide what she wants more—obscurity, revenge, or the woman who makes her feel alive. (978-1-63555-624-7)

On Second Thought by C. Spencer. Madisen is falling hard for Rae. Even single life and co-parenting are beginning to click. At least, that is, until her ex-wife begins to have second thoughts. (978-1-63555-415-1)

Out of Practice by Carsen Taite. When attorney Abby Keane discovers the wedding blogger tormenting her client is the woman she had a passionate, anonymous vacation fling with, sparks and subpoenas fly. Legal Affairs: one law firm, three best friends, three chances to fall in love. (978-1-63555-359-8)

Providence by Leigh Hays. With every click of the shutter, photographer Rebekiah Kearns finds it harder and harder to keep Lindsey Blackwell in focus without getting too close. (978-1-63555-620-9)

Taking a Shot at Love by KC Richardson. When academic and athletic worlds collide, will English professor Celeste Bouchard and basketball coach Lisa Tobias ignore their attraction to achieve their professional goals? (978-1-63555-549-3)

Flight to the Horizon by Julie Tizard. Airline captain Kerri Sullivan and flight attendant Janine Case struggle to survive an emergency water